Summer Snow

William T. Hathaway

Lightning Path Press
www.lightningpathpress.com

D1247518

An Avatar Book
Published by Avatar Publications
St Albert, Alberta. Canada
www.avatarpublication.com

For information on bulk purchase discounts contact
Avatar Publications at sales@avatarpublication.com

Library of Congress Cataloging-in-Publication Data

```
Hathaway, William T., 1942-
  Summer snow / William T. Hathaway.
        p. cm.
  ISBN 978-0-9738442-3-8 (acid free paper) -- ISBN
978-0-9738442-4-5 (PDF e-book) -- ISBN 978-0-
9738442-5-2 (Microsoft Reader)
  1.  Americans--Middle East--Fiction. 2.  Terrorism-
-Prevention--Fiction. 3.  Iraq War, 2003---Fiction.
4.  Women mystics--Fiction. 5.  Nonviolence--
Fiction. 6.  Sufis--Fiction.  I. Title.

  PS3558.A738S86 2005
  813'.54--dc22

                    2005025951
```

For Daniela Rommel

The author would like to thank Bob Schuster, Michael Sharp, Gina Ratkovic, Lisa Hayden Espenschade, Anika Weiss, Susannah Morrison, Jim and Herdis Burkard, Christopher Ladner, Keith Parker, Jim Karpen, and the wonderful people of Kyrgyzstan.

The first chapter appeared in *Consciousness, Literature and the Arts*, a journal of the University of Wales.

Cholpon sang as she hoed the earth by the honeydew melons, chopping the soil and heaping it up around the vines. The Sufi women working with her sang too; their voices swelled in unison, creating a vibrant hum that filled the space between them. "*Apavitrah,*" the altos led. "*Pavitro-va,*" the sopranos answered. Their chant echoed off the rocky cliffs and returned to spill over them like the overlapping rounds of a canon, suffusing the valley with music. As they sang the ancient verses, mantras whose vibrations cleared their minds of thoughts, they merged with the life around them: translucent green leaves, curling tendrils, floppy yellow blossoms, melon globes swelling from the calyxes of withered flowers. They became the singer and the song, the hoe and the earth, the bug and the leaf, all moving to the rhythm of the hymns. The August sun fed them with its radiance. They knew they were this sun too and its million sister stars, all working together.

A man walked down the path leading from the adjoining farm; Cholpon saw he wasn't their neighbor but a stranger. As he came closer, she could tell from his long face, full beard, and cloth headdress that he was a refugee from nearby Afghanistan. Thousands had fled the fighting and bombing, and some of the more shell shocked had then fled the refugee camps and were now wandering the countryside of Kyrgyzstan. He carried an ax over his shoulder and a bow saw in his hand and wore a pack frame to which were strapped a few dead tree branches. He's probably trying to make a few *soms* selling firewood. He walked with a bit of a lurch. Was he injured? No, it looked more like alcohol.

He stopped and regarded the women, puzzled. His eyes traveled back and forth searching for something that wasn't there. Oh, of course, Cholpon realized, he's looking for a man—the boss, no doubt. He snickered then threw back his shoulders and stood straighter. Ah, she thought, it just occurred to him that as the only man, HE was the boss. Middle-aged, he was dressed in a torn Pashtun tunic whose once colorful geometric design was now soiled and stained.

"We have no dead wood here," Cholpon told him in Kyrgyz, "but farther up the canyon you can find some." She didn't know if he understood the language, but she spoke no Pashto. She could try Russian or English, but that might trigger hostility.

He turned to Cholpon's voice, jutted one hand on his hip, and surveyed her as if she were an upstart rival to his new-found authority. He pointed his ax at a nearby walnut tree and narrowed his eyes.

"Our trees here have no dead limbs," Cholpon said. "We use them ourselves for firewood."

When he started toward the tree, Cholpon knew there would be trouble. Her Sufi sisters stared at the intruder, clutching their hoes. Cholpon thought her mantra while gazing around his head, to read his aura. The light coming from him was mostly muddy brown, but the green flares showed he wasn't totally vicious. Overloaded by stress—nothing but chaos to return to in Afghanistan and no future here. His surly stride told her this made him mad, made him want to bully someone, someone weaker than himself.

He whacked the tree with the ax, lopping off a green limb.

"That's not firewood," said Cholpon. "That's a living tree." Her indignation was mixed with fear: if he was crazy enough to hack a green tree, he might hack them.

The man leaned on his ax, mouthed a kiss at Cholpon, then thrust his hips at her.

She stood about ten meters from him—that felt a safe distance, on the fringe of his dark field. The women stood where they'd been working, watching in fright and repulsion, and she motioned them to draw together. As they moved, the man hefted his ax, not yet brandishing it but gripping it to show his power.

"We will not harm you," Cholpon told him.

He snorted, then suddenly pivoted back to the tree and brought the blade down on another limb, severing it.

"We know how to handle this," Cholpon said to her sisters. She named the more experienced Sufis standing in the melon field around her and told them to meditate; the others would chant the peace prayer. Although she'd been at the Circle of Friends from its beginning, she joined with the singers: she needed to keep her eyes open in case he attacked. "*Aum Shantih, Shantih, Shantih,*" they sang

2

from the heart *chakra* at the center of their chests. The droning waves of sound surrounded them, held them suspended in soothing reverberations, and penetrated even into their bones.

The meditators sat cross-legged on the ground in lotus position, eyes closed, silently thinking their mantras. Cholpon could feel the effect in her mind as theirs settled towards the transcendent. Her thoughts became fewer but clearer. Her fear dissolved, replaced by compassion for this ignorant man with an ax who thought he could get rid of his own suffering by forcing it on others. If they could reach him with their mental coherence, build up a strong enough field of transcendental energy to get through to his sputtering, miss-firing brain, he might wake up to what he was doing. Fortunately the human mind, even his, responded like a tuning fork to thought vibrations around it. If the sisters could generate a higher frequency, it would make him change his tune and hear the song of his own inner silence. Even a moment of that could snap him out of his stupor and let him know that any harm he does to others just bounces back on himself. This little shift in consciousness—a stroke with a feather of peace—had been enough to pacify other belligerents, at least temporarily. It had worked last year with a burglar and the year before with two drunken sheepherders intent on carnal conquest. Ax man didn't seem any worse than them.

He howled in mockery of their chanting, spat, then swung at the tree again. Thrap, went the ax into the trunk. The tree shuddered; chips flew; walnuts showered to the ground. From the grace and power of his stroke, Cholpon could see that swinging an ax was probably what he did best in life. Unfortunately no one needed ax swingers anymore, especially the tree.

The women continued chanting, the man continued chopping. Cholpon visualized Djamila in her mind and questioned her. Their teacher's aged face shone calm and beatific as ever. *No danger*, came the answer. *More meditators.*

Cholpon told the chanters to stop and meditate, and she continued the song alone. He tried to ignore them. Cholpon could feel her level of inner silence deepen as the new group settled in. Her voice became more resonant.

The man whacked again, then let go of the ax, leaving it quivering in the wood. Head nodding a bit, he looked up at the tree for a long moment. He wiped off his hands and widened his stance for another blow. He blinked and shook his head, then seized the ax and gave two quick chops, cutting deeper into the trunk. Frowning, he pulled the ax out and stared back up at the tree. His face softened a bit and he shrugged. He looked at the ax, then tapped the trunk with the handle, wood on wood. The man put the ax back over his shoulder, started to walk away, then whirled and swung the ax in a savage arc at the women. All but Cholpon had their eyes closed. She met his tormented stare with as much calm as she could muster. He roared to make the others open their eyes and look at him, then laughed as if he'd pulled a practical joke on them. He slapped his thigh, stamped his foot, and strode away with a swagger.

The women sighed with relief. "Meditate a little longer," Cholpon told them. "This time for us."

Afterwards they made a paste of chitilani root to heal the walnut tree, then returned to tending the melons.

A woman approached on horseback. Cholpon was glad to see Acel, a carpenter who'd been repairing the main house, mounted on Talas, their roan stallion. The workers paused to rest, leaning on their hoes and drinking from water jugs. Acel reined the horse in and called in Kyrgyz, "Cholpon, Djamila wants to see you."

Cholpon wiped her forehead with the sleeve of her cotton shift. Maybe she wanted a report on what happened. Djamila could usually sense an overall situation from a distance but not the details.

"Come." Acel extended her hand to help Cholpon onto the horse. "You can ride behind."

Cholpon gave her hoe to a sister who had been working with just a trowel. She reached up for Acel's hand, felt the woman's strength as she hoisted her, gave a springing leap, and vaulted up onto Talas's broad, bare back. The horse whinnied and pranced his hooves on the flinty path. Cholpon's wide-brimmed straw hat fell off, and another sister handed it up to her. She snuggled in close behind Acel, wrapped her arms around her waist, and gripped Talas's ribs with her knees. Like most rural Kyrgyz, Acel had been raised on horses, but Cholpon was a city girl. Although she loved the rocking sway of the animal beneath her, its warmth and smell, and the wordless communication of their

4

minds, Cholpon didn't feel quite steady perched up here, especially without a saddle. She clung tighter. The breeze of their trot dried the sweat on her skin, bare beneath her long dress, and she luxuriated in the coolness.

Cholpon's ebony hair was twisted and pinned in a spiral to fill the crown of her hat. Her eyes—pools of gleaming darkness, slightly slanted, almond-shaped—shone from an oval face with high, broad cheekbones, a short, straight nose, and full lips around a small mouth. Her pale-gold skin glowed from her labors.

From horseback Cholpon could see how much they'd accomplished in planting this hectare of melons. Since the spring thaw she'd helped to dig out rocks, cut down bushes, and plow the earth behind the bay mare to turn this hardpan canyon into a field. She'd hauled sand from the lake shore to build proper soil for a melon patch, scooping it up from the beach in two earthenware jugs and carrying them on both ends of a wooden pole that pinched her shoulders all the steep way up, shuffling with a straight back and bent knees. Then she'd shoveled dung—cow flops, sheep splats, horse apples—from the corrals and mixed it with compost—webbed with mold, steaming with the reek and heat of fertile decay—and pitchforked load after fragrant load of it onto the donkey cart. She'd led little patient Noumi clip-clopping with the full cart up the stony path. Cholpon had spaded the humus into the field, turning it over and over, making a loamy soil. She'd dug a channel to divert water from the stream and built gates to control the flow. She'd planted seeds from last season's melons, thrusting them deep into hillocks of dirt, watering and tending them, rejoicing at the first sprouts. She'd weeded and thinned and hoed, plucked bugs and shooed rabbits, and she'd done it all side by side with the other women, her Sufi sisters, singing together, joined with each other and all of nature.

Cholpon knew, though, that work was secondary to *sadhana*—their spiritual practice of meditation, yoga, chanting, and dervish dancing. That expanded their awareness. It showed them they were living in and around their bodies, each a teeming microcosmic universe in itself, on this farm at the shore of Lake Issyk-Kul in Kyrgyzstan, north of Afghanistan, west of China, on the round blue earth in this solar system of the Milky Way galaxy of the teeming macrocosmic universe. It let them know they were

5

little cells of the great body of God, each with a job to do.

The rewards of their physical labor would soon arrive. Some of the honeydews had grown to their full round glory and rang under Cholpon's knuckles with the right hollow thunk. She looked forward to her favorite breakfast of melon and tea, and to the new beds the Circle could buy with the sale of the crop.

Cholpon and Acel rode out of the canyon, its granite walls rising steeply on both sides and the stream coursing down the middle. In August the flow was a trickle that seemed incapable of having cut this sheer notch into the mountain, but each spring the snow melt swelled it to a roily torrent that flooded the narrow canyon, leaving no doubt of its force. Last summer Cholpon had hiked up the stream for two days to its source beneath a glacier high in the Tien Shan range, using its burbling plash as a mantra to wash her mind of grief from her father's death. She had done *puja* at the foot of the glacier, offering wild raspberries, lupin, and thirty-five years of memories up to *Parvati*, the mountain Goddess. She had stared at the blue-white wall of the glacier until it glowed amethyst in star light, then fell asleep wrapped in felt blankets and awoke covered with snow and finished with mourning.

"How did Djamila seem?" she asked Acel.

Acel didn't turn her head. "Not so good."

Cholpon brooded. Djamila was almost always fine. Maybe there was some other problem. The teacher rarely summoned someone from work. The day's events, even an event like ax man, would usually be reported after evening meditation. What else could it be? Cholpon mulled over things she could have done wrong. Perhaps a food wholesaler in Bishkek had complained about the quality of their produce. When she wasn't working on the farm, she handled the sale of their crops in the capital. Haggling with the businessmen was her least favorite activity; they were always griping about something, nothing was ever good enough. In contrast to her sisters here, they seemed empty pits of unmeetable needs, always grabbing for advantage and stuffing their ravenous senses. Maybe they'd convinced Djamila that Cholpon had made a mistake.

She glanced around for something to take her mind off the meeting. Her eyes rested on the silver shimmer of birch leaves along the stream and the deep needle green of pines at the edge of the canyon, and she drank in the sight. But wasn't that similar to

6

what the men in Bishkek were doing: craving sense stimuli as an escape from themselves? What would the teacher say about that? Probably that we should enjoy the senses but not be dependent on them. Djamila taught that our sensory perceptions and thoughts form a screen that separates us from the transcendent, the source of all this manifestation.

Cholpon and Acel dismounted in front of the main house, which stood near the shore of the lake with a craggy horizon of mountains behind it. To Cholpon the house embodied the past century of Kyrgyz history, from outpost of the Russian empire to independent nation. It had once belonged to a family of Russian *kulaks*, peasants who had grown wealthy under the Czar. After executing the family, the Bolsheviks had collectivized the farm, then added annexes to the graceful frame building, turning it into a rambling hodgepodge. The new additions were boxy and merely functional, some of unpainted plywood with tin roofs. Now the women were gradually renovating the place.

Talas saw two fellow horses at the water trough in the corral. As he headed toward them, it became Acel's turn to trot to keep up with him.

Cholpon walked between the two carved wooden columns which gave the entrance of the house pretensions of grandeur, which she rather enjoyed as a trace of frivolous luxury. The porch and its roof, though, slanted with age.

Most of the large rooms had been subdivided to make a dormitory for the farm workers. The salon, however, had been kept as their dining hall. Stalinists had purged its chandeliers and cornices as bourgeois ornament, but its high, coffered ceiling remained. Filled with cushions and prayer mats, it was now the Circle of Friends' meeting room, where Djamila led *dhikr*—meditation and discussion, and *sama*—singing and dervish dancing. The walls were painted an ancient proletarian gray, which the Sufi women had covered with colorful textiles: Kyrgyz felt, Indian cotton prints, Uzbek silk.

Djamila's group had bought the property during the first wave of privatization in the early 1990s. Before that, they'd been an underground circle of Sufi sisters, banned by the communist government and scorned by Muslim fundamentalists. They'd met secretly in small cells around Kyrgyzstan, with Djamila traveling among them teaching. The suppression had welded them into a tight congregation, and now since the collapse of communism they'd been thriving under the new religious freedom.

Djamila's office contained a table draped with white cloth and a desk that held a scattering of papers, a vase of roses, and a bowl of fruit. A purple-and-gold Bukhara carpet, worn but still vivid, covered most of the creaky wooden floor.

Djamila sat near the open window on a couch decked with multicolored pillows. To Cholpon she seemed like an ancient baby: her plump body was small in proportion to her head, white hair fine and flossy as a new-born's crowned her round face, her clear, luminous skin was unwrinkled except around her mouth, and her eyes projected outward in a big open dazzle on the world and inward as deep as Lake Issyk-Kul. Most of her teeth were gone, but she said she preferred her food soft and mushy anyway, so it didn't matter. The skin of her mouth was gathered in puckers, but they disappeared when she smiled, which was most of the time. She wore the same unbleached cotton shift as the others, and her only jewelry was a necklace of coral beads. She held a rose in her hand, waving it about while talking to her secretary in Kyrgyz.

On the wall above her hung pictures of her two teachers, Maharishi Mahesh Yogi of India and Shayk Rais Yasavi of Kyrgyzstan. With the same deep eyes and blissful smile, she looked like them without the beards.

In college Djamila had won a scholarship to study physics at the University of Allahabad. While in India she'd met Maharishi, who had a degree in physics and who showed her that what she really wanted to learn was *meta*physics, going beyond the physical to reach the source of the universe. She'd become a *chela*, an aspiring yogi, and studied at his ashram in the Himalayas. He'd taught her transcendental meditation and *sidhis*, higher mental powers, and then, once she'd mastered them, how to teach them to others. He encouraged her to return to Kyrgyzstan, remain a Muslim, and use these Vedic techniques of consciousness to re-enliven the mystical spirit of Sufism.

Back home, she had apprenticed to Shayk Yasavi at the Sufi center in Osh and immersed herself in Islam. When she finally felt ready, she founded the Circle of Friends and devoted herself to teaching.

Ranging from the Koran to the poems of Rumi to quantum

physics, her lessons integrated spirituality and science. She taught ancient meditation methods but used an electroencephalograph to study their effects on the mind. The scientific aspects of her teachings appealed to the many educated, nontraditional women who had come of age in Soviet times and were now seeking something deeper than the materialism of either communism or capitalism.

Cholpon waited hesitantly at the door until the secretary, a severe, efficient woman in her mid fifties, a former school administrator, noticed her and motioned her in.

"Ah, Cholpon! Yes, come," said Djamila in her birdlike chirp, her face suddenly tinged with worry.

Cholpon brought her right palm up to her forehead and made a sweeping bow onto the carpet, saying, "*Assalam alaikum*"— Peace to you.

"And to you, my dear. And to that sad creature who caused such a disturbance. Were there any more problems with him?"

"No. We re-synchronized his brain waves," Cholpon said with an ironic smile. "He didn't exactly thank us, but he left."

"Good. That's the only way to handle people like that. Opposing them on their level is useless. Now sit here"—Djamila plumped the cushion of the easy chair beside her—"for we must have a proper chat."

Relieved by her friendly tone, Cholpon began to relax. If the purpose of the meeting was a reprimand, it wouldn't have started this way.

But as Djamila looked at her, the sparkle in her eyes faded and her mouth tightened like a drawstring purse. Cholpon's stomach did the same. "But peace for you may have to be postponed for a while." The teacher's voice dropped. She gestured with the rose to her secretary, who left the room and closed the door. "I must tell you what I saw in trance this morning." Djamila frowned and gummed her lips. "It is not good. The astral channels are now very dark...so the vision was dim. But these troubles in Afghanistan and Iraq seem to be flowing over to us. We may all end up wandering around like that man out there. There is danger approaching. I could see it like a black fire...with flames that did not burn but crumbled all they touched into gray ash." She leaned closer, her forehead knitted. "And you were in the middle of the

9

fire, dancing the dervish rings, around and round, and a wind came up from you, fanning the flames so they covered you. But you did not turn to ash. Then your wind blew the flames smaller...into flickers. And they disappeared under your feet as you danced them away. Then you disappeared. And the evil was gone."

The vision scorched Cholpon, made her cringe inside; she wasn't ready yet to disappear. "I am evil?" was all she could ask.

Djamila shook her head with loving patience. "No, my dear. You are quite good. Of all our Friends here, you are closest to enlightenment. With you, the knowledge is not just in your mind...it is in your breath. But this fact is just for you and me, nothing to tell the others. We must have no favorites here...since Allah has none. But you have special abilities...and that is why you have been given extra duties."

Cholpon thought of all her trips to Bishkek: driving the produce van the five hours, paying the militia their bribes at the highway checkpoints, hassling with the merchants at the market, enduring the men leering at her breasts, spending a lonely night in her apartment there, then shopping for supplies for the Circle and driving back, all the while feeling she was wading through mud out in the world, yearning never again to leave the sacred atmosphere their *sadhana* had created in this valley. She had grown up in Bishkek, in that same apartment, but now after being with Djamila for eighteen years she felt alien in the capital, her weekly trips a burden.

"I know it has been difficult," Djamila responded to her thoughts, "but it has been necessary...for us and for your own growth. We all need activity...we can't always be turned inward. Remember when we dye cloth, first we soak it in the color. That's our meditation, merging our mind with Allah."

Cholpon settled into the cushions and prepared herself to be talked to.

"It's most important, but there's another part too. We must take the cloth out and spread it in the sun...to fade the color. That's like our work...in the fields, the city, wherever. Then dip it again into the dye...in and out...some of both every day...until finally the color is fast. After that you can wash it, wear it in the sun, doesn't matter. It won't fade. So we go back and forth between the inner and outer worlds...until we can be anywhere and it's all the same to us. Then we're free. Nothing can overshadow us."

Cholpon nodded and tried to conceal a flash of irritation. She'd heard the analogy a hundred times, and each time Djamila spoke as if she'd just invented it. There was probably some lesson in this, one Cholpon wasn't yet ready for. Maybe something about every moment being new...or the enlightening effects of boredom.

Djamila ignored the irritation. "But with you there is still some dipping in and out to be done. And so...we must lay you out now in the hot fiery sun. And we hope it doesn't burn you up." She gave one of her mirthless cackles to remind Cholpon of the stark impersonality that went hand-in-hand with her tenderness. "But if it does, so be it. Just remember, you are eternal."

Cholpon's fears rose again, but she asked, "What must I do?"

"Go back to Bishkek."

"I was just there."

"You must go again."

Heart sinking, Cholpon bowed her head. "How long?"

"A while. You will know...it will become clear."

"If danger is approaching, I want to stay here...to defend you."

"The danger is not here. It's in Bishkek." Djamila swung the rose with perplexity. "I'm sending you into the danger."

Cholpon's black eyebrows arched up into her creased forehead, and a knot formed in her chest. Djamila seemed to be foretelling her doom, and cavalierly at that. "Why?"

Her teacher's eyes rested on her in a way that left no doubt as to how much she cared about her. "It is your *dharma*. That which cannot be avoided is better met head on."

Cholpon bowed again.

"You are a fine ancient soul...we have been together in many lifetimes...and I love you very much." Djamila let the flower drop to her lap. "See, the rose falls, but it lands somewhere else. There is no loss. Our bond is so strong it goes beyond physical space. It goes beyond even this life. You don't have to be close to me...to be close to me."

Thinking of the dozens of times the teacher had been right in the past, Cholpon mustered her courage. "Yes. I will go."

Djamila bowed to her. "*Allah-aum*." She took Cholpon's hand. Although the *Shayka*'s face was mostly unlined, her hands were wizened and wrinkled. Their touch, though, gave Cholpon a surge of energy that flooded her brain with light and her heart with calm. Just being in Djamila's presence, or even looking at her picture, had a powerful effect, but her touch was concentrated *Shakti* force. "Something else was in the vision," Djamila continued, "something about a man."

Cholpon winced. More trouble.

"It is not clear...but there is some tie between you, some karma to be met."

"What sort of a man?"

Djamila gave one of her cosmic shrugs. "Just the man you will meet. I wish I knew more. The times are very bad right now. I could not see clearly." She dropped Cholpon's hand and stretched her short, plump arms. "Or maybe I am just getting old."

Leaving this sacred valley to plunge into some unknown danger with a strange man—that was as appealing as eating ashes. What had Cholpon done in a past life to bring this on her? No way to tell. As Djamila often said, "The ways of karma are unfathomable to the unenlightened...and irrelevant to the enlightened." All she could do was meet it—head on. Or maybe head off.

Cholpon pushed her fear aside: Djamila had steered her through enough problems to have earned her trust. Last year she had foreseen Cholpon's father's unexpected death, and once his symptoms manifested the *Shayka* visited him on the astral plane to help him prepare for the great transition. Her father, a lifelong atheist, had told Cholpon his wonderful dreams of an aged angel floating above him, caressing him and relieving his dread. He died peacefully.

"When should I go?"

Djamila smiled in approval of her student's obedience. "Today...after lunch. Now we will pack the van with what crops we have ready." She paused, ruminating. "Cholpon, I love you. But the Circle of Friends comes first. There is danger where you are going. I don't know what, I don't know why, but it is coming." She searched for a tactful way to say it. "The money from the merchants...make sure you put it in the bank as soon as you get it. We don't know what might happen."

Cholpon shuddered inside and nodded. Djamila, the ever practical. For the *Shayka*, individual desires, even individual existence, always came second to preserving the knowledge she had to give, to building the community that would continue her teaching after she was gone. This attitude—detached, hard, yet loving—was the only way she had been able to sustain her group here over the opposition of the communists and the Muslim *mullahs*. The communists had recognized her as a threat to their materialist creed and tried to get rid of her as a religious agitator, a fomenter of counter-revolutionary superstitions. Djamila had used subterfuge, bureaucratic delays, and diplomatic influence to fend them off and eventually outlast them.

During that time Cholpon had been able to persuade her father, a Party official, to block several efforts to jail the *Shayka*. He had thought the old woman ridiculous, but he'd been one of those fathers who couldn't resist giving his daughter what she wanted. Cholpon had pleaded and wheedled with him, and he had intervened.

Lately the *mullahs* had become a problem. To them, Djamila was a heretic. Her first teacher had been an Indian yogi. She blended the Koran and the Veda into her own version of Sufism, and this eclectic approach was anathema to orthodox Muslims. Sufis were the wild, mystical, rebel fringe of Islam, open to techniques and beliefs from other religions, so they had often been persecuted for their nonconformity. Djamila was on the liberal side even among them. She revered Krishna, Christ, Mary, and Buddha as well as Muhammad, so the Muslim establishment, under pressure from fundamentalists, was trying to purge her. Her being a woman, and a successful one, was a particular thorn in their patriarchal hides.

Cholpon agreed that the needs of the Circle had to be first priority. She'd seen too much of the aggressive, greedy, ego world for it to have any value to her. Basically the same under communism or capitalism, that world ran in mad circles of insatiable, ever-multiplying desires, getting nowhere. Through Djamila she'd experienced the other realm, the transcendental source of all this diversity, the unmanifest unity from which the relative differences emerge. Thanks to meditation, her mind had been saturated with the energy and bliss of this underlying consciousness. The feeble charade of what people smugly called the real world—just matter and its abstraction, money—couldn't compare to the unified field, the wellspring of creation, the infinite mind of God. Djamila lived there all the time and was showing her followers how to reach it too. Their Circle and the *sadhana* they practiced were a structure necessary for the journey, like sandals needed to walk the rocky path out of ignorance, and a lamp to light the way. These had to be maintained, or the darkness of materialism would reign everywhere.

"Yes," Cholpon said, "I'll deposit the receipts first thing. Then we'll see...what else will happen." She swallowed.

"I want to give you some inner reinforcement...for what lies ahead," Djamila said. "We've been working on your upper *chakras*, but now we must strengthen your lower centers. It's a lower energy that is coming towards you...and you need to be able to repel it." She unfolded her legs from the lotus position, massaged her arthritic knee, and stood up stiffly, steadying herself on Cholpon's chair. "First we will do *puja*." The sparkle returned to her eyes.

Djamila shuffled to a shelf of pictures in gilded frames and picked one out. "For this sort of business you need Durga's help...the slayer of demons." She held up a picture of a naked brown-skinned Goddess with red eyes, long matted black hair, curving white fangs, brandishing a bloody crescent sword, dancing on the chest of a huge, bearded, very male, very dead demon. Rather than triumph or malice, her face showed only peaceful joy. "Durga knows how to handle the dark forces. With her, your soul will be protected. Your body, though...well, we'll have to see." Her expression held a savage drollery that said death and other shifts in physical reality weren't worth worrying about.

Cholpon's heart beat faster.

Djamila set the picture on the white-draped *puja* table near a cluster of brass ceremonial implements: a candlestick, camphor lamp, incense holder, offering tray, bowls for rice and water. She pulled six red roses from the vase on the desk and a sprig of cherries from the bowl. "Stand beside me," she told Cholpon and gave her a flower.

They faced the puja table, and Cholpon followed the *Shayka*'s lead in bowing before the picture. Djamila dipped a rose into the water bowl and began chanting the 108 names of the Goddess as she waved the flower and sprayed water drops over them in ritual purification. Standing crookedly to take the weight off her painful knee, roses clasped in front of her, she sang the

14

Vedic verses in her little bird voice while staring at the picture.

The words filled Cholpon's mind in a way that ordinary sound didn't, permeating it completely, dissolving her thoughts, leaving her empty and immense. Her heartbeat slowed; her breath quieted, then almost stopped; she felt her outer self fading, and she clung to the chant to keep from disappearing. The picture began to vibrate and glow as if alive. Durga's eyes became beacons, and as Cholpon gazed into them, this fierce deity seemed to devour her, but with kindness instead of cruelty.

Cholpon's surface personality fell away, revealing her inner being that enlivened her body but was independent of it. Energy poured from the Goddess into her. As the chanting continued and Djamila offered rice, water, fruit, and flowers to Durga, a current of vitality spread through Cholpon, overrode her fears, let her know she was beyond all harm.

The *Shayka* stopped singing, took Cholpon's flower, and offered it with hers in front of the animate picture. They both knelt into a vast inner space, freed from thoughts and filled with the Goddess's reverberant presence.

Djamila spoke softly. "Now we learn how to use this *Shakti*. First we straighten the back." Cholpon sat up on her heels. "Then close your eyes and breathe out...all the way." Cholpon tightened her diaphragm to press the air out. "Into that hollow...pour a sound." Djamila paused, then whispered: "*Meera-ma.*" The mantra rang through Cholpon as a tap on a gong fills the huge dome of a mosque, faint but everywhere. The *Shakti* force became livelier, a glowing field within her. "Now draw this fire in from the different parts of your body...gather it all at the base of your spine, where you sit." Cholpon's mind brought the impulses together, collected them, concentrated them into an inner sun. "Good." Her tailbone grew warm and she squirmed with discomfort. "Now bring it quickly up your spine...but only as far as your ribs." She could feel it rising, but it stopped after a few inches and spread into her pubis, exciting it. "Don't let it stay there," Djamila said. "Gather it back and draw it up. It belongs higher, between your ribs and your stomach." Embarrassed, Cholpon collected the energy together, moved it up, and released it. It flowed across her torso like molten steel that did not burn but radiated vigor. "That's its home, your power *chakra*. From there you can project it out. Now raise your arms." Cholpon did so. "Higher...and extend your fingers. Let half the energy flow down into your legs and half up into your arms...all the way to your fingers." A kinetic wave surged through her limbs and sprayed from her fingertips. She felt she could lift the world.

"Am I this strong?" she asked in amazement.

"*You* are...but your muscles aren't. This is your heart shield. If dark spirits attack, it will repulse them. You can sense when evil is approaching and avoid it. But its effects are more on the astral than the physical. No, you can't lift the world."

Cholpon nodded in disappointment.

"Each morning and evening you meditate with this new sound. Afterwards, you sit straight in lotus and collect this energy into your power *chakra*. Draw it all in there. Then go out and meet the world...unafraid. The *Shakti* will flow wherever it's needed. Your inner self is protected."

Cholpon pressed her tingling palms together and bowed to Djamila, fearless now, resonant with force. "How will I find this evil?"

Djamila blew out the candle on the puja table. "It will find you." She gave Cholpon one of Durga's flowers. "You are ready for it. Go...meet the flames of your *dharma*...then come back to us."

Cholpon bowed again, this time in farewell. "*Allah-aum.*"

She packed her suitcase, helped load the old Moskvich van with cabbages and a few ripe honeydews, and set out on the 250-mile drive around Lake Issyk-Kul, over the Bistrovka Pass, and down into the Chu Valley where the city of Bishkek waited in the shadow of the Ala-Too peaks.

Late that night in Bishkek a man and a woman lay sleeping. The bed was small, and their sighs and dreams and murmured rollings intertwined.

The sound of a gunshot woke the man. Groping for consciousness, he didn't know where he was or who the warm, softly breathing woman snuggled next to him was. Maybe he'd dreamed the shot. He closed his eyes and spooned in closer to her, hoping it had been a dream and she was real. A short burst of gunfire. Not a dream: the unforgettable hammering of an AK-47. A scream from outside. That was no dream either; it was death, as familiar as the AK. A kill shot sounds different from a wound, more abrupt; the cry doesn't come out of pain but the shock of farewell.

Where were they? Where was his rifle?

Light filled the room, searing his eyes. The Oriental woman looked lovely but death-pale in the shadowless flash. Concussion fell on them in a smothering slap, then fled, taking the light. The room wobbled. Satchel charge. Sappers must've broken through.

In the darkness the woman wailed.

It was one thing for the bastards to try to kill him; those were fair rules of the hard game: he was the foreign invader. But they'd better leave her out of it. As he sat up, she clutched his waist; her long black hair flowed over small breasts. She babbled a language he didn't understand but knew said, Protect me.

Where was his rifle?

Machine gun bursts, long and ripping. Brass casings plinged onto pavement. She clung tighter. But these shots were outgoing: maybe the machine gun was friendly.

Shouts from down in the street—Russian. Soviet advisors with the North Vietnamese? Penetrating downtown Nha Trang, Tet Offensive. How many? Had to be at least a battalion to have Russians with them. Then his odds were low. If now was his time to die, he was ready; his bags stayed packed. But until then...he'd see what he could do.

What were they blowing? Something down the block.

Jeff Madsen rolled out of bed, naked, vulnerable, groping for his M-16. Not there...nothing. Now he couldn't protect her.

Trucks revved. Metal screeched, pushed over concrete. More shouts. The machine gun tore holes in the night.

The sounds weren't close, though, and no rounds were coming in their direction. The danger wasn't critical, unless the VC started a house-to-house search. In that case she'd be better off without him.

He held her to him, stroked her shoulder, and kissed the corners of her liquid eyes. The dark delta between her legs caught his sight.

The memory of a few hours ago brought back a flood of others. There's nothing like the primal act of mating to put reality into perspective. A third of a century returned in a flash, jamming the pieces of his life back into place. This wasn't Vietnam, it was Kyrgyzstan. He didn't meet her in a Special Forces bar but at the embassy...Ainoura. And he wasn't in his twenties anymore but in his fifties. Instead of an infantry advisor, he was now a State Department foreign aid official. But somebody out there was turning Bishkek into a combat zone.

Jeff picked his slacks and polo shirt off a chair and put them on. They were civilian, felt flimsy. He stepped to the window to pull back an edge of curtain; she hissed no, but he did it anyway. It was her curtain, but he had to see how close they were.

He looked out over the sprawling Central Asian capital and the Kyrgyz Air Force base across the street. At the corner a metal gate had been blown open. It had been part of a walled perimeter, had blocked a road leading into the base. Next to the guard house lay a soldier, chest dark with blood, a stubby rifle strapped across it. Two trucks—a pickup and a semi—were driving over the runway. A machine gun was sandbagged atop the cab of the pickup, and the men behind it wore ski masks and long robes in the eighty-degree heat. He moved toward the door. To defend her, he had to get the rifle.

"Don't go," said Ainoura, her English returning. She folded her arms over her breasts.

"I'll keep them away from here." The force of ancient reflexes was propelling him out. His brain knew he was in Kyrgyzstan, but that didn't matter, part of him was still back in Vietnam, had always been there, and that part was in charge now. Combat again. No choice.

"I'll be back." He waved, but it was half a salute; then he was out the door, running on automatic pilot.

A full moon filled the hot, deserted street with silvery light.

18

Rows of ramshackle three-story apartment buildings stopped at the wall of the air base. Wisps of cordite smoke floated and swayed; the acrid incense of death, its odor brought back airstrikes in rain forests, mortar barrages in rice paddies. The war of his youth seized him and dragged him back into battle.

The Kyrgyz soldier at the gate was dead, staring upward with eyes dull and distant. Thirty-five years ago, John Randall had lain like that in a rice paddy while Jeff held his hand and apologized to his corpse. A wave of remorse, still fresh, swept over him.

Most of the sentry's tan uniform was stained ruddy brown, and without blood his skin was pale. About eighteen, he'd been trying to grow a mustache. Even in death his expression held the hopeful curiosity of youth. The boy would have wished other than a chest full of holes for himself. So would his family.

Jeff could see human figures behind the curtains of dark apartments, but no one came out. He peered through the twisted gate. Across the runway the raiding trucks halted in front of a building. Toward them, down the airstrip, drove two Kyrgyz police jeeps, sirens shrilling.

From the back of the pickup a raider leveled a recoilless rifle, a long tube for firing rockets, at the police jeeps. Fire spewed from both ends. The round skipped off the runway and exploded in the air, a brief yellow blossom in front of the jeeps.

The defenders swerved and turned. They fired pistol shots, their little pops puny compared to the recoilless rifle.

On the invading pickup, the RR loader slid another rocket into the tube; the gunner corrected his lead and shot. This round hit a police jeep broadside, knocked it over, swallowed it in fire. Bodies tumbled through the blaze and black smoke. Flames danced on the concrete; in their orange light a man writhed and screamed, the sound high and airless.

Jeff wished he could snuff out the fire, cup the dying man in his hands, and blow life back into him. Take him home, God. Take us all home.

The other jeep turned 180. As it fled, machine gun tracers chased it, ricocheting off the runway like shooting stars. The gunner found his range, and lines of light plunged into the jeep. It drove faster, trailing wails, until the driver slumped over the wheel.

As it veered and slowed, a policeman leaped out, fell, staggered to his feet, and ran. Lights sparked toward him, seeking him; he whirled, arms waving, a dervish in the stars. Jeff thought he would be hit, but he kept running and finally disappeared in shadows.

Jeff nodded his congratulations after the running man.

Machine gun tracers skipped back to the jeep, silencing the cries. The Kyrgyz Air Force troops shot up a mortar flare, which burst open in the purple sky and cast a stark, swaying glare onto the land.

A dozen raiders in gas masks leaped from the back of the semi. One of them threw something against the door of the building; the others flattened against its wall.

The door blew in. Two of the raiders ran to the hole, tossed in grenades. Instead of an explosion, gray smoke curled out: tear gas. Coughing soldiers emerged from inside the building. A machine gun burst dropped the first three in the doorway; the other two raised their arms in surrender. They paused, gagging, until their need for air pushed them forward. They stepped over their piled comrades and raised their arms higher. The machine gun crumpled them over onto the others.

The raiders ran across the bodies and into the building. Jeff was starting to dislike them.

Air force troops peered around the corners of barracks, shouted back to those hiding, all of them confused and frightened. One hoisted his automatic rifle around a corner, sprayed a full magazine wildly at the trucks, then ducked back. More sirens...the chuffing of a helicopter.

Jeff checked the civilian streets and saw they were quiet; there was no assault outside the base. Ainoura was safe.

The raiders emerged from the building carrying a heavy object on a wooden pallet. Straining, they lifted it into the semi, then climbed in after it.

A Kyrgyz Air Force helicopter, louder now, flew around a hangar and passed low over the trucks. The thieves on the pickup swiveled their machine gun skyward. The chopper hooked back, leveled out, and opened fire on the pickup. Phosphorescent streaks met in both directions as they dueled. The rising tracers from the truck fell behind the chopper: the pickup gunner's lead was off. He corrected, sparks flew as he hit the fuselage, but he was too late. He jerked as the chopper riddled him, then slid limply down. The chopper widened its fire to the rest of the pickup. The recoilless gunner and loader crouched and covered their heads before they died. A spatter of dark holes appeared on the roof of the cab.

A raider leaped from the back of the semi and lifted a long cylinder from the bed of the truck. He adjusted the firing tube over his shoulder and aimed its missile at the chopper; a flash illumined his masked face. A blazing dart reached the aircraft, which exploded into a furious sun, silhouetting its frame and four humans in fire, and fell to earth, crashing with a whomp of aluminum on concrete. The chopper bounced once, rotor still whirling, tail breaking loose and dangling, then crunched down into a flaming hulk. A door gunner freed himself, stumbled out, and hobbled a few steps before fire covered him and brought him to the ground. The blaze filled the cockpit; strapped in, the pilot flailed his head and arms. Jets of light sprayed from the wreck with loud cracks as rockets and cartridges cooked off in the inferno. A rocket spurted along the runway and exploded against a hangar. The pilot sat still, turning black.

Another dad who won't come home, thought Jeff. What happens to the kids? His father—killed in Korea after the peace talks started. He saw again his mother's face that never lost its grief. Here he was, still at war, caught in the grip of the fever again. That's what happens to the kids: they grow up to be soldiers.

Aviation fuel flames washed over the runway, spread toward the trucks. The pickup burst ablaze from its own leaking gasoline. A wounded raider tried to limp away, but his robes caught fire. He stumbled and fell, then crawled frantically before being engulfed. Chanting aloud, he raised his hands beseechingly, then prostrated himself in a final bow of prayer.

Al-Qaeda? Could be. Or maybe Taliban, Jeff thought. The *jihad* comes to Kyrgyzstan...spreading like those flames.

Whatever they were stealing, he didn't want them to have it. Especially terrorists. He had to try to stop them, even if they killed him. Death might be an improvement. Lots of things were worse than dying, and he'd been through some of them lately.

The chopper burned next to the pickup, the two enemy crews side by side. Gouts of flame burst from the hangar as a plane inside ignited.

The tide of fire on the runway reached the semi; the truck

was rolling, its wheels blazing circles. As it raced beyond the fire's edge, the SAM man ran and leaped onto the back; comrades' arms pulled him in. The truck turned and drove towards Jeff.

Stop them. No matter what it takes. Jeff looked down at the young sentry; flies had found his drying eyes, and he smelled of the decay we all carry inside us.

Since you won't need this, maybe I can settle a score for you...and for lots of other people, Jeff told him as he pulled off the submachine gun, still warm and wet from his gushed-out life. He unbuckled and took the web belt holding the ammunition pouches; it was too small, so he hooked it over his shoulder.

The submachine gun looked like an Uzi, but its rough metal work showed it to be the Czech prototype the Israelis had adapted. Jeff had fired the Israeli improvement at Bragg...a long time ago. He couldn't remember where the safety was. He found a switch and flicked it. The barrel was too short to be accurate at distance; he'd have to wait till they were close. A dark exaltation surged through him as his combat instincts took over. Death was no big deal. Not theirs. Not his own.

In the sky the flare sputtered and went out, leaving them in moonlight. The troops lofted another, a soaring stem of sparks that burst into a radiant blossom. Jeff glanced toward the air force barracks, hoping for signs of a counterattack, but saw only soldiers huddled in shadows. *Guys, it's good you can see, but it takes more than looking. Fight back, damnit!*

Jeff darted into the street and tried to push the blasted metal gate shut. Still hot, it burned his hand. He pushed it with the gun butt; it closed but swung back open when he released it.

He returned to the sentry: *Need your help.* He dragged his limp body to the gate and laid it against the metal to prop it shut. The boy didn't mind. From their side it might look barricaded; they'd at least slow down.

The wooden guard house had been scorched and half blown down by the initial explosion at the gate. He took a chair from it, leaned it against the concrete wall, and stood on it. It wobbled but held his 190.

Stop them.

At sixty meters, the semi was close enough for him to see a masked face behind the wheel. He aimed at it, squeezed off a burst, and punched holes in the hood. Either the battle sight was

22

off or he'd lost the skill. He aimed the next burst at the roof. It shattered the windshield and the face behind it. Must be the battle sight.

As the truck swerved, the man next to the slumping driver grabbed the wheel. Jeff tried to give him three across the chest to match the sentry's. He missed. The man lowered his head to a crescent above the hood and kept steering. From the back a guy hung out and fired a rifle at Jeff, but his aim was shaky. Jeff emptied the magazine at the cab, bracing into the satisfying jolts of the recoil. The crescent disappeared; the truck slowed and stalled.

A dozen raiders jumped from the back. With their ski masks and AK-47s, they looked to Jeff like hooded priests of a religion of death. As he reloaded, his adrenalin rush overrode the fear. He was back in action. All that mattered was the mission: Stop them.

Several thieves leaned against the truck to steady their aim as they fired their AKs; Jeff ducked as chips of concrete stung his face. They were good. He didn't want to look back over the wall, but he had to. When he did, a man in rippling robes and black mask was running towards him holding a grenade. He stopped and pulled the pin, but as he raised his arm, Jeff sent him a burst. The raider fell, the grenade rolled away, and he crawled for it as Jeff traded fire with his comrades by the truck. Although the man's wound was interfering with his crawling, he was trying very hard to reach the grenade. As he seized it, it went off, taking his arm and half his head away.

The others redoubled their fire at Jeff, but now their bursts were too long to be accurate. His proto-Uzi wasn't as good as their AKs at this distance, but their truck offered worse cover than his wall. He could see one thief's knees as he knelt by the corner of the semi. When he hit them, the guy toppled away from the truck. The man's legs just flopped when he tried to move them, so he pulled himself toward cover with his forearms. Jeff hesitated. This crawling creature was a human being, like him, like the sentry. But his side had started the killing. Jeff raised his submachine gun and held the man in his sights. A voice inside said, *Don't kill him.* But another voice yelled, *They're trying to kill you!* He forced his finger against the trigger and hit the raider again.

A comrade darted out to rescue the man. He bent down, grabbed his hand, and dragged him to the truck, then his body twitched from Jeff's bullets. He fell on top of the other, and the two lay humped together.

Instead of Enemy, Jeff saw them now as pathetic humans. Ex-humans, thanks to him. He wished he hadn't shot them—too much death in the world. A feeling of dank foulness crept over him, but he shook it off.

The others pulled men out of the cab, one screaming, one still. They tried to start the truck.

Jeff shot at the tires. Sparks flew from the hubs, but the rubber stayed firm. He fired at the grille to puncture the radiator, but no water ran out. Battle equipped.

Troops from the base, dark figures in firelight, gathered at the building and began shooting at the semi.

Another raider ran towards Jeff, his shawl flapping like a cape, and threw a grenade. Jeff glimpsed its trajectory, jumped down, and dived into the remains of the guard house, hoping the plywood would at least slow the shrapnel. He lay head covered, afraid to die. The grenade thunked to the ground. Just as he thought it was a dud, it exploded.

A blast of white heat singed his body; concussion lifted him into the air, slammed him against the wall, jabbed his eardrums. The roar battered them and popped his eyes open. A wall was falling on top of him, the floor heaving. He closed his eyes and saw a spray of light as a plywood slab crashed into his head.

He crawled out of the splintered guard house. He could hear nothing. The smoke smelled like a thousand Fourth of Julys. Running men could be almost on him. Expecting a grenade, he glanced around the gate. The semi was rolling towards him; those thieves who could move were jumping into the back.

Seared and bleeding from shrapnel punctures, Jeff limped across the street and hid behind a building. The semi slowed at the gate, then pushed through, its Mercedes emblem gleaming like a peace symbol. The gate nudged the sentry's body and scraped past, leaving it in the road. The wheels of the truck rolled over it, compressing it so that each tire bounced less than the one before. The limbs jerked under the wheels.

Jeff ran, too afraid to shoot. As he fled, he remembered a saying of General Giap, the North Vietnamese commander who had outsmarted the Pentagon: "Knowing when to quit is half the battle."

"Go away," Ainoura said through the door when he knocked.

"I'm hit. Let me in." He pushed the submachine gun around to his back so she wouldn't see it.

"No. Men find you here...kill both us." Her voice was choked with fear. "I no want die."

Jeff knew the feeling, but he was in need. He was bleeding from helping her country's air force, and she didn't want to get involved. An old story. "They're gone. They got what they wanted. They won't be back."

"Then police come. Lose my job, maybe jail."

"I'm on the police side."

"No...go away please quick." Her voice had become a hiss.

OK...she could have it her way. It was her place. He'd already left a dribble of blood at her door.

"My watch." His voice showed his resentment.

"What?"

"My watch...I left it."

She padded away. He waited, listening to sirens from the base wailing uselessly. The door opened a crack, chain on; fingers extended his ancient Rolex, bought on R&R from Nam. He took it; the door closed, dead bolt clicked in.

Jeff's jaw clamped shut and his chest burned. He hadn't expected a ticker-tape parade, but he'd hoped at least for a place to wash off the blood...a gentle hand to soothe the brow, maybe even thanks for trying to stop them from stealing it...whatever it was. Had to be something major for that kind of operation. But he hadn't stopped them: they'd got away with it, they'd won. He'd failed, and now she was through with him. He raised the edge of his hand in a kiss-off salute and started down the steps, woozy from shock. His ears throbbed and ached and rang with sadistic electronic music.

The door across the hall opened a sliver; a woman's voice, Kyrgyz accent softening the edges of her English, asked, "Are you hurt?"

He nodded. He didn't want to go back out on the street.

Cholpon opened the door wider; her eyes took in his singed and wounded body. Who was this tall, bleeding man? His coarse, glowering expression repelled her but something else about him drew her. Underlying the violent red flaring from his aura were the blue and gold of spiritual potential. He gave off none of the dense, opaque murk that had surrounded the men he'd been fighting. He was very much in need of help that she could give. She gestured him in.

Grateful for sanctuary, Jeff stepped into her hall. Her lustrous dark eyes enveloped him with attention. The gaze was too intense for him, so he looked away, then stole a glance back at her and, despite his pain, was pleased by what he saw. Her face held a delicate symmetry of Oriental eyes, high cheekbones, a little nose, and a small, shut mouth. Straight black hair spilled over the shoulders of her silk robe. The robe curved generously over her breasts, in at the waist, and out again at the hips, alternations of abundance and leanness. She stood erect with her arms down and her hands cupped in front of her. A little over five feet tall, average for Kyrgyz women, she came up to his shoulder.

Seeing the submachine gun on his back, Cholpon's lips pursed into a frown; her hand moved trembling to the collar of her robe. The man's a killer. You saw him kill.

Jeff needed to reassure her. "*Spasibo*, thank you...for helping me," he said in his lame Russian.

"You are welcome," she said in her much better English. She stared intently into his face, then widened her focus to take him all in. Pondering, Cholpon pressed her palms. He was violent but not cruel...not hateful. He had much light shining beneath much pain. He was the one Djamila meant. It had begun—meet it head on. "Come," she said and walked down the hall.

Jeff followed her, appreciating her shelter, intrigued by her gaze, wondering why she was helping him. They stood awkwardly in her living room. He dropped his arms to his side to look less threatening, but when she saw the shredded, blood-soaked sleeve of his shirt, she winced and clutched her arms. She gave him that appraising stare again, first focusing deep into his eyes, then out to see him whole. As he met her gaze, Jeff could see that stronger than any fear in her was a quiet self-composure. He had the eerie feeling she was examining his thoughts. She motioned him into the

26

bathroom.

He unstrapped the submachine gun and ammo and set them near the door. She chose not to look there.

In the bathroom he took off his shirt and was greeted by the battle-stink of his armpits and the torn flesh of his triceps. Bits of plywood stuck out of the gash. The arm had shielded his head; its hair was burnt away, skin reddened. He thanked it for its fealty.

She wouldn't touch the splinters, so he jerked out a bunch, then yelled and gripped the sink. As pain chased away shock, his fear returned, rushing up in waves. Again he heard the thunk of the grenade, saw the flash, felt the blast, his helplessness as the shack blew apart. Back then, it had been too fast and vivid to be frightening, an existential instant. Now was the time for terror, swelling out of the belly, making him shake and cringe.

Seeing his desperation, Cholpon overcame her squeamishness and began to rub his neck and shoulders. Her small firm hands soothed the tremors. Her murmurs salved the spasms away and calmed him. She held his hand. The dread was still there, but it no longer ruled him.

The prospect of more pain decided him against washing the wound. He'd have to get pumped full of antibiotics and tetanus serum tomorrow anyway. The US embassy doc was on leave, so he'd need to find a local *vrach*.

As Cholpon wrapped the gauze bandage around his shoulder, he appreciated the shapeliness beneath her floral robe, the brush of her breast on his arm, her hip against his leg. Her woman's fragrance wafted a promise of stronger scents and tastes below. He was suddenly glad he'd lived...although lately he hadn't much cared to.

Cholpon tried not to brush against him. *He stinks of sex and he's already sniffing me, the randy old dog.*

"From the window I saw you." She forced her nervousness away and spoke in her business voice. "You were the only man who went out there. Everybody else stayed inside and hid. I thought, maybe you are Russian soldier and work on the base. But you are American. Why did you fight? You have friends there?"

"No," Jeff said. "Terrorists...I didn't want them to get away with it." His voice turned rueful: "But they did."

She pulled out a strip of tape and began fastening the

bandage. "Don't care about yourself?"

He started to say, Not much, but changed it to: "Some things are more important."

"Oh?" She stepped back and beaded him with a look he translated as, Cut the crap.

Jeff mulled over the jumble of reasons that had sent him out there. "I did it...just to do it."

"You do these things before?"

"Not for a long time."

Cholpon returned to taping the gauze. "I am glad they did not hurt you more." She glanced up at him wryly. "We have not so many bandages."

"I'm glad too," he said. "What do you think they took?"

"Maybe...money?" she replied.

"Always a good bet. Could be a safe with the air force payroll...couple of million *soms*. That'd be worth it for lots of people."

She cut a final strip of tape and finished the bandage. "How long you been in Kyrgyzstan?"

"Oh, about eight months."

"Such things like this...they usually don't happen here, even now with the changes." Her voice flowed with musical cadences and the lilt of her accent. She put the medical supplies back into the tin cabinet.

"Good news," Jeff said. "Actually they don't usually happen in the US either. But we put them all on TV. Everybody sees them and thinks they happen all the time." His voice rumbled with bass notes and long Wyoming diphthongs.

The klaxons of emergency vehicles grew louder as they approached from several directions, medleying with the sirens from the base. A police car screeched to a halt out on the street by the gate, its radio blaring frantic dispatches.

He told her he'd like to take a bath. She was embarrassed, flustered, then maybe relieved. Only death reeks worse than fear. She started the tub. With medical authority, she warned him against getting the bandage wet, then left quickly.

Jeff stepped out of his slacks for the second time that night. Aside from the worst headache of his life, the damage wasn't too bad, since the plywood had stopped most of the grenade. He had more shrapnel punctures down his left side, but they weren't

28

bleeding much, already puffing closed, but red and stinging inside. The thought of probing tweezers tomorrow made him clench his teeth. He remembered mortar fragments being plucked from his pulpy arm at an aid station near Ban Me Thuot.

A knock on the door was followed by her hand holding a towel and sheet: his winding cloth, perhaps. Or the closest thing she had to a man's robe.

Soapy water smarted as he washed off blood, stench, and her neighbor's perfume. He wondered if they were friends and if Ainoura knew she'd asked him in.

He came out of the bathroom wearing the sheet like a toga; now it was his turn to be embarrassed. The separation had made them strangers again. Cholpon had brushed her hair and set out cookies, tea, and aspirin. She held up a bottle. "I have some of my father's old brandy. You need it?"

He hadn't wanted a drink this badly in the nine months since he'd quit. Fighting back a thirst that was centered in his throat but scourged his whole body, he resisted the urge to grab the brandy and down it. The liquor would put his ragged nerves to rest, chase away the fright, but after that he knew what it would do to him. Been there...much too often. He'd spent only one year in the bottle, but it'd been enough to break his life wide open. He shook his head. "No, thanks."

She nodded in approval.

They sat in sagging chairs in her living room and sipped the tea, weak and sweetened with raspberry syrup, from white porcelain bowls. His fingers shook so much the tea sloshed out, so he gripped the bowl with both hands. He ate a cookie. It was a local brand from the bazaar, usually bland, but now it tasted fine. He munched several, then swallowed four aspirin. When they hit his stomach, nausea seethed up. He gripped the chair arms and resisted the urge to retch as his mouth filled with salty saliva. Gradually the queasiness passed, and he was able to swallow. Vomiting on her rug was the last thing he wanted to do.

His head swirled with clangor and pain, and he wanted to cry. *Don't do that either.* Trying to grope out of it, he pulled his chair closer to hers and ventured a glance into her eyes again. Their depth and softness drew him; he seemed to fall through her wide-dilated pupils into a shining black mystery. He saw his own tiny image splashing and playing there. It was too much, so he shifted his gaze to her irises, which were rings of dark brown not as deep as the pupils. He felt dizzy, so he looked out to her face, nestled like a bud in its sheath of black hair. He liked the contrast of her short straight nose to the curving lips below it. She was smiling slightly, and he could feel himself smile back. Her smooth, fine-pored skin was the light yellow of almonds, except for a reddish-brown mole on her cheek.

Nervous and self-conscious, Jeff looked around the apartment. Although clean, it had been cheaply built, probably in the 1950s, and then not maintained: water stains blotched the ceiling, cracks ran down the walls, gray linoleum surrounded a thick rug, its blue-and-red beauty out of place amid the drabness. The furniture was old but could never be called antique: mass-produced functionality in the Soviet style. A *stenka*, a dark wooden mass of cabinets and shelves, covered one wall.

On a table next to a lamp sat a gold-framed photo of an old woman with mountains behind her, wind fluttering her shawl. Her eyes were like Cholpon's, and looking at her calmed him.

"Your mother?" he asked.

Cholpon glanced at the picture and smiled. "My *Shayka*. But in a way my mother too."

He looked at her puzzled.

"I'm a Sufi Muslim," she explained. "She is my spiritual teacher."

Jeff thought about the rippling robes running at him and the prostrating prayer of death on the airstrip. He imagined the teacher to be a female *ayatollah*. He fought back a giddy wave of panic. Wanting to change the subject, he asked Cholpon where she worked.

She hesitated, then said, "On a farm." He made the mistake of telling her about a USAID program he worked on that gave insecticide and nitrogen fertilizer to farmers. She looked at him as if he'd turned into a monster. "*Nyet!*" She sat straighter, chin out, ebony hair cascading back, eyes now blazing, arms open, square hands with short, ringless fingers reaching at him. "No good." She gave him an impassioned mini-lecture about the virtues of manure and natural bug chasers. The chemical way was poison, genetic engineered seeds a fraud. Organic farming made better sense, especially with so many people unemployed.

As Cholpon got more worked up, she slipped into Russian and Kyrgyz, so he understood only part of what she said, but he enjoyed watching her. People always look their best when they're talking about something they believe in. She could well be right. But all he believed in now was his yearning for her, for the refuge she offered from the death outside. Her womanliness was the opposite of the killing out there, and she brimmed with a balm that could wash it away and restore him.

But his attraction to her was more than that. She had an intriguing quality, a fascination he'd never encountered before. Jeff stood up, took her hand, and said, "Let's talk about it on the couch."

They sat together on lumpy springs, and he told her he'd like to discuss it sometime when he could focus on it more. He tried to hold the sheet closed without much success. It was stippled with blood. Seeking solace, he bent to kiss the full lips of her little mouth, more out of neediness than lust. Just to hold her and feel her affection would be enough.

Cholpon flinched and turned away. Part of her wanted his embrace, but not now, not yet. Djamila was right—there was a tie between them...something unfinished. Despite the differences...a deep pull towards this strange man. She'd known him before— another life. But what had he become since then?

As she stroked his hand, a charge of *Shakti* energy flowed from her into him; too much for him now, it shattered his defenses. The tremors seized him again, but worse. He shuddered and gasped, inner sirens wailing louder than any outside. He closed his eyes to block the tears.

The battle returned in instant replay. Every muzzle flash, each hurtling grenade was aimed at him. A horde of hooded men strove with all their skill to kill him—and he them. They were all death's devotees, serving it worshipfully, eager for their turn to partake of the sacrament. This time there was no high, just the certainty of annihilation.

Out there, part of him had been craving that. Now, touching her, it seemed insane. Wasn't this human creature beside him enough? Didn't her caring make up for the dreck?

His lack of answers made him clutch her like the spinning earth. His sheet fell away, and he was just a naked man, sick of life yet afraid of death.

Pushing her fear aside to tend to his, Cholpon rolled him on his stomach and knelt beside him. She ran her fingers through his heat-crisped, gray-brown hair, and his scalp tingled as it relaxed. Avoiding his puncture-speckled left side, her hands stroked his body in long sweeps, then sought out old horrors knotted in his flesh, thrust into them, kneaded them away. But as they loosened, they spilled long lurking memories. Nam again. Gray men rushed from the bamboo, fleeing the globe of napalm his side had sent them, firing their AKs. As they charged his patrol, he made the same stupid mistake all over again, and John Randall bled to death in the rice paddy because of him.

That brought another, deeper wave of anguish. It was always after him, usually just the grip of withered fingers, now a full-blown strangle. She rode this one too, rubbing his quivering body, purring ancient sounds of comfort, turning off the lamp. Her voice became a song, part lullaby, part chant, its clarity penetrating and soothing—a song he'd needed to hear all his life.

He reached for her. She gazed at him for a long moment, his face glowing in the revolving red and blue lights of the police car outside. Moved by his need and their reawakening bonds of long ago, she gathered him in her arms and held him to her, draining his trauma away.

He sought her ravenously, one hand clutching her, the other parting her floral robe to reveal a nightgown covering her breasts. He touched them, caressed their softness, and finally felt safe: they could erase the memories and heal the wounds. As his lips moved eagerly towards them, Cholpon pulled away and touched her fingertips to his temples with a pulsing motion. She placed one hand on the crown of his head and the other on his forehead and massaged in hard circles, then pressed sharply between his eyes.

Jeff's brain flooded with a rush of clear white light. He shuddered, sighed, and fell asleep smiling at her breasts.

He could tell she had doubts about how this was going to turn out. She was trying to be optimistic, but her face showed her qualms. As Jeff broke an egg into the saucer of milk, poked the yolk, and mushed it all into a yellow glop, her expression approached revulsion. She'd never had French toast before. She looked interested as he sprinkled cinnamon on the bread, then glanced away with puffed cheeks when he dunked it.

Jeff felt tentative around her, unsure how last night had ended. He hurt worse today, the gash in his arm burning, shrapnel punctures along his left side red and swollen. His body was a sack of aches, and his torn, bloody shirt stank. He'd had to cut off fused-together clumps of singed hair.

Cholpon seemed calm but a little distant; her face was tranquil except for darts around her pursed lips and oblique eyes. "The police pounding on the door last night...wake you up?" she asked him.

Jeff shook his head. "I was out."

"They ask what I saw...what I knew. I said nothing."

"Good."

Cholpon made the tea while thinking about her guest. How strange...he just lurched back into her life. After who knows how much lost wandering. So far apart, so different...and now together again. Brought an old closeness back with him...not really memories...traces from a farther past. But who was he now? A warrior this time...took a dark turn...foolish game. So naturally he was like a hurt child. But still a good heart. She could handle him.

Jeff plopped two slabs into the hot butter; the sizzle and aroma revived her interest. After he flipped them, her expression said they didn't look too bad.

When one was on her plate, covered with rose petal jam, she was willing to give it a try. She bit a piece with small white teeth, smiled.

They ran out of bread before she ran out of appetite.

In her tiny kitchen they sat on wobbly stools, too short for comfort. The pans were battered aluminum, and the oven door was held shut by a bent coat hanger. The place was definitely Soviet, but she'd managed a few gracious touches. They ate with silver forks from plates of antique porcelain with a design of flying cranes. An embroidered cloth covered the rickety table. Violets bloomed by the open window. Another photo of her teacher, standing by a lake, smiling serenely, was propped near the table with a fresh rose beside it.

Cholpon noticed his glance and set the picture in front of him. The old woman stared up at him as if there, tiny but powerful. When Cholpon fixed him in the full gaze of her dark-brown eyes, pupils large even in morning light, he was caught in the crossfire of their attention.

"Her name is Djamila."

Reverberating into him, the name expanded a huge, hollow cavern inside. He felt the floor drop out from under him, and he swung suspended but safe in another kind of gravity. Although he liked the feeling, he had to glance away from both women. Must still be in shock.

His chest began to ache, and a tangle of images flowed into his empty mind. A woman transplanting rice in Vietnam, the graceful dip and sway of her body as she thrust the new shoots into the paddy, wading knee deep in brown water, pants rolled to her thighs, a bag of shoots hanging from her shoulder, a conical hat of rice straw shielding her from the sun, her work becoming a dance but without flourishes, just simple beauty of motion. A young boy, probably her son, crouching on the earthen dike, hunting crabs with a dip net. Jeff led his patrol of Vietnamese and Montagnard soldiers, all of them tired and scraggly, past them. One of their troops had been killed in ambush, and they carried his body wrapped in his poncho, suspended like a sagging hammock from a bamboo pole. The woman met Jeff's eyes with a mixture of curiosity and fear, then looked away and continued planting. The little boy stood up and saluted as they marched by. At the bend of the trail Jeff glanced back at them silhouetted in late afternoon shadows against the sun-silvered paddy water.

He hadn't thought of the incident since, but the woman and boy were suddenly here in Cholpon's kitchen, filling him with loss. He wanted to hold them, to apologize to them, but for what?

He tried to find a reason for his sorrow, to put his rational mind back in control. He hadn't harmed them or any civilians. His battles had been against other soldiers, and he respected them as fellow warriors, recognized their prowess. But maybe he felt guilty for losing the war, for leaving the mother and boy to be taken over by a communist dictatorship.

Thinking in these abstractions was comforting, let him draw away from the pain. He stole a glance at Cholpon, who was staring at him in silence; her glistening dark eyes spurred other thoughts: He hadn't harmed them directly, but he'd been part of a death factory that had turned millions Vietnamese into corpses...and no mention of them on the Wall in Washington.

Now hundreds of thousands of Iraqis and Afghans killed.

He had to force his breath, and his chest seemed to cave in. Trapped, he glanced again at Cholpon, whose face had turned ancient and sad, whose eyes were dark and slanted like the woman's in the rice paddy, and whose mouth broke in a slight smile of great comfort to him.

As he looked at her, though, the ache increased. His face contorted, and he bent over, gasping. Suddenly the little boy was him and the woman was his mother. Instead of on the dike, he was playing on a couch at home. Hearing a cry, he looked up to see his mother reading a slip of yellow paper. A yellow telegram envelope lay on the rug. With a wail she let the paper fall and clutched him in her arms. He could feel her tears and tremors, and he became very afraid.

Wrapped in a poncho, his father floated by. His father used to call him Champ. Jeff hardly remembered him.

That is why you hurt, an inner voice told him, and why you hurt others.

Jeff screamed and jerked his body rigid. Cholpon shuddered but kept her eyes fixed on him.

Don't overload him with trauma, she thought. Enough for now.

Cholpon's face soothed him, unlike his mother's then, which had spread her terror into him. Jeff trembled and broke out in a sweat. He could see his father's Purple Heart in its velvet case, the medal's enamel worn away from Jeff having touched it so often. His father had started World War II as a private, fought his way across the Pacific, and mustanged up into the officer ranks. He had returned to Wyoming after the war, then got drafted again for Korea. He wrote letters home about the bridgehead at Pusan and human-wave attacks at the Yalu River, which Jeff's mother read to him. She told and retold him stories about his father, then made them up when he demanded more. After cease-fire negotiations began, he wrote that he'd be home soon, but in one of the many flare-ups, he was shot in the throat by a sniper near Panmunjon.

Jeff wailed as his mother had, then caught himself. No! Shut it off. Don't go crazy in front of Cholpon. That was half a century ago, no point in wallowing in it. If you get stuck in all that, you'll always be a weak little kid. He dragged his mind away from the feelings, as if pulling himself out of quicksand. He tried to hold himself tight, to make a shell out of his skin, so he didn't turn into a jellyfish. Think about something else. Look at something else.

Out her window he could see the remnants of last night's destruction on the base. The chopper and pickup truck lay on the runway, blackened hulks surrounded by guards. He'd killed five men out there last night. They'd been human beings just like him and his father, little packets of woes and joys. Jeff chewed on his lip. In his mind five accusing faces confronted him. He saw a veiled widow in a black robe wailing over a casket in a hot stony village while another little boy watched. And would later become a soldier.

Jeff moaned but choked it down. He brushed tears from his eyes. Don't slide back into that muck. Life is hard, you have to be hard. Stay rational, stay in charge.

Sorry, he told the widows, but next time keep your tough guys at home. They came here to kill, left other wives and kids crying.

Jeff closed his eyes and prayed: God, Allah, whatever they call you there, please comfort them. Was I wrong to kill the killers? I don't know. If I was, I'm sorry. There must be some better way than this. Please help us all to find it.

He blinked his eyes open. Near the twisted gate, now chained shut, he saw the stain of the young sentry's blood and a chalked outline where his body had lain. *Peace, lad, they never gave you a chance.*

Jeff imagined his own silhouette there. How did he feel today about being alive? Confused. Death might have brought relief, an early out from a life turned sour. But then he never would've met Cholpon.

She was standing quietly beside him, looking away so as not to make him self-conscious.

Policemen were measuring distances and taking notes. The

security van from the US Embassy was parked off to the side, and next to it several men in suits were conferring.

The sting of the shrapnel was now anguishing, and his punctures oozed. His face was flushed with a low fever from the beginnings of infection. The grenade was still doing its job, festering its fragments into his flesh. No wonder his thoughts were weird. He'd get over it. Switch channels.

Back at Bragg he'd seen a dismantled grenade; wrapped around a core of white plastic explosive was a wire coil segmented to explode into thousands of jagged bits. Once in an assault near Cung Hoa he'd hurled one at a VC foxhole, seen a helmet loft up in the blast, and later found a mangled body. This time he'd been on the receiving end...but luckier.

A bird flying in front of the window drew his sight. It landed at a feeder attached to the casement. The chickadee, head as black as Cholpon's, clung upside down to pluck a sunflower seed, then flew to a nearby branch, held the seed between its feet, and pecked at its breakfast, chattering all the while.

Cholpon stole a glance at him. What stress, she thought. This man has a load of karma. All that suffering stored up inside him. Let him draw back. Better that he gradually open up.

Her trim but shapely form moved next to his lanky height. "You like birds?" she asked, her accent gliding the words together into a purr.

He thought of all the pheasants he had blown out of the sky and then eaten and said guiltily, "Sure."

"Let's see if birds like you." She picked up a jar that sat near the window. "Hand." He held it out, and she poured a few peanuts into his palm. "Put it out there, don't move." He rested his hand on the concrete sill. She whistled two high, piping notes. "Peanuts are their favorite," she said. They waited but no bird came. She looked at him dubiously and whistled again. From above a chickadee circled and fluttered, landed on the sill, then hopped on his hand with a brush of feathers and tiny feet. Avian toenails gripped Jeff's finger like a twig. The pert little bird cocked its head to examine the choices, knocked them about with its beak, picked out the one it wanted, then sprang back into the air and flew away with a chirp.

Jeff gazed after it, delighted. "I could feel it push

away...powerful little thing. So light...but still strong."

Cholpon nodded at him as if he had passed a test. "Different kinds of strong," she said.

Jeff sprinkled the seeds on the sill and looked back at her, avoiding her eyes. As he took in the feminine fullness under her coral blouse and tan skirt, she turned away, but then lowered her eyes and allowed him to look at her. He yearned to trace the geography of her curves, the swell of breasts and hips, the plunge of her waist. He tried to recall the press of her limbs, the smoothness of her skin last night. Her face held a peacefulness that drew him. He wanted to stroke her ebony hair, pinned up in a chignon. He liked it better down, but with temperature in the mid eighties it was probably cooler this way.

You shouldn't be making love to any woman besides your wife, a voice inside him insisted. But Valerie wasn't his wife anymore, he countered; she'd filed for divorce. *It's not final yet,* said the part that still loved her; *they could get back together.* Dream on.

Jeff and Cholpon talked awkwardly, trying to ease the tension. He told her Wyoming was a lot like Kyrgyzstan—high mountains, dry plains, extremes of hot and cold—but didn't have a city as big as Bishkek.

She sneaked a glance at her watch. She had to leave; he had to go to the doctor. He wanted to stay, but it was time to say good-bye. She didn't have a phone, so he gave her his number.

He stepped closer to her. She's not the kind you just grab, he told himself, struggling with desire. He leaned his face into hers, brushed his lips against hers. It was a morning kiss, light and dry. He wanted to kiss the space between her wide-set eyes, but held back. She touched him carefully, knowing that he hurt. She smelled of gardenias and garlic. They pulled apart. Her hand, small with closely-trimmed unpainted nails, stroked his unshaven cheek.

"Can I come back and see you?" he asked.

"Yes," she said.

A smile crinkled the corners of his hazel eyes.

"But you must leave your gun at home."

He folded his hand, scarred from a VC mortar barrage, around hers and pressed it to his chest, then kissed the top of her sleek, dark head.

The farewell door loomed. He turned and picked the submachine gun off the floor; she frowned. Trying to look peaceable, he pointed at it and at the street. She got him a plastic shopping bag, and he put it inside.

Cholpon wouldn't kiss him with the gun, but she waved and so did Jeff. "Thanks...for everything," he said.

What am I getting into? she wondered.

What a woman! he thought.

Jeff yelled as the Kyrgyz doctor probed in his arm for shrapnel. The doc must have been of the Marxist medical school that disdained local anesthetic as bourgeois luxury. "More Novocain" topped the list of all the things Jeff wished he could say in Russian.

He hadn't realized pain came in so many colors: pink splashes, crimson blossoms, lavender washes. The worst, though, was clear white light, the same he'd seen last night when Cholpon had touched his forehead. Then it had been delight, now it was agony, sharing the same tint. He tried to divert himself with thoughts of all the colors emerging from white.

The doctor pushed the pincers deeper into the meat of his shoulder; Jeff cursed him and gripped the table. Shoved to the depths, his mind reached for Cholpon. The image of her face formed, then her body. Her hands seemed to cup his head. At her touch, he knew that everything, not just the colors but the universe itself, comes out of this light.

He got some comfort from this insight but would have traded it for more Novocain.

The old Russian woman, blue eyes clouded by cataracts, smiled when Jeff handed her a blanket. The old man behind her, square chin stubbled with gray, just took his and glanced away. Both of their lined, stolid faces showed eighty years of endurance. All the old plans of workers' paradise and the new plans of consumer paradise had left them with nothing but resignation and a stubborn strength.

Jeff looked down the line of elders waiting for blankets and felt better: giving things away to people who needed them was the best part of his job. And the painkillers he'd bought at a sidewalk pharmacy were starting to take effect. Today his team was working at a senior citizens' center. A faint rectangle above the door marked where the portrait of Marx used to hang. Some of the old timers missed him.

Jeff ruminated on what the Kyrgyz were going through. For the retired, the change to capitalism had brought disaster. "Difficulties of redundant sectors in transitioning to a market economy." That's how the PricewaterhouseCoopers business consultants from the US labeled their ordeal. Jeff avoided them whenever he could. The people themselves called it *bednost*—impoverishment. Before, they'd had very little, but at least their basic needs had been met. Since the scrapping of the old system, their pensions had stayed low while prices soared, so now they were destitute. Compared to that lost security, freedom was irrelevant, just a word. Like the hordes of unemployed, they were paying a high price for free enterprise. They were too old now to become capitalists; all they knew about supply and demand was that their supplies were gone and their demands ignored. But although their material lives were grim, they were used to tough times; with grit and savvy they survived.

Foreign aid helped too. The US had spearheaded the drive to bring down communism, and now, since chaos in Central Asia wasn't in its interest, it was trying to patch up some of the problems caused by the collapse. The aid programs were mostly loans for the purchase of US-made equipment, a subsidy to our corporations. Jeff worked in the small humanitarian assistance program; he saw himself as a foreign aid Band-Aid stuck on a gaping wound. He could do only a little, but it was better than nothing.

He needed the job, too. It had been a lifeline that hauled him out of his deepest pit of self-loathing after the divorce. It still held him together, gave him a purpose, kept him from slipping back onto the sauce.

He handed a blanket to a frail Kyrgyz lady who chattered at him happily. Even with it, he knew she'd still be sleeping in her coat and cap.

August was early to give blankets away, but winter could sneak in fast here. Icy winds blew south from Siberia and north from the Pamir Mountains, catching Kyrgyzstan in the middle. Heat was a luxury most of the retired couldn't afford anymore. When he'd arrived last January, old folks, the more hardy ones, had been out with sledge hammers and wedges, breaking up tree stumps for firewood. Fortunately, Bishkek had lots of trees. The less hardy seniors sat on doorsteps with hats outstretched. Fortunately again, small change trickled into those hats, often from people in need themselves.

The blankets would help. They were US Army issue, and he might have slept under one of them, many long years ago.

"Hear anything about the shooting last night?" he asked Lance, his assistant.

"Shooting?" Lance perked up, switching from boredom to interest. "What was it?" In his mid twenties, Lance had blond hair, blue eyes, and a constant smile. He was almost great looking, which made his few flaws more noticeable. His face was square and rugged with broad cheeks, a low forehead, wide jaw, and small, upturned nose. His hair—too long for a crew cut but too short to comb into anything else—was strawy and tousled. His teeth, like those of many blonds, had a faint yellow tinge, but they were straight and even, set between lips stretched thin by his smile.

"I'm asking you." Jeff looked at him deadpan. "I heard there was some gunfire out around the airfield."

Lance's face showed a blank. "Oh that. No, that was just Erkin farting. Hey, Erkin." He didn't want to admit to not knowing. Lance was just out of the navy, which he'd joined after dropping out—Jeff guessed flunking out—of college. He'd enlisted on a four-year hitch for language school, where he'd learned Russian. That skill plus his veteran's bonus points got him this civil service job with USAID, but his plans were to angle his way into a big company expanding over here. The former Soviet Union, he said often, was the new frontier for business opportunities.

Erkin, their thirty-year-old Kyrgyz counterpart, glanced up from his client roster and shook his head in the obligatory it-wasn't-me look. A shock of straight black hair dominated his slim face and overhung his keen narrow eyes. Five-feet-six and wiry, he wore the traditional Kyrgyz black pants and gray-and-white striped shirt. His skin was the color of wheat, and his features were a blend of Middle-Eastern and Oriental: nose long, broad, and aquiline; eyes canted slightly upwards. The only person in his extended family lucky enough to have a job, he supported a network of relatives, everyone eking by. "Somebody shot chopper down, blew up whole place. Killed twenty. Nobody know why." His Kyrgyz accent, thicker than Cholpon's, blurred his English.

"No shit?" Lance was enthused. "Who was it...the Muslims?"

Since he was Muslim himself, the question embarrassed Erkin. "Nobody know," he said, spreading the fingers of his slender hand.

"Must be some reason," Jeff said and gave away another blanket. It was patched and spotted with cigarette burns, but it'd keep a body warm. He wondered how the Pentagon decided whether to fix a torn blanket or surplus it. Somewhere in the books must be a regulation, researched by a committee of captains, that spelled out how many patches it could have and how big a rip was worth mending. They needed to balance out repair vs. replacement costs, the morale of the soldiers vs. the morale of the congressional budget subcommittee.

Jeff was glad the blankets were light. If they'd been sacks of rice like last week, he would've been in trouble.

Usually they didn't hand out the stuff themselves but just gave it to social agencies to distribute. The local officials stole a certain amount and sold it; that was inevitable. But when USAID figured that over a quarter was getting ripped off, they cracked down and put the thieves out of business for a while by giving it to the people directly. USAID didn't have enough staff to do that for very long, and the local officials would make their lives miserable by finding all sorts of reasons to complain to the US Embassy, so after a few weeks things slipped back to the old routine. Jeff preferred handing it out personally.

When he had come to work this morning, he'd decided not to mention his involvement last night; he was ashamed of his failure and also wanted to avoid hours of bureaucratic reports. To explain his damage, Jeff told his two assistants his camping stove had exploded while he was trying it out. Since the injuries entitled him to a bit of help, he asked Lance to carry over a fresh box of blankets.

"Getting old and weak?" Lance jibed, always aware that thirty years but only two pay grades separated them. Lance matched Jeff's six feet but was heavier. His muscular wedge of a body tapered from broad shoulders and chest to narrow hips and legs that were a bit short in proportion to the rest of him.

"Could be." Jeff was weary this aching morning, but he was also ready for whatever it brought. He hadn't been so ready, though, for Cholpon last night. He hoped to get another chance. The echoes of her presence were still ringing through him. Already he missed the serenity that dwelt in the symmetry of her face. She was a shower of welcome rain in his desert.

Fred Garcia walked into the building. Usually the boss was too busy at the office to show up on site. He was wearing a suit—

unheard of. Brown eyes peered out of a round, soft-featured face that was disrupted by a jutting nose. The droop of his walrus mustache was countered by the smile of broad lips around uneven teeth. "We gotta shut it down for the day." He was using his boss voice, its gruffness countering the smile. "Got a briefing at the embassy."

They drove through Bishkek, which looked a bit like Washington: wide tree-lined streets, plazas with white public buildings, green parks. But the streets were potholed and clogged with cars burning gas that turned the air to acid, and the buildings were dilapidated. The government couldn't pay the garbage men, so mounds of uncollected trash were growing in the parks. Despite more poverty, though, Bishkek didn't have as many vagrants and thieves as DC.

For Jeff, the best thing about Bishkek was the mountains. South of the city soared a range, the Kyrgyz Ala-Too, that made the Tetons look like hills. Sheer granite peaks white with snow even in summer loomed above the capital and thrust their ragged silhouette into a sky of deep blue. At the foot of these mountains lay the steppe, an immense arid prairie sprawling down from Siberia.

Kyrgyzstan seemed to Jeff like Wyoming at the opposite side of the world, and not just in the raw power of its landscape. The people were as blunt and laconic as those back home. They had a passion for horses, riding them with great skill and panache, eating them with zest. They drove their cars faster but with less skill than they raced their horses. Some of them were still nomads, herding cattle and sheep and hunting with eagles. They were Central Asians who'd had a Turkic language and Muslim religion imposed on them in the seventh century by invaders from the Levant. Much later, Russian colonizers forced their Cyrillic alphabet on the language and tried to replace Islam with their state religion of communism. Now the Americans were here, bringing free enterprise, English, and Christian missionaries. The Kyrgyz adapted and endured.

Jeff felt both at home and totally strange here. Since he and Kyrgyzstan were making new starts, it seemed the right place to be. And he liked the challenge of getting along in a culture of which he hardly knew the language.

Jeff shared the back seat of the small Lada with Fred, who

was bulky. The boss's yellow foulard tie dangled short of his belt on his generous middle, its other end tucked into his blue oxford button-down shirt. His graying black hair curled thickly despite his fifty years, and his bronze cheeks showed the blue-black sheen of whiskers on the rise. The driver was dodging potholes, which kept bumping the boss against Jeff's arm. It hurt. Fred was an old Soviet hand, had been stationed in most of the republics and visited the rest. Kyrgyzstan was his favorite, but he didn't think it was much of a league. A new BMW zipped past them, ignoring the lanes and honking, its horn playing the tune to "Oh, Susanna." Fred scowled at it; sweat beaded his salt-and-pepper mustache. "In some ways it was better in the old days." He loosened his tie, knocking Jeff's arm. "First they'd lecture you on the virtues of communism, then they'd try to buy your jeans. Now they just try to sell you Herbalife."

Fred could stand to lose a few pounds, but Jeff couldn't see him drinking a diet shake. The USAID honcho gauged his moving up in the world by his switch from Jim Beam to Jack Daniels. Starting as a dirt-poor, whip-smart Texan from a tangled lineage of Mexicans, Indians, and cowboys, he'd gone on scholarship to the university at Austin. After a Ph.D. in political science and a brief, unhappy stint of college teaching, he'd ended up in the State Department. USAID wasn't the fast career track at State, but Fred had burned himself out striving in his youth and was now comfortable at a plateau.

The embassy was a small, but to Jeff a pompous, building with concrete columns painted to look like marble. It had formerly been a health clinic for the Party elite. Oak trees rose above it, dappling the sunlight in a way that camouflaged the crumbling walls and giving the building a pleasant, secluded look, despite the guards and heavy traffic on the street.

The briefing room was packed; all the USGs and half the ex-pats in town seemed to be there. Hating crowds, Jeff found a place at the edge against the wall. He stood straight, hands at his side, with something of the military unconsciously ingrained in his bearing. Lance fell in next to him.

Creigh Townsend, the civilian defense attaché, stood up front beneath the flag, a tall, tailored blade of tension. His blue-and-gray pinstriped suit and white shirt seemed to Jeff to have same expensive blandness as his rep tie. Beneath sparse black hair, his high forehead—smooth, bare, and pale as a reflecting shield—beetled over and dwarfed the lower triangle of his face. He drummed the podium with his long fingers and cleared his throat. "So, uh...we'll start." Over the drone of an overworked air conditioner, he spoke in the clipped style of the Chesapeake Bay gentry. "There's no point in beating about the bush, so I'll get right to the point. One of State's worst-case scenarios just happened. Gentlemen...ladies and gentlemen, that is...." He flicked his sharp blue eyes over to his boss, Ambassador Sarah Ettinger. "We're looking at a whole new ball game. We've got a loose nuke. Last night somebody stole one of the nastiest pumpkins ever. Broke into the air base...left twenty-three dead." He paused, sweat gleaming on his expansive forehead. His late-thirties hairline was receded toward vertical. "If this thing goes off, it'll take everybody in Bishkek."

As a murmur of alarm spread through the room, Townsend stood with jutting chin and tight lips. Jeff could tell he liked his power. "What they got was a Gagarin-9, a Soviet IRBM warhead. Back in the bad old days it was targeted on China. It's actually rather modest megatonage...but a real dirty blaster. The main kill operant is contamination, more than the fireball. Everyone—everything—within thirty miles contracts radiation sickness. Most of them will be fatals, but slow. As you can imagine, it totally overloads the medical infrastructure. Renders the area uninhabitable for about 40,000 years...unless you're a mutated cockroach." He looked around the room as if expecting a few wry chuckles, but this wasn't the MI audience he was used to. They were stunned into frightened whispers.

Jeff crumbled inside. He could have saved it. He should have stayed there, shot the driver as they came through the gate—stopped them. They would have killed him, but it would have been worth it, it would have meant something. The bomb would be safe, and he'd be out of this crap. Instead he ran to save his sorry ass. If he'd known what it was.... Ach, he'd probably still have run.

"What's your intel on who took it?" Bruce Watson asked. Half standing and hunching forward, the portly embassy logistics officer looked ready to grab whomever it was.

Townsend glanced at his notes. "We've got eleven bodies at the airfield, Arab dress, prayer beads, a couple of blood-soaked

Korans, no IDs."

"That's ID enough." Watson sat down heavily. He wore a white short-sleeved shirt and a red tie; the slightly frayed collar wouldn't button because of his expanded neck. A silver flat-top crowned his pink, jowly face, and meandering blue veins lined his round cheeks and nose. As people nodded at him, a friendly and confident smile lit his face and he hiked his pant legs up a bit.

Townsend's hand jiggled in his pants pocket. "Al-Qaeda and Taliban would love to have a firecracker like this. They've got active units in Kyrgyzstan, but we don't know for sure it's them. Could be what's left of Saddam's Amn al-Has...Iran...the Chechens. The Russian mafia could've stolen it...sell it to the highest bidder.

"This thing would be high on the wish list of lots of terrorists. If they didn't take it themselves, they'd pay major money for it. It's not too big, you could bring it anywhere: New York, DC, Tel Aviv. Use it for blackmail or just set it off. Get another revenge on the great Satan."

Lance nudged Jeff, who winced. "That's you and me, buddy."

Spare me, Jeff thought.

"Important thing is not to panic. We've got a good chance to get it back. The borders are sealed, every road out has troops on it. Delta Force is flying in. We're offering a ten million dollar reward. Somebody out there has seen something and knows where it is. Since Kyrgyzstan's Islamic, there'll be some sympathy for the perpetrators. But ten million dollars speaks pretty loud."

"I'd take it for that," Lance whispered.

"The Muslim element here may account for the good intel these guys had. Somebody told them the when, where, and how." Townsend grimaced. "This nuke was the last one in country...waiting to get shipped out and dismantled. Next week it would've been scrap."

"Instead, we all may be scrap," Ambassador Ettinger said over tented fingers. She spoke in the flat, regular tones of the Midwest. Her green silk suit and gold brooch contrasted with a plain white blouse. The lines of worry etching her forehead and mouth and the dark blotches of fatigue under her eyes made her look older than her forty-five years. Her nostrils dilated as she

47

breathed under the pressure. Jeff got the impression that the lives of at least everyone in Bishkek were weighing on her. She was a large-boned, strong-framed woman, and the suit had padded shoulders, but not for that kind of load.

"Possible but not likely." A smirk showed Townsend enjoyed contradicting her. The word was he was CIA, so she didn't have much leverage over him.

"What if they're cornered, Mr. Townsend?" she asked acidly, peering above her brindle reading glasses. "If they're fanatics, they'd rather set it off than lose it." Her hair was less neat than usual this morning, and she pushed a light-brown strand out of her eyes to stare at him.

Townsend tapped the podium impatiently. "Probably won't set it off in a Muslim country. Allah wouldn't approve."

"You hope." She kept her large blue-green eyes fixed on him.

He looked away, enough of a diplomat to let her have the last word. She frowned, uncapped her fountain pen, and began writing on a yellow legal pad.

"What about that chopper?" someone asked.

"Yeah. The Kyrgyz fought pretty well." Back in his element, Townsend grew more lively and leaned his lanky frame over the podium. "They almost won. Their chopper shot up the lead truck, killed six...till it got taken out with one of those sharp new little SAMs. The bad guys were equipped and they were pros.

"The gate sentry damn near stopped them. They wounded him going in, but he stood up to them coming out...killed five before they got him. They had to run him over. He's being put in for the Kyrgyz Medal of Honor." Townsend's eyes, raptor sharp under thick black brows, surveyed the audience as if to inspire them. He buttoned his suit jacket before stepping away from the podium.

"This briefing is non-classified, ladies and gentlemen. The cat's already out of the bag. At this point, better the truth than a lot of crazy rumors."

The group broke into anxious, talking clusters, and Jeff split, too down to want to see anyone. Finally he'd had another chance to do something right, but he'd blown it. He could picture fallout descending like snow on this hot summer day, flakes of death sticking to everyone, shrouding the city in lethal isotopes.

This damned world gave us few ways to make a difference in it and few ways to die well. To have stopped them would've been both. Now what did he have ahead of him? Thirty more years of this shit. Or, if the men in the ski masks got uptight, six months of radiation sickness. Either way, better to have stayed and fallen.

Out on the sidewalk people streamed by him, bound on missions urgent to them, trivial to the others. Jeff joined the throng, wanting urgently to go home and sleep. Taller than most of the crowd, he walked leaning forward, leading with his shoulders, the posture a holdover from the days when he'd been eager to get wherever he was going. Now the eagerness was less but the habits of body remained. He kept his left arm against his side, sweating in the green corduroy shirt he'd worn to keep the bandages from showing. His curly brown hair—frosted with gray, thinner than it had once been—riffled in the breeze. He wore it longer now, trying to cover the increasing bareness of his temples, an attempt that was vain in both senses of the word. Slightly crooked from being broken, his large nose gave a raffish, off-center cant to his long face. His hazel eyes, set deep under ginger brows, scanned ahead, alert to avoid collisions with his arm. He still hurt under the blur of painkillers, so his wide mouth was clamped shut, lips disappeared into a resisting grimace. The antibiotic shot was starting to take effect, so he felt less feverish.

Then he saw her, and his skin flushed warm. His hopes soared, denying the miles and misery that separated them, until a closer look sent them into a dive of disappointment. No, it wasn't Valerie; but the tall blonde Russian looked so much like her that he couldn't catch his breath. He felt like he'd swallowed a rock. She had the same sensuous stride and raised chin, avid blue eyes taking in the scene, face open to it all. As she passed him without a glance, he could see the differences, but he stared after her, mouth sagging with yearning and regret. Maybe someday his wife might take him back...if she ever got over what he'd done to her. He forced himself to look away, then stubbed his toe on a sidewalk slab that had been buckled by swelling tree roots.

The faces were a mix of the world. The pure Kyrgyz were northern Orientals of a stock similar to Native-Americans. Both groups had long ago gotten fed up with Siberian winters. The original Americans had crossed the Bering Strait, and the Kyrgyz

49

had migrated southwest till they reached the mountain spine of Asia. They'd prowled the valleys as nomads for centuries, enduring the newcomers who kept charging through: Mongols, Muslims, Europeans, from Genghis Khan to Tamerlane to Stalin. When the invaders weren't slaughtering the locals, they were fucking them, and these faces showed the blend.

Bishkek had been on the ancient Silk Road. Westbound cloth-and-spice caravans weary after trekking the mountains from China, eastbound gold-and-fruit caravans thirsty after weeks on the steppe, they all pulled in. Drivers and camels and horses rested here by the river; sometimes a driver liked this valley at the foot of the mountains and stayed.

Later the Russians came, first the Czar, then his killers. They'd moved into Kyrgyzstan in force, making it a colony then a Soviet Republic. For generations they'd dominated the Kyrgyz, but since independence the natives had turned the tables, discriminating against the ethnic Russians. The more things change....

Jeff grabbed a bus for home. A rattletrap made in Hungary, it was named Ikarus, after the Greek boy whose journey had ended in death. It was jammed, as usual. The great-grandmothers of the world, wrinkled babushkas wrapped in scarves and long, dark dresses even in this heat, were muttering into their whiskers. Next to them chattered kids in T-shirts made in Singapore with odd bits of English on them: "Racing Ahead, Eternal Image, Mr. Cowboy." An old Russian man hung on the rail, wearing canvas boots and his medals from the Great Patriotic War pinned to what looked like torn pajamas. A busty middle-aged Kyrgyz woman swayed back and forth; she'd indulged her new consumer freedom by dying her hair a punk shade of purple but still wore it in a bun. Bathing wasn't a priority here, so the air was a bit ripe.

Jeff gazed at his fellow travelers with a pained tenderness; he saw them all, this whole little jalopy of a world, covered with the gray, bleeding sores of radiation sickness.

Passengers paid as they left, and the driver was busy making change at each stop. A pile of bills, most worth about a dime, filled the open glove compartment, and above it sat a little lamp with a shade made from a Coke can. The dashboard was covered with pictures of fast cars—formula-one racers, Jaguars, Corvettes—and the sun visor with a photo of a naked blonde straddling a motorcycle. The windshield was a spider web of shatter marks.

Last night's semi, its windshield shattering under his bullets...where was it now?

The driver sat in broiling sun, shirt unbuttoned to his waist, and swabbed his ochre face and chest with a cloth he'd dipped into a pan of water. He lurched the bus through the traffic in search of open lanes and pavement without potholes.

Jeff didn't care for the way he was driving, but there was nothing he could do about it. He was like the guy who was driving his life. For the past two years Jeff had been a backseat driver in his own life, trying to be in charge, but something else had been at the wheel, sending him down dark streets, along freeways to nowhere.

But up until a couple of years ago things had gone pretty well for him. After the army he'd attended the University of Colorado on the GI Bill and taken a B.A. in history. His studies led him to the conclusion that with such a past, humanity can't expect too much from the present, so he tended to accept things other protested. He was too rebellious to be a conservative but not optimistic enough to be a liberal.

The war was a helpless sadness gradually fading. He tolled the names of dead friends in a litany of remembrance.

The harsh solace of the land drew him back to Wyoming, and he worked at various jobs to be able to keep living in Jackson Hole. He became a ski instructor in the winters and a back-country guide in the summers and ended up managing an outdoor equipment store. But a couple of years ago the booze took over and before he knew it he'd lost Valerie, the kids, the job.

And last night he'd lost the chance to save the nuke. But at least now he had one hand on the wheel of his life: he'd been sober for nine months...and some days.

An Oriental man, wearing sunglasses with the label still stuck on one lens, brushed by him to get off, hurting his arm. Instead of paying, the man elbowed the driver aside, snatched the bills from the glove compartment, and jumped out the door.

The driver screamed after him in Kyrgyz.

The guy was fast, but a big Russian waiting to get on grabbed him by the collar. The thief tried to jerk loose, then shoved the bills into his jacket pocket and raised his fists. The

Russian chopped the edge of his hand across the sunglasses, breaking them. As the thief grabbed for his eyes, the Russian jabbed him in the belly.

The Oriental doubled over but came out of it in a karate pose. Yelling, he made a few feints with his hands; the Russian backed away. The Kyrgyz moved like he'd had some training a few years ago and was trying to get his reflexes back. He kicked threateningly. People on the bus and street gaped at the entertainment.

The Russian sized him up—he stood a head taller than the thief—and snorted with contempt. He moved in, looping a roundhouse punch; the Kyrgyz ducked and kicked at him. It was clear what he was aiming for, but since he was kicking from a crouch, his shoe landed below the crotch.

He ran, but the long-legged Russian caught up. The big man gripped the smaller one around the head and rammed his knee into his side. The Kyrgyz yelped and tried to twist away, but the Russian lifted him by the neck and whammed him into the bus. Jeff felt it rock, and a few women cried out in protest. He shoved him to the ground, spat on him, and raised his boot. To protect his groin, the Kyrgyz rolled over; the Russian kicked him in the kidney. Snarling, he jumped on him with knees driving into his back, then lifted the smaller man's head and smashed it into the sidewalk.

The Kyrgyz groaned, tried to push him off but couldn't. Face blanched, he babbled a surrender; people watching seconded it. He was bleeding out of one eye.

Jeff hadn't been fond of the thief from the moment he'd knocked into his arm, but this was too much.

Instead of stopping, the big man turned the Kyrgyz over and hammered his fist again and again into the cringing face, like he was pounding a nail. He cursed him and lifted his hand for another blow. The Kyrgyz shrieked. His twisted nose was spewing blood.

The Russian had no skill, just size; he fought like the ranch hands Jeff used to bounce out of the bar in Jackson. But that had been twenty years ago. Jeff's bad arm gave the guy another advantage, but he didn't know it. If Jeff came on threateningly enough but left him space to get away, he might take off. "Stop it!" Jeff bellowed and jumped out the door. "Enough!"

People backed away. The Russian probably didn't understand English, but he saw someone his own size coming at him. He clamped one hand on the thief's quivering chest, reached the other into the jacket pocket, pulled out the money, leaped up with a sneer, and ran away with bills balled in his fist. The crowd watched him go and so did Jeff.

The driver muttered something, closed the door of the bus, and pulled away. The crowd switched its stare to the first thief, who was holding his hands to his face and jerking spasmodically.

Jeff walked the six blocks home, his long, doleful but determined face bobbing above the stream of his fellow pedestrians. He hadn't gotten the driver his cash back, hadn't even paid his fare. But he'd done what he could, and he could stand himself a little more.

Jeff stood among the thirty people waiting outside the Kyrgyz Air Force terminal. A US military cargo jet, hugely sleek, taxied past them. The American flag was emblazoned on its lofty tail, and as it passed by, Bruce Watson saluted. The others just stood in the heat. The C-141 Starlifter, silver wings sagging now without wind to support them, pivoted away from the green cinderblock building and stopped, gushing torrents of exhaust back over the reception party. Its turbines slowed from a roar to a high, hollow whistle.

Clothes flapping, eyes squinched, Jeff was reminded of the first instant of parachuting, the leap into the windy blast that blew everything, even fear, from his mind. It'd been a long time since he'd jumped, and he missed it. After the army, it had reminded him too much of the military, so he'd let it go and gone back to mountain climbing. Now he wished he'd kept it up: his mind could use some free-fall ventilation. A few years ago a friend had combined the two sports by climbing the Grand Teton and base-jumping off. Before his chute could open, winds drove him back against the granite, smashing his spine. Jeff and three others had climbed up and recovered the body, lodged in a spur. Hanging there, his face wore a faraway smile, as if he had seen something very beautiful just beyond his grasp.

The Central Asian heat shimmered on the concrete. Jeff looked at the burnt-out hangar filled with blackened skeletons of airplanes and at the blown-open armory from where the bomb had been stolen. Kyrgyz soldiers, laden with guns and grenades, sweating in flak jackets and steel helmets, guarded all the buildings, which now held nothing worth stealing.

Jeff thought of their comrades who'd been guarding the bomb. They should've come out the door shooting, not just coughing from the tear gas. They would've still died...but it would've been a better way to go.

Stray rounds had blown out a glass door on the terminal, leaving a gaping hole rimmed by shards. The guards now stepped through it rather than opening the door, ducking their heads under a guillotine-like slab of glass.

Jeff felt better today after sleeping for twelve hours. The fever was gone and the pain had subsided into a bearable ache. He glanced around at the embassy staff, a dozen Kyrgyz civilian and military officials, and a few diplomatic guests, hoping none of them would bump into his shoulder.

The Starlifter's clamshell rear doors opened with hydraulic smoothness, revealing a cavernous cargo bay filled with men and equipment. Ambassador Ettinger, wearing a dark-blue suit and an orange scarf, hair churning in the turbine wind, walked toward the plane. A trim black man with an eagle on each epaulette strode down the ramp and saluted her. She nodded formally and shook his hand. They stepped to the side, and the Delta Force company double-timed in two columns down the ramp.

The troops wore desert camos, helmets, and full rucksacks. They carried submachine guns at port arms, and each turned his stubby weapon upright in a rifle salute as he passed his commander and the ambassador. The fifty men jogged into a rectangular formation, a bit uneven by strict military standards. Jeff smiled, thinking back to the similarly lax formations in Special Forces compared to the tightness of regular infantry divisions. Commandos had to be given more slack than conventional troops, they weren't as moldable. They were more willing to die, but it had to be on their own terms, not blind discipline. Jeff could see, though, that the Delta Force's jungle boots were spit shined and their fatigues starched. He shook his head in weary memory. The army was still cranking out violent guys and then forcing them to be obsessed with their clothes. He could handle the violence OK, that was the point of the whole thing, but the prissiness drove him up the wall.

In a dress shirt without a tie, linen slacks, and running shoes, Jeff stood in the shade of the terminal building, glad not to be in the army, yearning to be in the army. Part of him tried to hold on to the peaceful afterglow from Cholpon from yesterday morning, but the sight of soldiers ready for battle pulled him back into his military past. He had hated the pointless make-work of stateside duty—painting jeeps, polishing barracks floors—but had liked the extremity of combat patrols, the heightened pitch of life on the brink.

His thoughts wandered back through a maze of might-have-beens. If he had stayed in, he could've switched over to SOG and done recons into Laos and North Vietnam. He could've spent a couple of tours in El Salvador with a little cross-border action into Nicaragua. Jumped into Grenada and Panama, done a few clandestines into East Berlin, sky dived into Iraq to spot Scuds, called in air strikes in Kosovo, torn up the al-Qaeda and Taliban in Afghanistan, then back to Iraq to dethrone Saddam. Now he could be here, one of these mean dogs on a short leash, on his last mission before retirement. Or—anywhere along the line he could've bought it, gone out in a quick flame. Either way might've been better. At least it seemed that way now, looking down roads not taken.

The ambassador and colonel walked slowly through the ranks for the ritual inspection of the troops. Each soldier snapped to attention as they approached, saluted, then snapped to parade rest when they had passed. We who are about to die salute you, Jeff thought.

The chief of staff of the Kyrgyz Army, General Osmonaliev, a short burly man whom Jeff had met once at an embassy reception, welcomed the troops and thanked them for their assistance. With their help, he said, Kyrgyzstan would continue to enjoy enduring freedom.

Delta Force began unloading equipment. They carried off M-60 machine guns, 60 mm. mortars, crates of rations and supplies, and a bundle of stretchers. Next they drove the vehicles down the ramp: two jeeps, four camouflage-painted dirt bikes with almost silent engines, a two-and-a-half ton truck, and a Fast Attack Vehicle—a stripped-down jeep frame mounted with a machine gun and recoilless rifle.

The soldiers stood at parade rest around the equipment to cordon it off on the runway. All these great toys, Jeff thought, fighting back another wave of nostalgia and regret. But now maybe he could have them and still have his freedom, a civilian warrior, his own free ragged self, the best of both worlds. He pulled himself together, stood with as military a bearing as he could muster after all these years, and walked over to the colonel, who was standing by the plane talking to the pilot. *Whatever you do, don't say Sir*, he told himself.

When the pilot left, Jeff stepped in. He quickly read the name on the starched fatigues. "Colonel Hobbs, I'm Jeff Madsen, your USAID liaison." He didn't mention that his position was entirely self appointed. He'd learned that in times of confusion it's better to assert authority even if you don't actually have it.

Hobbs was a small man with intense dark eyes set deep between high cheekbones and a ridged forehead. His nose had been flattened, in contrast to Jeff's, which had been bent. He wore a green beret with a colonel's silver eagle on it, a Delta Force patch on his left shoulder, and a Special Forces patch on his right, indicating he currently commanded Delta Force and had seen combat in Special Forces, Delta's parent organization. The colonel extended his hand; his grip was solid but not the exaggerated crush some soldiers affected. "What'd you say your name was again?"

"Madsen, Jeff Madsen. I'm ex-Special Forces, spent a year on an A-team in the Central Highlands."

Hobbs' interest switched from casual to keen. "Which camp?"

"Cung Hoa...up near Ban Me Thuot."

"I know the place. Beautiful country up there. You had Montagnard troops?"

"Sure did."

Hobbs smiled, a sudden flash out of a dusky face. "Best damn people I ever met...and we left them there for the NVA to grind down. Worst thing about the whole sorry mess was what happened to the Yards afterwards."

Jeff nodded, thinking about Lo-ee and M'noc, his friends and fellow warriors, hoping they'd survived the "re-education" camps.

"When were you there?" Hobbs asked.

"Sixty-seven to sixty-eight."

"Tet, huh?"

Jeff held up his scarred hand. "You got it."

As they talked, Kyrgyzstan slipped away, and it seemed as if they were standing on a runway in Vietnam, ready to be helicoptered into the jungle.

"I was a lieutenant with the Mike Force then," the colonel said. "What a time."

Jeff thought back to the Tet Offensive, when his A-team had been pounded by North Vietnamese cannons and nearly overrun by their infantry. His captain, gut-shot with artillery shrapnel, had radioed a request that the Mike Force, the elite Montagnard unit commanded by Special Forces, be air-dropped into the camp. The reply came back negative, they were already committed to battle. His team had fought off the NVA at Cung Hoa but lost a third of their men. Jeff asked the colonel: "You guys were fighting up around Pleiku then, weren't you?"

Hobbs winced at the memory. "Yeah...with no air support. We couldn't even get medevacs. Not enough choppers to haul all the wounded...no room in the hospitals even if we could get them there." The colonel gave him a probing look, to test if they were on the same wavelength. He smiled slightly and said, "I'd do it again in a minute."

"Know what you mean. Nothing quite like it," Jeff said. Their eyes met across a third of a century. "I thought you might need another hand here."

"You're with USAID?

Jeff nodded. "I know the country and the people...how to get around and deal with the hassles."

"Might could use you, Madsen. You coming to the briefing this afternoon?"

Jeff smiled. "Yes, sir." It was the first he'd heard of the briefing, but he'd definitely be there.

"See you then." The colonel turned to Sarah Ettinger, who was waiting to introduce him to the Russian ambassador.

Jeff walked away kicking himself for letting the word of subservience slip out. Those reflexes were pounded in so deep. At least he hadn't saluted.

Jeff noticed a man on the edge of the group. The thin Oriental stood facing Jeff but staring beyond him at the Delta Force equipment. Rigid in a blue blazer with a crest on the chest pocket, he tightened his elbow into his side, then relaxed and glanced casually around. He shifted a bit to the left, stood still, and again pressed his elbow into his side. The movements were hardly noticeable but nonetheless strange. Jeff looked behind himself and saw a dipole antenna mounted on a mast. He looked back at the man, who was now facing other electronic gear.

Maybe the guy was snooping the new equipment...a hidden camera. His blazer swelled a bit beneath the crest, but it could be just a wallet and pack of cigarettes. Jeff watched him repeat the procedure several times, covering it with other motions. If Jeff grabbed him and turned out to be wrong, it wouldn't go well. Plus his arm wasn't up for much grabbing. But he couldn't just let him spy.

Jeff walked over to a Delta trooper standing nearby. "Sarge, we got a problem..." He explained the situation to the tall, black soldier. They looked at the guy together for a minute, and the sergeant thought it over, scratching his closely trimmed mustache with his thumbnail and appraising Jeff with oxblood eyes. He gave a quick nod and the trace of a smile.

They circled around and came up behind the man as he stood facing a cluster of satellite dishes. Jeff felt like a hawk swooping down on its prey. The thin man sensed their presence and stiffened.

As he passed him, Jeff pretended to stumble and lurched into his side. "Sorry," he said, groping at the guy to steady himself and clutching the crest of the blazer. Underneath was something hard and rectangular, too firm for a wallet or cigarettes. He pulled the blazer open and saw a wire at the inside pocket.

"Grab him," he called to the sergeant.

The man tried to pull away, but the sergeant pinned his arms. "Diplomat!" the man screamed. While the trooper held him fast, Jeff yanked the blazer down over his shoulders and reached into the pocket. With a slice of pain Jeff felt a stitch tear out of his wound.

Jeff pulled out a camera and wire. The spy acted the victim, shouting, "Let me go! Police, help!" He strained against the blazer, trying to snatch the camera back, but couldn't move his arms enough. His skin flushed carroty. As he held his fury in tight control, it seemed to spray from him. "You attack an embassy officer," he hissed.

A group of staring, murmuring onlookers formed. Jeff called to them, "Get the ambassador...the US ambassador."

The sergeant followed the wire down the man's side to the shutter release. He yanked it out along with a piece of his shirt that it had been fastened to.

"You thieves!" The spy's eyes flared.

"Pat him down for weapons, sarge," Jeff said.

While the guy squirmed and more people gathered, the trooper searched him, finding no weapons but a diplomatic passport from the Democratic People's Republic of Korea. Ambassador Ettinger arrived, followed by Colonel Hobbs and Creigh Townsend.

The man spoke immediately to the ambassador. "This is an insult to my government. Your men attack me, steal from me."

59

"What happened here?" Sarah Ettinger gave Jeff a look that said, You'd better not have messed up. Her emerald earrings brought out the green in her large aqua eyes, but her light-brown hair stuck out in tufts from the turbine wind.

Jeff explained the situation, over interruptions from the spy.

The ambassador looked through the passport. "Mr. Roh works at the North Korean embassy here," she said. "Let him go."

I could get burned for this, thought Jeff as he and the trooper released him.

The man straightened his blazer in self-righteous dudgeon. "My property," he demanded.

The sergeant, holding the camera, stared questioningly at the ambassador. "Give it to me," she said, and the sergeant obeyed. She asked, "Is this yours, Mr. Roh?"

The man thrust out his hand. "Your men steal it."

She held it beyond his grasp. "And what's inside?"

He remained silent, mouth a tight line.

"Maybe they stole something from inside," she explained. "We want to make sure you get everything back that was stolen...so we should check inside." She turned the small, black camera over and began pressing and twisting things, trying to find the latch.

"Give camera now...or I protest to Kyrgyzstan government."

"These things are hard to open, you know. Not as user-friendly as an Instamatic," she said, fiddling with the camera and ignoring him. He lunged for the camera. The sergeant grabbed for him but got the blazer instead; its blue silk ripped up the middle but stopped him. The trooper wrenched the man's arms behind his back, loured over him, and asked, "Where you goin'?"

"Now, now, Mr. Roh. Be patient. I'll just be a minute," the ambassador said, unperturbed. "Mr. Townsend, take his name down in case we need to get in touch with him."

The CIA chief's venatic blue eyes fixed on the slender Korean. "I already have a file on Mr. Roh. We know he's with UFD."

She glanced up at the spy, said, "You see, we do care," and returned to working on the camera. "Ah...there we go." The back popped open. "Good! The film is still there. They didn't steal that." She held it up to show it to him. "Let's make sure the pictures are OK." She pulled the film out of its case in a long curl and held it up to the sun to look at it. "Hmm...I can't tell." She turned to Colonel Hobbs. "What do you think?"

Hobbs peered at the gray strip and shook his head. "Doesn't look like they came out. Maybe they're over exposed. You ought to have your camera checked," he told Mr. Roh.

"Good idea," said the ambassador. She held the camera out to the spy, then pulled it back. "Did he have any more film?" she asked Jeff.

"No," he replied, "and no weapons."

"Good, Mr. Roh. Here's your camera. Let him go, sergeant."

The trooper released him. He shook himself, glowered at the gawking crowd, and took the camera with trembling hands.

"Give my greetings to your ambassador, Mr. Roh...and tell him I'll be in touch." Sarah Ettinger turned and walked away, followed by Hobbs and Townsend. Roh stalked off.

"Good work," Jeff said, extending his hand to the sergeant. "Thanks for your help." They shook. "I'm Madsen."

"Blake," said the trooper. He gestured to the equipment the man had been photographing. "The North Koreans would love to know more about that stuff."

"Can't blame them," Jeff said. "They want to know what to expect...when we go after their nukes."

"I'll be there." With a wave, Blake walked off to rejoin the Delta Force.

Jeff headed across the runway. Stroll away and disappear like the Iraqi Republican Guard, he thought. The sun cast an iridescent sheen over the fuel stains where the chopper and pickup truck had burned. Death by fire—probably the worst. But maybe you just lose your air and the shock blocks the pain and it's over quickly. For the sake of the chopper crew—and the hundreds of thousands who'd died under US napalm and the dozens of Buddhists who'd died protesting it—he hoped so.

Jeff pulled bits of singed skin from his burnt arm. It was starting to itch as the skin sloughed off.

Farther on, fading chalk marks outlined the bodies he'd killed, and their blood stains formed Rorschach blots. What does that shape remind you of? An nuclear bomb exploding. And that one? A fatherless child. Jeff's chest tightened, but he fought off the remorse that was starting to swamp him. Hell, he'd just moved those guys one step ahead of the rest of us. Better a few of them than all of Bishkek. We can't have fanatics running around with nuclear bombs.

The ceaseless wind from the Asian steppe was already erasing the chalk outlines of their bodies. It had also blown drifts of trash against the concrete wall at the far side of the base. Newspapers, plastic bags, aluminum cans, Styrofoam—Kyrgyzstan was getting modern.

The metal gate the raiders had blasted open was unrepaired but now chained shut and guarded by a squad of soldiers in full battle dress. Typical military response. The bomb was already gone, it was the only one. Were these guys out looking for it? No, they were standing around making a show of force. As Jeff approached, they closed ranks. The majority were Kyrgyz but a few were ethnic Russian. Most looked like the sentry who'd been killed here: young and full of potential that would never be realized. The sentry was probably their friend...now a martyred hero.

A stocky Kyrgyz sergeant strode toward Jeff waving his arms rejectingly and speaking loud Russian. Any Caucasian was assumed to be Russian. Jeff understood enough to know the gate was closed and he'd have to go around. That would mean a forty-five minute walk.

Jeff said, "*Amerikanski?*" and pulled his ID card from his wallet. "*Kartochka.*" He handed it to the sergeant, who perused it, his bristly mustache twitching on the broad disk of his face. The Kyrgyz government issued all foreign officials a card that was supposed to cut through bureaucratic hassles. Usually the minor authorities were intimidated enough not to harass anybody carrying one. They didn't want complaints that would cause the foreign ministry to jump on their boss, who would in turn jump on them. But the sergeant was a brave and greedy man. He was paying more attention to Jeff's wallet than the card.

In his fumbling Russian Jeff tried to explain that he needed to see someone on the other side of the gate.

"*Nyet,*" the heavyset sergeant said. Short arms akimbo, he strode back and forth ranting about how foreigners had broken into the base, killed Kyrgyz soldiers, stolen Kyrgyz property. He stared at Jeff accusingly, then at his wallet.

Jeff kept a sheaf of one-dollar bills there for minor

extortions like this. A successful bribe called for delicate diplomatic skill; it needed to be offered discreetly or it would give grounds for insult, which would lead to demands for more cash. The briber had to make a pretense of concealment in order to acknowledge the higher position of the bribee; otherwise it might seem like tipping a lackey. Jeff lowered the wallet to his side, pulled out a couple of bills, and palmed them in his hand. He stepped next to the sergeant and pressed them into his waiting fingers. The sergeant glanced down at the bills and shook his head curtly, mustache wiggling. Jeff sighed, took out two more dollars, handed them over, and slipped the wallet back into his pocket.

Two corporals walked up to stand on either side of Jeff. The privates then also moved toward them, but when the sergeant barked a command, the privates fell back in line. Rank hath its privileges, Jeff remembered. The bottom troops needed to be reminded of their lowly status, to give them incentive to servile their way into promotions so they too could share in the booty. With a scowl that was mostly ritual, Jeff took his wallet back out and gave each corporal a dollar. He didn't enjoy giving them the money, but they needed it a lot more than he did. They all had families, and inflation had made their wages barely enough for one person to live on. Most people were poorer now than they had been under communism, and he was here as part of the victor's foreign aid program.

The corporals exchanged glances with the sergeant, then held out their hands for more. Jeff shook his head. The sergeant folded his arms across his chest and shook his. Jeff thought about walking all the way around the base. Definitely worth a few more dollars to get to her place now. He gave the corporals each another bill. They nodded contentedly, having just made more than their day's pay, but the sergeant blustered in, demanding more to show his superiority to his subordinates. Jeff forked over another George, but the sergeant, eyes gleaming under thick lids, gestured for more. He stared at the wallet, mouth open. "Nope," Jeff said, shoved it back in his pocket, and walked toward the gate, avoiding eye contact with the sergeant so as not to seem to be defying his authority. As he approached the troops, they parted and let him pass.

A Russian private caught his eye in Caucasian camaraderie.

He was older than the Kyrgyz, with a Sad Sack look that said he knew he'd never get promoted now but just had to stick it out until he got his pitiful pension.

When Kyrgyzstan had been part of the Soviet Union, the ethnic Russians here were on top, holding more than their share of power. Like all privileged groups, they thought they deserved it, and many looked down on the Kyrgyz, calling them *chorniye*—blacks. Now after independence the Russians were at the bottom of the list for hiring and promotions. Some were philosophical about it, but most thought it unjust—they'd never personally done anything to harm the Kyrgyz, so why should they suffer. Jeff had heard it before, from whites in the US who didn't think they should have to sacrifice anything in reparation for centuries of slavery.

He stepped over the chain that held the twisted gate closed, wondering what these troops had been doing during the attack. Probably lying low, waiting for orders, hoping someone else would die and not them. And someone else had. The sentry's bloodstain still darkened the macadam. His corpse was probably lying next to his killers' in the government morgue. Rigor mortis was gone and they were all settling in for a nice relaxing rot. And the boy would get a hero's funeral, Kyrgyz Medal of Honor around his neck, for not firing a shot. Jeff felt jealous and resentful, then ashamed of it.

The rubble of the guardhouse where he'd dived away from the grenade had been carted off. The blast had torn a larger-than-average pothole in the pavement. Near the wall lay brass casings from the shells he'd fired.

Twenty-three dead. But people are dying all the time, he told himself. They probably haul that many stiffs out of the hospital every night. We're all getting blown away by all different kinds of wind, so what does it matter?

But while we're still here.... Which apartment was Cholpon's? He scanned her building, one of a row of three-story stacks of gray concrete whose drabness was only accentuated by red-painted bas-relief figures of factory workers, farmers, and soldiers. He found her balcony; geraniums bloomed on the balustrade and potted bamboo grew in the corner. The curtains were closed. He hoped she was home. But what if she was with another guy?

Climbing the stairs, he saw that his blood drops had been

scrubbed away. He rang her bell, imagining her face and eyes. No answer. He knocked on the heavy wooden door. After a minute his spirits sank. He wrote her a note: "Sorry I missed you. Thanks again for your help. Give me a call—89792. Jeff." He had an urge to kiss the note, then felt foolish and just slid it under the door.

A door across the hall opened. Jeff turned to see Ainoura standing in it, and he flushed with awkward embarrassment. She must have recognized him through the peephole. She managed a strained smile and said, "Wrong door...I over here. I glad you come back." In the heat she was wearing next to nothing: a yellow T-shirt barely covered her underpants. One long leg protruded, the other hid timidly behind the door. He thought of how they had wrapped around his back. Her expression was both apologetic and inviting. "Sorry I so mean. You forgive me? I so scared." The yellow silk of her shirt emphasized her cascading jet-black hair and the points of her small breasts. She gestured him with a tilt of her head, her lips a pale rose invitation on her ivory skin, her eyes a dark allurement. "We talk inside."

She had flirted with him when he had met her at the embassy where she was applying for a visa. Jeff knew it had more to do with his nationality than with any irresistible qualities he might have. She was looking for a ticket West. And he'd asked her out more for her pretty face and sleek body than her personality. Such shallowness had to end sometime, he thought, and their half a night together was probably the best they had to offer each other.

"Actually...." Jeff faltered. "I came to see Cholpon."

Ainoura's expression changed from coquettish to quizzical to crushed. "Her?" She pointed towards Cholpon's door.

"Yes."

"But...she's...." Her features condensed into anger as she stood speechless. Finally she shouted, "You go to the devil!" and slammed her door.

Jeff gave her another salute and started down the stairs, smiling this time. *Ainoura, I guess we're just not meant for each other.*

"This man! Why am I supposed to be with him? I don't want him," Cholpon said in Kyrgyz to Djamila. "He's...well...he tried to...."

Djamila gave her an indulgent, even encouraging smile. "And did you enjoy this?"

"Enjoy? I didn't let him!"

They sat together on a bench shielded from the sun under a wooden pergola covered with morning-glory vines. The heart-shaped leaves and curling, twining tendrils shone translucent green in the strong light, and the funnel-shaped flowers held the same clear blue as the sky.

"But did you enjoy his trying?" Djamila asked.

Cholpon blushed and turned away, wanting to dissolve into the cool shadows and splashes of green light filtering through the leaves. She'd never heard Djamila speak this way before. Jeff's opening her gown, the touch of his hand on her breasts, his eager expression had been with her ever since. In dreams, driving back to the Circle, even while meditating she had played out the possible next steps, unable to stop herself.

But unable to yield to it either. For years she'd struggled to free herself from that need, and now she didn't want to get dragged back into it. During her apprenticeship in the Circle she'd fought a long battle with lust and thought she'd won, but now it was flaming up again, stronger than ever.

In her late teens and early twenties, before becoming a Sufi, she'd gone along with the orthodox communist view of sex: the glass of water theory. The Party, to hasten the eradication of bourgeois puritanism, had declared that sex was just another bodily urge, like thirst. If you want a glass of water, just drink it. Sex is no different. If you want it, just do it.

As a student at the Kyrgyz National University and as a young teacher of music and English, she'd downed quite a few glasses. The more she drank, though, the thirstier she became, ending up miserable and unsatisfied. She kept expecting there to be something more to it than a quick slug.

Eventually she saw a pattern in her relationships: At the beginning he wants her but she doesn't want him, but gradually his desire excites hers and she lets him. Then she starts wanting him, but at that point he stops wanting her and looks around for somebody new. After repeating this cycle, she'd come to the bitter conclusion that most men didn't want to *have* a woman, they wanted to have *had* her, another drink, another name on the list.

But in fairness not all men were like that. There's also the kind who just flops over on his back, throws his arms and legs up in the air, goes goo-goo, and expects you to take care of him forever.

When she realized she was addicted to something she didn't enjoy, she'd met Djamila, who'd lifted her out of those cravings. Meditating put the brief joys of girls and boys into perspective. Within the deep pool of her being lay depths of divine bliss, a fulfillment that didn't evaporate.

During her first years as a Sufi she had a few more unsatisfying affairs. After deciding for chastity, she was beset by lurid dreams and fantasies that became increasingly depraved as she ignored them. This just strengthened her resolve, though, and she became scathingly antisexual to defend against them. Eventually she won and they faded. Somewhere along the line her prudery must have faded too, because for years she'd been at peace about the whole topic. Now Djamila seemed to be urging her to plunge back into it all.

Not again. She couldn't bear to be dependent on a man, to worry about how he's thinking about her, when will he stop wanting her.

But a Westerner, an American...maybe they're different. Maybe really able to communicate and share as equals, to see you for who you are, not just assume the whole universe revolves around their needs.

Somehow she doubted it.

She looked at the lush vines and made herself think about them instead. Morning-glories thrived in this sunny, arid climate, spreading in rampant profusion. The astral being who dwelt in them and drew power from their psychedelic seeds effused a wizard-like presence around the plants, a vapor of enchantment Cholpon respected but avoided. Some Sufis chewed the seeds for the visions they produced, but Djamila recommended against this, saying they, like other drugs, use up your energy and leave you weak and dependent.

Come to think of it, she said the same about sex, so why was she now telling Cholpon to go ahead? So much for the

67

distraction of the flowers. "I thought we were supposed to be celibate."

Djamila waved a frail arm dismissively.

"'Supposed...supposed,' that's a word people fall down over. This celibacy here is just to build up your inner power. It's useful for that. But in itself it has no importance."

The *Shayka*'s expression was half a grimace, half a smile. "Sex is not something bad...it's like going back to being an infant, it can be fun but a lower level. And it reinforces duality, makes you think there's something outside yourself...that you need...in yourself." She sat drifting on distant memories. "If the desire is mild, we can let it go, but if it is too strong, if it takes over your mind, better to go ahead with it. Fighting against it makes people crazy." She laughed like one relieved to be beyond the struggle. "Doing it makes them crazy too, but at least they enjoy life a little more."

Cholpon raised her bare feet on the bench and wrapped her arms around her knees, black hair falling thick and straight around her face. Jeff...her objections were just thoughts. Her yearning was a feeling. According to the Veda, feelings were a better guide than thoughts; the emotions, when not confused by stress, were a more refined tool than the intellect. "So...I should...be with him?"

"'Should'—that's another one like 'supposed.'" The teacher flapped her wizened hands in scorn. "Useless words." Her eyes locked fiercely on Cholpon's. "Who are you? What do you want? That's all that matters. You *are* with him, right now. He is always in your mind. You want him. There is a reason for that. It is too strong just to let go. So enjoy it...if you can."

"But what is the reason?"

"Just some karma." Djamila wrinkled her lips. "Somewhere...sometime in the past you two built up deep desires for each other. So strong you couldn't finish in one life. Now you have come back together...to fulfill them. Just that."

"Will it be good or bad?"

Djamila shrugged. "Both, probably."

"Do you know what we had between us before?"

The *Shayka* shook her wispy white head. "Better not to know those past-life things. They just distract us. If the memories were helpful, we would have them. But they're just a muddle. It's a blessing to forget the past...a less evolved state than the present.

Better to focus on who you are now and what you want now."

Cholpon's mind leaped toward Jeff, then recoiled at the thought of leaving Djamila. "I am your *chela*"—her voice turned pleading—"and I want to become enlightened."

Djamila wrapped her in an all-encompassing look. "That you are...and that you will become."

"But I'm afraid he'll pull me away. He's not like us."

"You are not so easily pulled. Maybe you will pull him. We shall see. Now you have a chance to finish what you started...long ago."

"Being with a man...." Cholpon closed her eyes with a frown. "Especially in that way...after all these years...it seems so strange."

"It *is* strange, all this business of bodies...but apparently you need it. Some desires have to be acted out before they can be left behind. No harm in that. It generates a little more karma and slows you down, but you're not in any hurry."

"*He* is in a hurry...but not to get enlightened."

Djamila laughed, then her expression turned probing. "One reason I can tell there are such strong ties between you is that you keep speaking of him. He is not the main thing. This horrible weapon...that may kill so many people. You have quite forgotten about it."

Cholpon lowered her head in shame. It was true. She was like a teenager who can't think of anything except her crush. That bomb could kill everyone in Bishkek...poison the land and rivers...and she was day-dreaming about a man.

"Would you like to keep that from happening?"

She met the *Shayka*'s eyes. "Very much so."

"Then I will teach you a few extra things...to help with that. Come." Slowly and stiffly Djamila stood up. "First we meditate together. Out in the sun." She hobbled a few painful steps, while Cholpon restrained her urge to offer a steadying arm, knowing how adamantly self-sufficient the old woman was. As her joints limbered, Djamila strode out to the yard, her coral necklace swaying.

Even in the morning, the sun glared down, filling the sky and glinting off the sand that surrounded the pergola behind the main house. This was the ramshackle side, an annex of unpainted plywood and tin roofs. Their budget wouldn't yet allow the improvements they had planned. The older section still had ornate carvings on the eaves that reminded her of her grandparent's home. She liked this gingerbready charm, which was prevalent before the revolution but died out as utility replaced ornament in the socialist building crafts.

From here they couldn't see the lake but could hear its lapping, a sound that saturated them, waking and sleeping. The mountains, vastly blue with white peaks, soared above them.

Djamila prodded the sand with her gnarled feet until she found a soft area and said, "Sit here, face *Surya*."

Cholpon squinted at the sun. Strange, she thought, the only times they meditated in the sun was at dawn on festival days. The sand was warm through her cotton shift but cooler as she wriggled deeper. She pulled her heels onto her thighs in lotus position. The teacher sat beside her, lowering herself more quickly than she had risen, and scooted in close so their knees touched.

Strange again: they always kept to their own space when meditating.

The barn and stable were nearby, and the breeze brought them scents of hay and dung. Cholpon inhaled the blend, that crisp, herby odor of dry alfalfa and the dank heaviness of digested alfalfa. Good smells. It was only meat waste that reeked.

The breeze also brought them the mingled songs of women working the fields, the rising and falling cadences of the ancient hymns that joined them with each other, the earth, and Allah. When would she sing with her sisters again? Maybe never. She was getting swept away...by a dark wind.

Acel walked by, her carpenter's tool belt swinging from her hips. She stared at them, met Cholpon's eyes with a look of envy, then glanced away. More jealousies, Cholpon thought. All this special attention was bound to create them. Cholpon would talk to her later.

Djamila waited until they were alone before speaking. "This is a *sidhi* to develop your inner light...so you can see objects hidden from view. You don't close your eyes all the way. Leave them a little open, but let them roll back like you're looking into your head. Let the sun shine right in."

Cholpon's eyes fluttered uncomfortably at first, then relaxed.

"Within you is your own little sun, a connection to *Surya*," the teacher continued. "You are a microcosm of the universe, so everything is within you, including the sun. It's there on the subtle level, your astral body. That's what the scriptures mean when they say we're made in the image of God. The universe is God's body, so each of us has the universe inside us. This is God's great gift to humans...once we find it. The astrology works through there, but we want it now for its light." Her eyes shone from deep within.

"We will wake it up," the *Shayka* continued. "For this you use a special mantra. Let me know when you are free of thoughts."

Cholpon exhaled, allowed her mind to sink toward the silence of the transcendent, then nodded. Djamila leaned close and whispered: "*Agni melei.*" As the sounds plunged into her quietness, washes of orange and yellow flowed across Cholpon's vision. Flames roiled at the edge, and her brain seemed to blaze. She sat as if inside the sun, engulfed in hydrogen fusion.

Until now, Cholpon had experienced the inner world of meditation as a silent glow. This fire was glorious but dreadful in its devouring power. "Just be with the sound and the light," the teacher said, sensing her fears. "This is the astral *Surya*. Here only ignorance is burned." Through the linkage of their knees, Cholpon could feel an energy current running from Djamila into her, calming her yet supercharging her awareness, expanding her mental space out towards infinity. The mantra quieted to a hum, and the light diffused into a soft gold. Her empty mind glistened.

After what could have been minutes or hours, the *Shayka* spoke: "Now we will work on the body. Some asanas. First the cobra, the *kundalini* animal."

Cholpon pulled her mind reluctantly out of the ethereal light. She unfolded from the lotus, stretched out on her stomach and raised her upper body off the sand, then tilted her head back until the whites of her eyes met the sun. Its radiance poured into her. As she held the pose, her spine extended tautly, then each vertebra relaxed, sending starbursts across her vision.

"We're working with the second highest level of *kundalini* here. Its seat is in the forehead.

I know that already, thought Cholpon.

"Now the shoulder stand, to put some pressure on the upper *chakras*."

71

Cholpon rolled on her back and raised her legs into the air until she was almost vertical. Her long shift fell to her thighs. She wiggled her toes at the sun, and the breeze tickled the soles of her feet.

"Drop down into the plow."

Cholpon bent her legs over her head until her toes reached the sand, her body taking the shape of a plowshare. The blood pooling down into her head made it feel larger. The teacher leaned over her, touched one hand to the crown of her head and the other to the base of her throat, and began to massage. The pressure on her throat made her want to cough, but as she tensed, Djamila said, "Relax into it. Open up."

Light flowed between the *Shayka*'s hands, pulsating in waves that built in power. The tension eased and Cholpon's face seemed to burn. The more she surrendered to the light, the stronger it became. As it approached overwhelming, Djamila licked her thumb and rubbed it on the center of Cholpon's forehead. Cholpon felt a coolness that drew the light toward it. As Djamila pressed down, it concentrated there in a small circle that flashed light and dark, on and off. When dark, it was ringed by a corona like an eclipsed sun; when light, it was a brilliant beam surrounded by darkness. The flashing seemed to go with her heartbeat, then it slowed and seemed to go with her breath; finally the dark phase stopped, and her miniature sun shone steadily.

Djamila took her hands away. "This is *Bindu Surya*, your inner light. It has always been there, but now you are awake to it. Would you like to see things with it?"

Cholpon nodded, mute.

"Then you will dance," the *Shayka* said, "in the dark room." Although tiny, she bristled with a force field; her flossy white hair stood out from her head and her dilated eyes were beacons.

With a long exhalation Cholpon lowered her knees and uncurled her body onto the sand. She lay for a few swirly moments in the corpse pose, then got up woozily. They walked back to the house, this time Cholpon the unsteady one.

They entered the plywood annex and went down a narrow corridor that separated two rows of dormitory rooms. The hallway was hung with *shyrdaks*, lengths of felt appliquéd with velvet and satin into colorful swirling patterns. They brightened and insulated the dim interior, as they did in the Kyrgyz yurts they were

72

originally made for.

The two women passed through a curtain of glass beads into the main house with its drably painted, high ceilinged rooms. Here the walls were also hung with fabric, but since insulation wasn't necessary, cotton and silk were used, in colors and forms that seemed to chase each other into intricate symmetries. The kitchen sisters were bustling with lunch preparations, and the aromas of baking bread and boiling cabbage filled the air.

In the center of the house, encased within its own set of interior walls, was a windowless room, its walls and door covered outside and in with thick brown felt to block noise and light. They entered it into a darkness so total Cholpon felt she'd disappeared.

Like all the Friends, she came to the dark room alone twice a week for trance dancing, a half hour of solitary whirling that took her beyond the senses. The absence of light, sound, and companions turned her perceptions inward, where she saw visions, heard silent music, and for ecstatic moments merged with the Divine. To Cholpon this room was a vortex, a cyclotron, a chute into another dimension. This was her first time here, though, in the dazzle of her inner light.

The *Shayka*'s disembodied voice was thin but musical: "Now think your new mantra and dance the dervish rings. At the end, when your arms are raised and you are whirling with the planets, that is the time. Then the inner and outer *Suryas* will be conjunct. You can look into the astral channels...and see."

"What will I see?"

"Whatever you want. Come tell me afterwards." Djamila abruptly left the room, sending a flash of light over the felt-covered walls and hardwood floor. As the door closed, blackness gobbled up the intruding rays.

Cholpon could feel her identity disappearing. Snuffed...like a little candle flame. Now just some smoky thoughts. Am I here? Is here here? Where is down? And up? She rubbed her bare feet across the wood for assurance. That's down. Up is here, where I'm thinking. Where who is thinking? There must be somebody in here. She raised her hand, then dropped it before touching her head. Leave the senses. Let the physical fall away. Don't resist...dissolve....

She saw Djamila's face, then her parents', but as she tried to

73

focus on them, they vanished.

Let it all go.

Cholpon—she clung to her name. Forget that...don't hold on.

But what's left?

Just this. She replaced her name with her new mantra and began to turn with regal slowness in the dark. Yes...unwrap me, uncoil me like a too-tight spring and spiral me out into what I really am. Out of my thoughts...out of my ego. Into...what?

Unity...with the cosmic Self.

But I'll never get there if I keep thinking. Back to the mantra.

Giving herself up to its sound, she orbited, first in a ring around the floor, then like a planet around the sun, and finally like the universe around its still center, the *Brahmastan*, the channel to the source. As she spun faster, centrifugal force furled her dress up around her, lofted her hair, and lifted her arms above her head, light as wings.

Her temples tingled as her brain waves synchronized and reinforced each other into coherent pulsations. The mantra faded away, leaving her alert with no thoughts. Since the ego was just a construct of thoughts, it dropped away along with them, freeing her from the small self.

In the silence beyond her shell, she became her soul, an eternal being attached but not confined to her body. This divine essence, God within her, both loved her and was her. She knew it had led her through countless incarnations and was now guiding her home to enlightenment.

With a rush of bliss, the boundary between subject and object disappeared and she expanded into unity with all creation. Beneath a billion disguises, everything was a single soul encompassing the universe, oneness aware of itself.

Gliding and pivoting on the balls of her feet, breathing in a thin stream that seemed to flow directly from her nostrils to her brain, stretching upwards, twirling in her own breeze, she ascended the dark in a luminous helix.

As her breath stopped, her last boundary dissolved and she merged into a still, deep ocean of being, the unified field. Rather than impersonal and distant, this too was her soul, God and Cholpon united in a joy so complete that any possibility of suffering was left behind with the hull of her ego.

From this oneness she knew all dualities were superficial. Male and female, pain and pleasure, life and death, good and bad, electrons and quarks, galaxies and black holes, Creator and creature were just polarities seeking, mating, and fleeing their opposite. That turmoil was the thin exterior of an unchanging sea of consciousness.

As she took a breath, her inner light intensified until she seemed to be spinning inside a diamond. She could see into its facets as if they were screens. She thought of Jeff, and desire leaped up. This clouded the gem, though, and she had to wait until it lessened and the diamond grew clear again. From one facet flashed a faint image, like a slide projected in a lit room. Jeff was sitting in the front seat of a truck with a black man, a white man, and a Kyrgyz. He looked worried. She wished she were with him, but this erased the vision.

She tried to calm herself so it would return, but thoughts and emotions poured in. As the diamond dimmed, she became aware of her body, the skip of her feet and weight of her arms, and she slowed to a stop. The room kept whirling.

She stood gulping air and sobbing, wanting to be with him. To be able to see but do nothing about it seemed a cruel gift.

She felt the felt walls, she felt her wet face. She was back in her small self. She left the room, shielding her eyes from the harsh light, walked dizzily to Djamila's office, and told her what she had seen.

"And the bomb?" the *Shayka* asked.

Cholpon put her hand to her forehead. "I forgot."

Djamila's tiny frame rocked with rueful chuckles. "It is him that you want. You must go to him. That is your heart's desire. Together you may be able to find it."

Feeling both ashamed and happy, Cholpon bowed her head in obedience.

"And the dancing in the light?" the teacher asked. "How was that?"

Cholpon looked up, her face bright. "The best dervish rings ever. So clear...and huge. I was one with God. Why does it have to end?"

Djamila looked at her reassuringly. "When you're

enlightened, it doesn't end. Then there's only one reality. But until then, reality is different in different states of consciousness."

Cholpon tried to focus her churning mind on the *Shayka*'s words.

"The dance put you into unity consciousness, just a taste of it. Now you're back in duality consciousness. Very different worlds. Each has its own rules...and needs to be respected for what it is. Here everything is split apart." Djamila's hand severed the air. "There's you and me and a gap between us. We're bound by the senses, locked into matter and time.

"But this relativity has its basis in unity. It manifests out of that." The teacher swept her arm around the room, pointing here and there. "All these different things are just one thing, God's awareness taking on forms. What you experienced in the dance is the ultimate truth. And that is what awaits you...permanently."

Cholpon bowed at the blessing of the *Shayka*'s knowledge. "*Allah-aum*," she said and left the room.

Before she could drive to Bishkek she had another duty, a job she loved. It was her day to be *muezzina* and sing *adhan zuhur*, the call to midday prayer. She climbed up the rusty iron ladder to the wooden platform they had built atop the water tower, their highest structure. They couldn't afford a minaret, so this was their substitute. Unfortunately it had caused them trouble with the Muslim establishment.

Last year Djamila had applied to get the Circle accredited as a *Zawiya*, a Sufi training center. This would have brought some funding, given them official recognition, and allowed their sisters to compete for the few laical positions open to women. A team of *mullahs* had come to inspect. Judging from the amount they ate, they seemed to like the food, but little else met with their approval. In their report they derided the wooden platform and cited the lack of a minaret as the most visible sign of a pervasive lack of respect for Islamic tradition. They also condemned the yogic meditation techniques, although these are widespread among the Sufis of India. Before they arrived, Djamila had hidden the pictures of Goddesses.

In her defense, she responded that the *mullahs*' attachment to minarets had more to do with their shape than with spirituality. The patriarchs' conviction, she told them, was, "No phallus, no Islam."

This did not go over well. The religious fathers took offense and denounced her as a heretic, ordering all the sisters to leave the Circle and return to orthodoxy. A few obeyed but most stayed.

Afterwards, Djamila said the incident had purged and strengthened their community and taught them again the value of the Sufi saying, Love the pitcher less and the water more—The outer form of faith is less important than its inner content.

Since then, these rough planks she was standing on had taken on a new beauty for Cholpon. The Circle had paid a price for them. She reminded herself, though, that this platform too was just another outer form.

From up here she could see the wholeness of this place she loved: The immense blue span of Lake Issyk-Kul, second largest mountain lake in the world, so huge its horizon showed the curve of earth and so deep the Soviets used to test submarines in it. Its fathomless waters were warmed by thermal flow from the earth's core, keeping it from freezing even in the coldest winter. Across it to the north rose the mountains of Kazakstan, their jagged blue silhouette faded over the watery miles. Behind her to the south, close and clear through the dry air, towered the peaks of Kyrgyzstan, colossi of rock and snow.

A road ran along the shore toward the town of Kara-Kol, a few of whose roofs she could see to the east. Around her spread their farm, its fields quilted onto the alluvial fan left by the stream that flowed from the mountains into the lake. Terraced into the slopes of the narrow canyon were orchards of fruit trees, and beneath them were beehives and grape arbors heavy with clusters of muscat. The canyon floor held plots of vegetables and pastures of their animals: cows for their milk, sheep for their wool, horses for their carriage.

Tending them were the Sufi sisters, working and singing, their voices reaching her in a weave of music. Despite the inevitable spats, she knew and loved all the women, the thirty in the fields and the ten around the house. They were her family. Now so much darkness was rushing at them. Would they be together? Even alive?

Closer in stood the barn, corrals, tool sheds, and racks for drying raisins and apricots. Beneath her stretched the roof of the house, where she noticed a few more missing shingles. Her mind returned to practicality. Budget or no budget, these had to be replaced before the first snow, which could come next month.

But now it was time to call the faithful to prayer. "*Allahu Akbar*"—God is most great—she began the Arabic invocation. Singing in her strong alto, she could sense her voice gliding over the lake, echoing off the mountains, permeating the universe, telling all who could hear that now was the time to stop laboring, face west toward Mecca, bow to the earth, and offer praise to Allah. Then come eat lunch.

Her voice soared into the coda, "*La ilaha illa Allah*"—There is no God but God. The verse was used by fundamentalists to exclude other religions, so Cholpon hadn't cared for it. But it became her favorite when Djamila had explained that it meant, Everything is God, nothing but God exists; God is the universe in synergy, the Whole that is more than the sum of Its parts. God is All-ah.

She was one of those parts, so nothing permanently bad could happen to her. Bring it on! Now she was ready.

Jeff listened to the gray-robed *muezzin* chanting the call to midday prayer from the minaret of the Bishkek mosque. The man's bass voice resonated from his stocky chest and carried over the city in plaintive ululations. The drawn-out, quavering sounds filled Jeff with an unfamiliar longing for the unearthly and made him think of Cholpon singing to him three nights ago. He could almost see her face as she leaned toward him, feel her hand as she stroked him.

Resisting the urge to float away on waves of song, he brought himself back to the front seat of the US Army two-and-a-half ton truck. Crammed in with him were Sergeant Blake at the wheel, Erkin as their translator, and Captain Justin Holmes riding shotgun. The GIs wore desert camos and jungle boots and Jeff a striped polo shirt, cotton pants, and running shoes. He was glad to be in civis rather the camos. The uniforms were part polyester, so patches of sweat were already breaking up the chocolate-chip pattern.

"The worst time to come here," said Jeff. "The place'll be filling up now, and they don't like infidels around the mosque."

Cars were wheeling into the parking lot and men were strolling into the plain, unornamented building. With a minaret instead of a steeple, it reminded Jeff of fundamentalist churches back in Wyoming, a functional place of worship rather than an architectural monument. A gift from Saudi Arabia, the mosque had been built after the collapse of communism, when the restrictions on religion had been lifted. The simple sanctuary of cream-colored ceramic tiles was dominated by its fifty-foot hexagonal tower of polished tin that swelled out into a cupola at the top, where the *muezzin* was chanting.

This was the main mosque, and one of the few in the capital. Most Kyrgyz weren't very religious; they didn't let faith interfere with fun. They boozed and went to mosque mainly for social occasions. In Bishkek almost no women wore veils, but in the more traditional towns in the south, a few did.

Being in the minority, though, made the fundamentalists all the more devout. Most of the men arriving now for prayers would be militant defenders of Islam.

"How about if we stay outside the grounds?" Jeff asked Holmes. "Can we do it from the street?"

The captain gauged the distance and shook his head.

"Negative. We need to be within thirty meters."

"Maybe we could come back later," Jeff suggested.

"Negatory. They might've noticed us already. Then they'll move it as soon as we go. Drive on in, Blake." Holmes's large body was solid muscle, the kind that would turn to fat if he stopped lifting weights. About thirty, he was prematurely balding and what hair he had was buzz-cut and blond almost to invisibility, so his head was a dome. The pink of his skin accentuated the gray of his eyes. His small, smiling mouth and plump, unlined face made him look to Jeff like a gigantic boy.

"Yes, sir," said the lanky sergeant, his dark skin, short brambly hair, and closely trimmed mustache glistening in the swelter.

"Get as close as you can to those outbuildings. If it's here, they're not going to put in on the altar." Holmes twisted around and spoke into the rear of the deuce-and-a-half. "Start the sweep now."

Jeff watched through the rear-view mirror as an electronics specialist put on a headset and switched on the ionizing radiation detector, a green metal box three feet high. The specialist adjusted its dials, glancing back and forth between wavering meters and a CRT screen.

It couldn't find anything in Iraq, thought Jeff, but maybe it'll do better here.

Around the detector sat a dozen sergeants mostly in their late twenties. Their manner blended eagerness, a quiet hardness, and a dash of fear. They held black submachine guns with silencers. Their helmets and flak vests lay in a pile on the floor, too uncomfortable to wear in this heat. For shade and concealment, a canvas top covered the back of the truck.

From the driver's seat Blake stared with yellow-tinged bloodshot eyes at the minaret, and his face broke into a sparkling grin. "Great spot to mount a fifty caliber. Man could bring pee on half the town from up there."

"If he's got a fifty up there," said Holmes, "it'll be your job to go get it."

"Nothing to it." The sergeant made a fist. "I'd just tell him I'm a Black Muslim come to join them. Climb up there with him and say, 'Brother, let's close our eyes for a moment of prayer.' Then I'd heave him over the side."

"Blake," the captain said, "if anyone could pull that off, you could."

"What if the nuke is here? What then?" Jeff asked.

"Depends," replied Holmes. "When we find it, we're supposed to, you know, just blockade it and call in the Kyrgyz Army, let them get it. That's the SOP." His scowl showed his opinion of diplomatic procedure. "But if the bad guys try to take it out before that, we can...Stop Them!" His large pink face and small gray eyes brightened at the possibility. "But if it's in an embassy...a whole other can of worms. Might even need the UN. And you know what good they are."

The men around the mosque were staring and gesturing at the truck and talking animatedly. A thin, elderly cleric detached himself from the group and approached the intruders; the others followed. The *mullah* walked with slow stiffness, and the laymen stayed several paces behind. The old man wore a brown robe woven with stripes of red, black, and gold and a skullcap of the same material atop his gray head. Below large dark eyes his cheeks were grizzled and sunken. His lips moved in prayer.

"Tell him we just want to admire his beautiful building...we won't get out of the truck." Holmes said to Erkin. "We'll only be a minute."

Erkin nodded, pressure showing in his slim tawny face and narrow eyes. Before he could translate, the *mullah* gazed up at Holmes and asked in accented English, "From where you come?"

Holmes patted Erkin and smiled, playing the naive, friendly American. "Well, this man here's from right here in Kyrgyzstan. He's been showing us the sights. I'm from Indiana and Blake here is from New Jersey. Where you from, Madsen?"

"Wyoming," said Jeff.

"So we're kinda from all over," Holmes continued. "How about yourself?"

The cleric folded his frail arms across his chest. "If you are not Muslims, must go."

Holmes raised his beefy hands in innocent bafflement. "We're just out seeing the sights. We didn't know about the rules."

"You not belong here."

"OK, have it your way," Holmes said. He turned to Blake and whispered, "You can't start the truck," then said louder,

"Sergeant, let's get out of here."

Blake ground the starter several times.

"What's the trouble?" Holmes asked him.

Blake ground the starter again. "Maybe it's flooded, sir."

Holmes shrugged helplessly at the old man. "Seem to be having a little problem with the truck. We'll go just as soon as we get it started." He forced a small-mouthed smile that made his pink cheeks even plumper. "Shouldn't be more than a minute."

The men behind the *mullah* were muttering and scowling at the profanation. Erkin was trying to placate them in Kyrgyz, a rapid, sibilant language that sounded to Jeff like a machete cutting tall grass. More onlookers began to cluster around the deuce-and-a-half. Bold curious boys were bounding up in the air to see in the windows. Most of the laymen wore black pants, gray-and-white shirts, and colorfully embroidered skullcaps. Jeff imagined a wife stitching a cap for her husband, setting it proudly on his head, and saying the Kyrgyz equivalent of, "No reason it can't be pretty."

Valerie...once she'd made him a bag for his climbing iron from the leg of an old pair of jeans, embroidering the denim with flowers and birds. Jeff had cherished it, liking the contrast of the sentimental decoration with the practicality of the pitons and karabiners inside. Where was it now? Where was she now? That wind kept blowing.

"Got it...clear," said the technician at the detector.

Holmes told Blake, "Try it again."

This time the engine started; Blake revved it.

"OK! Sorry to bother you folks," the captain said. "We'll be on our way."

Blake ground the gears into reverse, and they pulled out of the parking lot. The boys waved to them. "Next stop?" Blake asked.

Holmes glanced at the list on his clipboard. "The Iranian Embassy."

"It's not far," said Jeff. He directed them down busy thoroughfares and shady side streets to a two-story cube of polished marble that reminded him of a mausoleum. The new, almost windowless building was set amid a block of pre-communist-revolutionary mansions that were now run-down after eighty years of neglect. Two guards of the Islamic revolution stood at the embassy gate, and a large photo of a hard-eyed, black-bearded cleric with head wrapped in cloth adorned the entrance. So much for revolutions improving things, thought Jeff.

He wondered if one of the guards had thrown a grenade at him the other night. Both looked like they would've enjoyed it, and they carried AK-47s just like the raiders. Their glowering leader would probably love to revenge their sacred grievances by killing a million Americans with a nuclear bomb.

Jeff noticed three Kyrgyz soldiers ambling along the block. "You know, one thing we should check out," he told Holmes. "The militia patrol around the embassies...mainly to keep down street crime. It's embarrassing when an ambassador gets mugged. We can ask if any of them saw a truck like that...or something delivered, anything unusual going on that night."

"Can you take care of that?" Holmes asked.

"I'll do it," Jeff said.

Holmes spoke to Blake: "You can probably get closer from the back. Try the alley."

They turned at the corner and again at a narrow alley lined with overflowing trash cans, then stopped behind the embassy where a nine-foot concrete wall flanked a gated driveway. Inside stood two more guards. Tin storage sheds and garages rimmed the inner courtyard at the rear of the main building.

"Leave it running," said Holmes, "in case we have to get hat." He turned around to the technician. "Roll it."

"Roger," came the reply. The machine hummed as it scanned the air for decaying isotopes.

The guards, officious but bored, stared at the truck. One nudged the other and gestured at the US Army insignia on the side. "Americans?" came a hostile bellow.

"Tell them you're Kyrgyz," said Holmes.

After an interchange, Erkin relayed, "The others...are they Americans?"

The captain leaned out the window and grinned at the guards. "How you guys doing?"

One hurled a Farsi curse and jerked his AK-47 up to his chest but didn't point it. The other took a radio handset from his belt and spoke into it, then shouted at Erkin in Russian.

Erkin said, "He ask what we want."

"Tell them we're tourists," said Holmes. "Just driving

around."

Erkin and the guards yelled back and forth. "Cannot stop here," he interpreted.

"Won't be long," said Holmes.

The guards from the front ran around the side of the embassy. The rear door of the building opened, and two men in dark suits walked out.

"We got movers on the right," Blake said.

"Call the air force," said Holmes.

The older of the two men, distinguished looking with graying black hair, an aquiline nose, and thick mustache, approached the truck, followed by his assistant carrying a briefcase.

"Why are you here?" the ambassador asked. "This is property of Iran."

"We're in the alley," the captain said. "You don't own the alley."

"What do you want?"

"We're checking the place out," Holmes said. "Thinking of buying it."

"You must go!" The man drew himself to his full but modest height.

"We'll go when we want to. This is a public street. We're not on the embassy."

"Now!" the ambassador insisted, then spoke to the guards. All four pointed their AKs at the truck, but kept their fingers off the triggers.

Steady there, Jeff thought. He could feel Erkin trembling next to him. Maybe the bomb is here. Otherwise this guy's risking a diplomatic disaster.

"Makes me nervous, somebody pointing a weapon at me," the captain said to the ambassador. "Could you tell them to put them down?"

"Get out!" the Iranian replied.

"We'll just be another minute."

"No! Now!"

One guard began cursing the Americans in rhythmic Farsi. The ambassador spoke to his assistant, who opened his briefcase, took out a cell phone, pressed a button, and gave it to him.

From the rear of the truck, the technician said, "Done. Place is clear."

"Out of here," said Holmes to Blake and waved to the ambassador as the truck pulled away. "Say hi to the *ayatollah*."

Blake stuck his head out the window and called, "Yo' mama sucks Osama!"

The Iranians raised their weapons in the air and shouted with triumph at having chased off the great Satan.

When they turned the corner, Jeff patted Erkin on the knee and told him, "You see, nothing to it. But you're definitely earning your pay."

The troops blew off their tension with calls of, "Like to waste those ragheads" and "Fuckin' send 'em to Allah."

Jeff wondered how Erkin, as a Muslim, was reacting to the GIs' comments. Erkin's expression showed only relief at being alive.

Holmes exhaled heavily and laughed from stress. "Guess our ambassador will be getting a pissed-off phone call."

"She can handle it," said Jeff. "But I thought the Kyrgyz gave us a permission paper, like a search warrant, so we could check anyplace out."

"Yeah, I got something like that here." The captain tapped the papers on his clipboard. "But who needs it?" He gave Jeff a friendly whack on the shoulder; Jeff winced. "I thought you said you were Special Forces. You've been a civilian too long."

"Hey, I thought it was just fine. Most fun I've had all day," Jeff said, blanching.

"Where to now?" Blake asked.

"Some Arab-owned warehouses on the edge of town," Holmes said and gave the list to Jeff for directions.

"Turn left at the corner," said Jeff. "It's a ways."

They drove on a bustling, potholed avenue amid a menagerie of vehicles: small three-wheeled delivery wagons, battered Soviet coupes, spiffy German sedans of the new elite, tractors driven by farmers coming to town in their only vehicle, buses ranging from little jitneys painted with magic charms to long omnis jointed in the middle to go around corners, trucks from pickups to vans to diesels like the one used to steal the bomb. A few brave bicyclists rode hugging the shoulder, glancing anxiously to the left for turning cars. The rule of the road was the weaker yielded to the stronger, and some drivers wouldn't brake for a bike.

Men and cars, Jeff thought, egos on parade wherever you go. Pedal to the metal...with a tank full of testosterone. Look out, world. Here they drove with avid aggression, passing others and terrorizing pedestrians at every chance. Many of the pedestrians were equally bold jaywalkers, affecting the cool hauteur of matadors as they dodged the hurtling cars. It was sport, often blood sport. Jeff wondered if it was because communism had given them so few outlets for competition, for the macho assertion of me-first. Driving here was like business in the US. Just having a car set them apart.

The Delta Force truck rumbled on through downtown Bishkek. Jeff was glad the city had few skyscrapers, so the Ala-Too peaks—blue-and-white miles of snowy granite that filled the southern horizon—were unrivaled as they floated above the city, distant deities aloof in their own bliss.

The population of the capital was burgeoning towards a million, but it was spread out, so the city didn't feel crowded. Trees and parks kept it green. Modern office buildings, many with white marble facades that from a distance looked elegant but close up were thin and crumbling, fronted the main streets. Apartment buildings, most of them solidly built of brick and stone during the 1930s, lined the side streets. The business streets were bustling, the residential streets quiet, and people could walk to work—a good blend, Jeff thought, for a downtown.

They drove toward the outskirts, which were less pleasant, dominated by clusters of concrete high-rises that were just as ugly but not as dangerous as housing projects in the US. They also passed stretches of hovels, crowded shacks of wood and tin jammed together around meandering dirt paths. Jeff had walked through these slums with Erkin as his guide. There, running water meant you ran down to the communal faucet with your bucket, and plumbing was an outhouse in back. He'd been impressed, though, by the grace of the life going on. Children played, neighbors talked while sweeping their shared porches, somehow something got cooked for dinner. Kyrgyz and Russian alike, they were strong people, too stoic to slump into chaos and hostility.

A Kyrgyz in a shiny black Mercedes whizzed around their truck to pass against oncoming traffic, then darted back in to avoid a head-on. He switched his theft alarm on and off like a siren. A chicken foot dangled from his rearview mirror.

When they stopped at a light, a motorcycle behind them swung out between lanes and passed. The cycle with two men aboard pulled in front of them and stopped. The men wore black helmets and leathers. The one in the rear hopped off, pulled a pistol from his jacket, and aimed with both hands at the truck.

Jeff saw a squinting dark eye above a perforated silencer as he dived and crushed Erkin toward the floor. With a sting another stitch tore out of his wound. The windshield shattered; slugs shrieked in and struck with sharp thunks. Lying against Holmes's side, he could feel the captain jerk once, then again. Blake grunted and his leg kicked Jeff's. The motorcycle roared off. Jeff rose up covered with glass as the bike rounded the corner like a black hornet.

Holmes had a hole in his chest and another in his cheek; the back of his skull was spread over the ceiling of the truck. Blood pumped from the stump of his head and spurted from his chest, spraying warm over Jeff and Erkin. Spasms shook the captain's body, which was sopping and reeking with its crimson sap.

Impatient drivers blew their horns. The GIs in the back were shouting and grabbing their weapons.

Heart jackhammering and breath surging, Jeff rode a wave of adrenalin. Any others out there? Where are they? He looked out the windows but saw no enemies.

Erkin lay on the floor screaming, hands to his head. Blake slumped over the wheel, a red hole in his wet, twitching back. The truck rolled into a parked car. Jeff checked himself for holes—no new ones. He looked at the captain—nothing could be done: the pink had left his face and his eyes were wide and blind, their gray dulling.

Farewell, Justin Holmes, good soldier. Jeff sensed the great hawk of death, wings rising in undulant waves—slow, black, beautiful—carrying the perished away to feed to its young in their mountain nest.

He pulled Erkin, quivering and weeping, up from the floor and checked him for wounds—none. He released him and Erkin slid to back the floor. Jeff turned to Blake, saw an exit wound the size of a fist on his shoulder, pulled him upright and saw an entrance the size of a nickel on his chest. Must be a .45 or a magnum. At least it missed the heart. Sweat dripped from the sergeant's chin and blood trickled from his fluttering lips. He wheezed through his mouth. His face held an expression of deep puzzlement.

Jeff looked around again for foes. He felt like a boiling pot about to blow its lid off, wanting to shoot back to release hysteria.

A Delta trooper stuck his head in from the rear of the truck. Jeff asked, "Medic?" The soldier nodded, trembling. "Get Blake," Jeff told him. "He's got a chance."

Blake had slumped back over the wheel. Another GI hopped on the running board and opened the door. Jeff eased Blake over on his side and into his comrade's arms. "Well...son of a bitch," Blake whispered, blowing bubbles of red froth, gazing up at Jeff pleadingly but with a lack of register. He gasped for breath but couldn't inflate his lungs; with a soughing whistle he sucked air into the cavity as his blood burbled out. While the troops blocked traffic and held back a gawking crowd, the medic laid him on the pavement, ripped open his camouflage shirt, sealed the entrance wound with tape, and gave him mouth-to-mouth.

"Goddamned Iranians," a trooper said. "Must've followed us."

Two sergeants tried to get Holmes out of the truck. The door was jammed against the parked car, and he was too big to fit through the window. The bleeding from his chest, cheek, and cratered head had slowed; his uniform was drenched and ruddy, skin gray. The vibrations of his body had stilled, and his small mouth was open round.

"No use," Jeff told them. "Get Blake in the back. We'll get to base."

A traffic cop approached through the crowd, looking stern and in charge. He saw Blake sprawled in the street and shook his head with a manner that said accident victims were just part of his job. Speaking a stream of Kyrgyz, he walked around the truck and gestured at the damage it had done to the parked car.

Jeff darted into the cab and pulled Erkin up from the floor. "Come here. We need you." Erkin gazed at him quavering; Jeff shook him by the shoulders; Erkin's straight black hair fell into his eyes like bangs. "Get yourself together. You're not hurt." Jeff led him out of the cab. "Ask the cop if he saw the motorcycle."

Panting, Erkin clenched his slender fingers into fists and spoke to the man, then relayed back, "He say he need see your papers."

Jeff cursed in exasperation. "The motorcycle...did he see it?"

"No," came the translated reply. "Who belongs to truck?"

Jeff pointed to the crowd. "Ask the people here if anyone saw the motorcycle."

Erkin shouted to them, and they responded with mutters and head shakes. "No one see."

Sure, Jeff thought. He heard a siren approaching—more cops. It couldn't be an ambulance—only a patrol car could order one. More cops would just ensnare them and waste time Blake didn't have. They had to get him out now.

Jeff bent over the medic, who was tying a second compress around the exit wound on Blake's shoulder. "Can we move him?"

"Have to," the medic said, his mouth red with Blake's blood.

Jeff and three troopers lifted him up, keeping him as level as possible. "*Nyet!*" the policeman said, waving his arms and continuing a torrent of protest.

Erkin translated: "Man must stay here until police can look."

"He'll be dead by then," Jeff said.

They carried him toward the deuce-and-a-half, but the cop blocked their way, furious at having his authority ignored. A huge GI hoisted the policeman under the arms and set him aside as he yelled in outrage. They slid Blake—head lolling, eyes closed, mouth ajar—onto the floor of the truck.

With a look that said, *You've pushed me too far*, the cop put his hand on his holster and shouted at them. Erkin relayed: "Everyone arrested. No can go."

Jeff threw his hands down in disgust, then pointed in at Blake. "This man will die."

The siren grew louder. The policeman shook his head with righteous firmness and spoke to Erkin, who started to interpret, but Jeff cut him off. "We're taking him." He told the troopers: "I'll drive. I know the way. I want a shooter up front." He turned to Erkin. "You get in back...and stay down."

The sergeants exchanged glances, then nodded among themselves. Jeff could sense their thoughts: Holmes had been the only officer. According to chain of command, the highest-ranking sergeant would now lead. But Jeff was older and knew this strange place.

Jeff figured he was their best chance to get them out. Plus, better to be the leader than the led.

He and a young sergeant walked towards the cab, the others towards the back. Livid at this defiance, the cop rushed forward shouting commands. He started to pull his pistol out, but then looked around at the troopers. They weren't pointing their submachine guns at him...not yet. Stymied, he stood, face orange.

"Send me the ticket, chief," said Jeff as he swung up into the cab.

The captain was where they had left him, sprawled against the door, head and one arm out the window, inert. The seat was slick with blood, and Jeff could feel it warm and wet underneath him as he started the engine. In the rear of the truck the medic was rigging an IV for Blake, and the commo sergeant was radioing to Delta headquarters to have a surgical team ready.

Jeff backed away from the parked car, tearing off its door in the process, and drove away from the siren. A bystander cocked his arm back and threw something at the truck. Grenade, thought Jeff, getting ready to lift his legs away from the floor. A rock bounced off the hood.

As they rounded the corner, Holmes's body flopped over on the young sergeant, embracing him with a limp arm. The sergeant cried out and pushed him away with a shudder; the corpse slid heavily to the floor. Obviously a rookie, the trooper gazed appalled at his hands, now covered with blood. He moved them toward his pant legs as if to wipe them, then stopped. Although he was sitting in blood and the undersides of his fatigues were soggy with it, the topsides were still crisply starched, so he couldn't get them dirty. Finally he leaned forward and wiped his hands on the dashboard, but when he saw the gray-and-red lumps inside the captain's blown-away skull, he threw up over the top of his fatigues.

"You'll get used to it," Jeff said, and thought: Or die first. He imagined Holmes and Blake as they had been fifteen minutes ago, their energy and bantering humor. He liked them. Wished he'd known them longer.

An inner voice accused at him: You blocked off Holmes when you dived for cover. Holmes had to just sit there. You took the space and he took the bullet. Just like Randall in Nam...if you hadn't jumped up, he'd still be alive. You killed him...your stupidity.

Jeff writhed as his old tormentor lashed him. The wind through the gaping glass blew away a few tears but not the feelings.

Drop it, he told himself. You've got a job to do. Back to base. Now he knew how those guys in the semi must've felt when he shot out their windshield.

Leaning on the horn, Jeff plowed through the traffic and his thoughts. Every car, truck, and cycle held a potential killer. Anyone could shoot at them. Did the guy with the chicken foot have anything to do with it? A scout? Why a chicken foot? Voodoo?

Covered with a fetid stickiness now beginning to crust, hair glinting with glass nuggets, cheek twitching, Jeff bulled his way through to the Kyrgyz Air Force base hospital, where Blake, still unconscious, was wheeled into surgery and Holmes into the morgue.

A shower. Clean clothes. Coffee. Helped a little but he was still shattered...like the windshield bursting around him...like Holmes and Blake and their families...like his family...like the whole damned sorry world...shoot us all and be done with it.

He felt worse now than he had after trying to stop the raiders, mentally at least. This time he didn't have Cholpon to soothe him out. Plus he hadn't been able to shoot back. In Nam he'd found that blasting back at those who are blasting at you releases that storming energy, clears it out of you. Otherwise the fear clogs up inside, turns to poison.

Still jumpy, wanting to scream, he forced himself to go to the embassy for the after-action debriefing. The marine guard at the front entrance stood stiffly with his M-16 beside his leg at order arms. Glaring, he looked both ready for revenge and ready to duck. The receptionist, a chubby young Kyrgyz woman, normally relentlessly cheery, was red-eyed and sobbing.

As Jeff entered the briefing room, Sarah Ettinger was introducing Holmes's squad and the Delta Force officers to Jürgen Schulz, the German ambassador. Schulz gave his condolences to them for their fallen comrades, and Ettinger thanked him for arranging a Lufthansa jet to fly Blake back to the US military hospital in Germany.

Young for his position, Schulz had shaggy brown hair, hazel eyes, and wore a silk double-breasted suit that showed off his husky physique. In precise, formal English he said he very well understood the urgency of recovering this weapon of mass destruction. He had read the technical reports on the Gagarin-9 and knew the damage it could inflict. He sincerely hoped the Delta Force could get it back before some maniac set it off.

After he left, Ettinger motioned that the door to the briefing room be closed. She stood in front of the troops with Colonel Hobbs and Townsend seated on either side of her. Her long face was drawn and ashen, and lines darted her aqua eyes, which seemed smaller today because the lids were puffed. She wore a black suit, a white blouse, and her light-brown hair pinned tightly back. She told the troops she shared their mourning. The latest report she'd received was that Blake's condition was critical but stable; the next twenty-four hours should determine whether he survived. She had the men describe the attack, then asked, "So who are our suspects here?" She turned to Townsend. "Tell us about those Sudanese you had seized for interrogation."

Townsend, in a charcoal suit and tattersall shirt, crossed his legs and folded his arms across his chest. "That's classified."

She gave him a come-off-it look. "I heard about it from the Saudi ambassador. How classified can it be?"

Townsend glared at her to warn her off. "This is highly sensitive information. It could compromise an ongoing operation. If there's already been a leak, that's unfortunate but that doesn't declassify it."

Ettinger leaned toward him and spoke insistently. "All of us here have security clearances. We need to know."

Townsend held the long triangle of his face rigid. "It could endanger my operatives."

The ambassador shook her head determinedly. "The Saudis know about it, the Sudanese know about it...it's not a secret anymore. Just from us. You tell us, and I'll take responsibility for any security violation."

The CIA chief cleared his throat and straightened his tall, thin body in his chair. "That's out of your area."

Ettinger's face flashed with anger. "All right, Mr. Townsend, I'll tell us, then. The story I got was that your men, your operatives, not only illegally seized two citizens of Sudan off the street, but killed one of them."

"You're spreading rumors." Townsend's high forehead corrugated, his bushy black eyebrows pinched into a solid line, and his usually pale skin turned pink.

"Then give us the truth."

"The truth is...." He paused, breathing heavily, nostrils dilating on the thin blade of his nose. "What are Sudanese doing in Kyrgyzstan? They don't have an embassy, there's no trade. They're not tourists. We need to know if they're al-Qaeda." The CIA chief channeled his tension into his words, speaking with controlled emphasis and tapping the table with his long fingers as he made his points. "It's too important. We have to find out...even if that means violating the niceties of diplomatic protocol. There's too much at stake and time's too short."

The ambassador's face slumped. "So they did kill him."

Townsend made eye contact with the officers. "A suspect died in interrogation. It happens. This is the real world...not some idealistic make believe. The military understands that."

"And now al-Qaeda takes revenge," Ettinger said. "You gave them another reason to hate us. Didn't you learn anything from Abu Ghraib?"

Townsend shook his head curtly. "No way for them to know we were involved. This was a cut-out operation...all Kyrgyz."

"Don't be disingenuous," Ettinger said. "You know better."

The CIA chief avoided her probing, turquoise-sharp eyes.

"I don't mean to single you out," the ambassador continued, "but this is the kind of incident that just creates more terrorism. If your operatives can't get information without killing people, you need to hire some new operatives. Why don't they use sodium pentothal?"

"Not reliable."

"You have to come up with a better way."

"We got valuable information out of this," Townsend insisted. "They admitted they were al-Qaeda. We learned more about their organization."

"What do they know about the bomb?" the ambassador asked.

"They claim to be here looking for it...like lots of other people. Trying to snatch it from whoever's got it."

Thieves stealing from thieves, Jeff thought. Like the two guys on the bus.

"We need more sources before we can give that a probability rating, though," Townsend added, then lapsed into silence while the ambassador wrote with green ink on her yellow legal pad.

The soldiers sat with faces frozen in neutrality, too intimidated by the civilian authority to risk any attitudes slipping out, glad they weren't the one being grilled. Colonel Hobbs cupped his chin in his hand and stared at the ceiling.

After planning more sweeps with the radiation detectors for tomorrow, this time with two shooters in the cab of each truck, the meeting limped into adjournment.

Out in the embassy lobby, Jeff checked his mail slot and found one letter, from Clerk of the District Court, Teton County, Wyoming. Some old parking tickets from the drinking days, he thought, finally caught up with him. He tore open the envelope and read: Notification of Final Decree in the Suit of Valerie Anne

Olmstead Madsen vs. Jeffrey Keith Madsen.

Jeff sat down heavily. His chest felt as if a hole had been blown through it. He hadn't known how much he'd been holding on to hope...until now that it was gone. He had convinced himself that Valerie would relent and take him back, that she was just trying to punish him, to teach him a lesson: Never do that again!

He'd thought she would leave him hanging for a few more months, ignore a few more of his letters, then she'd write him back saying how furious she still was. That would be the sign they could communicate again. He would hear her rage out, tell her she was right but she should give him a chance to prove that he'd changed. He hadn't had a drop to drink. He'd missed her every day. It'd be much better for the kids. The family could get back together. There'd always be a scar on their marriage, but better a scar than a dead body. But no, she'd signed the decree, she'd pulled out a pistol and shot their marriage. He'd been the one to wound it, but she'd finished it off. Guess she thought she was putting it out of its misery, a mercy killing. But now another kind of misery was just beginning. The finality closed down on him like a coffin lid. It was really over. He felt plunged down to the freezing point of fire, love's absolute zero.

Out on the street he wandered confused and disoriented amid the pedestrian tumult. He passed a row of kiosks, sidewalk stands run by aspiring merchants. The beginners had only open-air tables, but they got robbed often, so everyone who could afford it had a little tin shed with their wares safely out of grabbing distance. They sold the staples: booze, cigarettes, candy, and condoms.

For distraction, Jeff ran his eyes over the stuff. The booze ranged from cheap local vodka and champagne to Chivas Regal and Mumm's. He hadn't had any hooch since he'd been here and didn't want to start now. He forced his eyes away, onto the cigarettes. They also ranged from bargain local to expensive imported, with Marlboro at the top. Marlboro's marketers had moved in big after the fall of communism, handing out millions of free smokes and plastering the region with ads showing their Men as the epitome of the West, the strong, successful, benevolent conquerors, whose ranks you can join just by lighting up. The candy featured Russian chocolate bars with fake US hundred dollar bills for wrappers and light, crisp Iranian cookies. These made Jeff see there must be another side to Iran that doesn't make the news—anyone who can bake good cookies must have something going for them. He'd never tried the condoms, all of which were local and packaged with pornographic flair. Having been warned in his State Department briefing about a lack of quality control, he'd brought a supply of Trojan Magnums with him.

Valerie...never again to see her, to touch her, to be one with her. He looked again at the liquor standing in femininely curved bottles with promises of warm, wet delight inside. Forgetfulness...pleasure...destruction...all so needed.

He saw Val's face, her big open smile turning to horror as she'd opened their bedroom door and seen him lying naked on top of her best friend, both of them plastered. Then he heard her sobs. They still wracked his life.

A young Kyrgyz soldier pushed past him and ordered a liter of vodka. He already smelled of alcohol. Had Holmes been a drinking man? The rosy flush to his skin said he might've been. Jeff had bottomed out on bourbon, Walker's Deluxe with water back. He could feel the sweet burning in his throat right now.

Before he could stop himself, he seized a bottle of Kyrgyz champagne, tossed the clerk a few bills, and strode off. Part of him screamed in protest: *Throw it away, give it away, you know what'll happen!*

His Swiss Army knife had a corkscrew. He sat on a park bench, popped the cork out, and gulped the spouting froth, sweet and bubbly like warm soda pop with a sting. It tasted like more, like there could never be enough. He chugged a third of the bottle so it'd be too late to stop. The effervescence switched him on bright and alert. "Hah," he said with a burp and a self-hating smirk. He looked around, hoping no one was staring. No one was. Several were sipping at bottles of their own. Tippling in public held no stigma here.

Jeff tried to muffle his inner disaster alarms by thinking about how Kyrgyzstan, like most of the former Russian empire, was a hard-drinking place. Only devout Muslims abstained. This was a good Topic, just what he needed to distract his brain. Alcohol was the state-sanctioned drug of instant relief under the Czar, the communists, and now the capitalists. Even with the changes, local booze had stayed cheap and plentiful, been encouraged to the masses as one of the good things in life. The new rulers, like the old, didn't want to risk an uprising. Neither did Jeff. *Na vasheh zdarovyeh!* Cheers!

He took a nip. Lighten up on yourself, old man. Holmes and Randall are better off out of this shit. And Val...well with some guys, she would've come home to find him on top of the daughter. At least you never did anything like that. Forgive yourself, you're not a monster. He took a deep swallow.

His daughter's birthday had been last month. He'd sent Tricia a bedspread made by village women in Naryn, a province in the Tien Shan Mountains known for its crafts. They had stitched colorful bits of silk and velvet into a circular design, a psychedelic mandala he thought she would enjoy, since she was one of those teenagers fascinated by the 1960s. He hadn't heard from her and didn't expect to. All his kids thought he was a louse. Val had recruited them as allies in her war against him. Daddy was a baddy. Case closed.

That was worth a good slug. This cruddy life just went on and on. Most people in their fifties were worried by how little time was left, but he was appalled by how much was still to come. Sure it was self pity, but he couldn't do anything about it...just kick himself for feeling sorry for himself. Everything was ammunition against him...and it all made him very thirsty.

Another deep draught. Off the wagon with a big bounce. The wine made the front of his mind twirl like an acrobat, but from the rear he could feel the numbness deadening his skull. Another glug or two and it'd be like pulling a sock over his head. Why would anyone want to do that?

He stood up and walked away, clutching the bottle. He noticed that the mounds of trash had been removed from the park. The government must have come up with the cash to pay the garbage men. Progress. It was again a fresh grove of grass and trees, an escape from cars and concrete. Strolling lovers, mothers with baby carriages, kids on roller skates, a few derelicts like him— all needing sanctuary. One more quick taste.

Near the entrance to the park stood a granite statue of Feliks Dzerzhinsky, stern-faced founder of Cheka, the Soviet secret police and one of Stalin's chief hatchet men. A giant statue of Lenin, arm outthrust pointing the way to the socialist future, dominated the skyline from a block away on the main government square. Some of the republics had torn down their communist statues after independence, but Kyrgyzstan had left them up, partly as a reminder against the totalitarian mentality, partly because it was easier.

At Dzerzhinsky's feet sat an old woman selling sunflower seeds from a burlap bag. Wrapped in a cotton shawl, smiling through her wrinkles, brown button eyes gleaming, she dipped a cone made of folded newspaper into the seeds. As she handed it up to a customer, a chickadee fluttered down, hovered above the bag, snatched a seed, and flew away chattering. The woman chattered a cheerful curse after it. Several other birds perched in the tree above her, awaiting their opportunity to raid her wares.

At Cholpon's window Jeff had fed one from his hand, maybe one of these very black-caps, vibrant with power, a mighty little creature, while she stood beside him.

He imagined Cholpon's trim but curvy shape, her tranquil face, her vast eyes. He tried to focus on her but the image faded. She didn't want him either. But maybe he should leave her another note. No...that'd be desperate. Admit it, she's just not interested. What did you do for her but bleed all over her sheets? But maybe she never got the note. Maybe...a mouse ate it. A tiny tornado sneaked under her door and blew it away. A....

Jeff bought a cone of sunflower seeds and walked home munching them. His apartment was in a sturdy old two-story building on a quiet side street. His landlady, the widow of a Soviet colonel, had lived here before him, and the spacious rooms still gave off the stolid ostentation of the communist elite. From the high ceilings hung a mix of bare light bulbs and cut-glass chandeliers, all of them dusty. The plaster on the thick walls was painted and polished to look like marble. The furniture and drapes were dark and heavy.

Under communism the government had owned all real estate, but as part of privatization in the early 1990s, the new leaders gave all apartments to the people living in them. With the influx of foreigners, many of the owners had moved out and rented their flats to the newcomers. Jeff's landlady now shared the one-bedroom apartment of her unemployed son and daughter-in-law and their three children. Jeff's $350 a month rent, ten times what a local would pay, maintained them all.

He opened the creaky French doors out to his balcony and

strewed the sunflower seeds on the tiles to tempt a few birds. Then he chose the widow's fanciest glass, a chipped goblet with a base of fused lavender marbles, grinned at its florid kitsch, and filled it with warm champagne.

Slurp. Slurpee attack. Slurpers of the world, unite! You have nothing to lose but your brains. Here's to you, Karl. A swallow to wallow in. Down the draino.

On his desk lay the captain's submachine gun and ammo belt, still crusted with blood, loaned to Jeff for the duration by Colonel Hobbs. Jeff took out some rags and solvent and sat down to clean it. Thank you, Justin Holmes, and *bon voyage* to a better world. And to you, John Randall, God rest your bones. Jeff toasted dead soldiers and drank deeply. Wish you were both still here...but maybe I'll see you soon. And maybe you'll forgive me.

He picked up the SMG and could tell at a glance that he'd moved up to state-of-the-art weaponry. Underneath the blood, the Heckler & Koch was matte black with a built-in silencer and a laser aimer mounted beneath the barrel. With the stock pushed in, it was scarcely bigger than a pistol, and like a pistol it wasn't made for accuracy at distance but for quick, close-in work. Jeff hefted its well-balanced steel.

He'd give the Czech Uzi to Erkin...if he didn't quit. Erkin did OK...considering he wasn't the warrior type. This was a new world for him...probably not the one he wanted.

As Jeff took a pull on the wine, the phone rang.

"Is this Jeff?"

He spluttered at the sound of her voice; champagne trickled down his chin. "Yes."

"This is Cholpon. I just got your note. I have been away for a few days."

He set the glass down and stammered, "Well...how are you?"

"I am fine."

They chatted, Jeff feeling awkward and elated, like a teenager. So she did care. Good, so did he.

When he asked her out to dinner that night, she paused, then accepted.

He hung up the phone with a smile that sagged into a frown as he realized he'd set himself up for disaster. He was half drunk. How could he see her this way? A Sufi wouldn't drink or be close to a drinker. Especially Cholpon—she wasn't the liquor type, that much he knew. He'd ruined his chance.

Panicking, he grabbed the glass and took a gulp, then caught himself and spit it out all over the table. *Hey*, cried a voice inside, *whaddaya think you're doin'? Makin' a damn mess. Have some more and clean it up.*

No way, he replied.

Then have some more and leave it. What the hell.

Shut up. Gotta get sober.

Look, you go there sober, you'll be a real deadhead with her. But if you have a little more, you'll sparkle and be charming. Plus, you shouldn't prejudge Cholpon. How can you be sure she wouldn't share a drink with you? After all, she had the brandy.

Come off it, conman, he told the voice. This woman's not a lush. She'll smell it.

Vodka. She won't smell that. Just a couple of snorts to set you up. You don't have to go off the deep end. It's the extremes that are bad. Being an uptight teetotaler is as bad as being a drunk. You've learned enough now to walk the middle road. You can have a few drinks and enjoy life.

That's bullshit. I'm not going to risk turning her off.

Bring her some liqueur filled chocolates. Women love 'em. Once she's got a little bit in her, she won't smell it on you.

You're not worth talking to. No wonder alcohol's called spirits. I'm possessed by one. Jeff raised the champagne goblet and watched the bubbles fizzing up.

Please! Those bright pops. You need them. Clear your head.

Jeff picked up the bottle in his other hand, walked into the kitchen, and poured it all down the drain while the demon screamed.

Have to sweat it out of my system before I see her. He pulled off his clothes except for his running shoes and put on shorts and a T-shirt. He ran down the stairs and onto the sidewalk. Pound it out of me...dust from a carpet. Lengthening his stride, he could feel the concrete slapping his soles. The shoes were too old and worn to be good for running, but they'd do the job.

He held his wounded arm against his side to reduce the jarring. Dodging pedestrians and buckled concrete, he ran toward less trafficked streets, where he switched to the asphalt, softer under his shoes, watching out now for potholes and cars. The locals never jogged, so people stared then wrote him off as another crazy foreigner.

He ran two miles to the Jirgal steam baths, two white-tiled domes, men's and women's, attractive from outside but dank and mildewed within. Breathing hot vapors and the scent of his naked neighbors, head swirling and stomach churning from agitated fermentation, Jeff did sit-ups on a wooden bench fringed with fungus. His mind kept sinking into an alcoholic miasma, but he dragged it out of the dregs and forced it to work.

Think about Cholpon. No, he'd spoiled it with her. She wasn't going to want him. What a time to fall off the wagon. Was there ever a good time?

Think about anything...where you are right now. These baths—belly of the whale...spew him out sober. The steam—by-product of the city's central hot water system. Huge underground boilers heat water for the whole city. Free for everybody. Nice communist idea. But they had to lay another set of pipes everywhere, then pump the hot water. The ground gobbles up the heat. In winter you can see where the pipes run because the snow melts there. Costs a fortune. City has to turn it off when they're short of cash. Then everybody washes in cold water...except the people at the top—they've got individual heaters they took over from the Party elite.

Sober yet? No...need...need a drink...drown myself.

Instead he ran back to the apartment, legs wobbly at first from steam bath low blood pressure, then catching hold and almost sprinting the last mile. He took a cold shower, letting it gush over him. His brain felt swollen enough to burst his skull. Congratulations, you're finally hungover. The fiend was still screaming for its chemical fix, begging for the burning, the numbing, the glory. He fed it two cups of black coffee. *Poison*, it protested.

He brushed his teeth, head throbbing. Alka-seltzer. Plopped into water, it fizzed like champagne, but the demon wasn't fooled. *You're killing me!*

Yep. Remember how we used to start the day? A shot of gin with Alka-seltzer instead of tonic. Sizzles as it hits the hot brain, doesn't it? Ethanol...definitely not one of the good things in life. Just an addicting drug, centuries of marketing behind it. I'm not going to feed you. Leave.

In case he and Cholpon ended up back here, Jeff changed the sheets and towels, tossed some dirty socks and underwear into his closet, and swept bread crumbs and dead flies off the floor. He considered wearing a coat and tie, but it seemed ridiculous in this heat, so instead he picked a pinstripe dress shirt, linen slacks, and business shoes. With his scabs and bandages he didn't look exactly chic. Oh well, nothing I can do about that. Time to go. I'll bring her flowers. No—too young and smitten. Just you.

Cholpon opened her door and smiled a greeting; her glowing dark eyes enfolded him. For a moment Jeff wanted to step back or glance aside, but instead he met her eyes and returned her smile and felt something gleam inside him. He tried not to breathe too hard. Her gaze shifted and she seemed to be looking around his edges. Finally she nodded. "You have survived."

"So far."

"Good, come in." He followed her into the living room, appreciating the involuntary sway of her hips beneath the long silk skirt, which was dark green and topped with a gold blouse and a necklace of coral beads. She'd dressed up for him...and put on make-up.

She motioned him to sit on the couch and took a chair across from it. "Tea...or coffee? she offered.

The spirit pleaded, *Irish coffee!*

"Thanks, I'm fine." Gazing at her face, he was pleased. An oval bordered by black hair, it wasn't gorgeous but was delightful to look at. Her large, canted eyes formed interesting triangles with her small nose, mouth, and chin. Her skin was clear and radiant, but her cheeks were wide and her teeth uneven. The brightness that shone from her, though, unified her features, blended what might have been flaws into a harmony that made plainness seem perfect. She looked about thirty, but it was hard to tell.

"How is your arm?" she asked.

"Getting better. No more infection. It's healing. It was just the muscle anyway, no damage to the bone. What we used to call a soft-tissue issue." He dipped his head. "Thanks for helping me. Made a big difference."

"I am glad I could." She paused, staring at him. "You are still in pain." A statement, not a question.

"Oh yeah."

"I hope that will soon be gone." Her accent beveled the edges off her words, smoothing the sounds.

"Thanks...it probably will."

"You are trying to find this bomb."

"Yep, still at it. Haven't got as close as that first night, though." He winced with regret of his near miss, then gasped as his mind filled with the image of blood burbling from Holmes's head and Blake's chest. He stood up abruptly; Cholpon stared at him, startled. Rather than explain it to her, he forced a smile. "I'm hungry. What's your favorite restaurant?"

She looked embarrassed. "I don't know them. I don't go."

"Well...I know a nice place."

They took a cab to Philharmonia Plaza, a downtown square with a lofty new sculpture of the Kyrgyz folk hero Manas astride his flying horse. To repress Kyrgyz nationalism, the Soviets had banned his image and the poem of his exploits, the longest epic in world literature. Now they were displayed and recited throughout the country.

Behind Manas stood a white marble building with the entrance to the fanciest restaurant in town, named with a bold red sign Flamenco.

A tuxedoed maître d' greeted them at the door with a nod of aloof hospitality. "Some place quiet," Jeff told him, and the man led them to a corner table. The room was filled with prosperous Kyrgyz and foreigners and their multilingual chat. Soft lighting gleamed on polished brass and wood. An empty stage covered one wall and a crowded bar the other.

Jeff nodded hello to Jürgen Schulz, who was dining with two men who looked like European executives.

The waiter brought them menus emblazoned with the name Flamingo. Jeff had learned on a previous visit that the original name had been Flamenco, but when the place had been sold last year, the new owners wanted to change its image. Replacing the sign was going to be too expensive, so they printed new menus with a name that looked different but sounded the same. Jeff thought that when he understood this reasoning, he would feel at home in Central Asia.

Rather than Spanish or tropical, the cuisine was a melange of Kyrgyz, Russian, Middle Eastern, and spaghetti. It was well-prepared, though, and he'd never been sick afterwards.

"What would you like?" he asked Cholpon.

She looked up hesitantly from the menu. "I don't eat the animals."

Vegetarian...hmm. He scanned the English side for meatless dishes. Even the borscht had beef. Salad and dessert were about it. Not much of a dinner.

Four young men in black leather came on stage and began playing Russian rock, homicidal guitars to a polka beat. It did Jeff's headache no good at all.

"Do you like this place?" Jeff asked her.

From the way she hesitated, he could tell she was torn between being tactful and truthful. "No," she said with an apologetic shrug, truth winning out.

He'd messed up again. Brought her here to impress her...like she was somebody he'd picked up. He should've known better. "Then let's get out of here."

Outside in the warm evening, the sky now velvet above the city lights, Jeff mulled over the other restaurants in town. None of them would be right for her. She certainly wasn't typical Kyrgyz: meat was their staple food. She wasn't typical anything, and that was one of the reasons he liked her so much. But what about dinner?

Bishkek had one pizza place, run by Turks and catering

mostly to foreigners. The crust was pita bread, and they used feta cheese instead of mozzarella and mint leaves instead of oregano, but it was passable, and they would leave off the meat. "You like pizza?" he asked.

"What is that?"

Hmm. This was not going to be easy. "It's...well...you just have to try it."

"Then I will try it."

Flash Pizza occupied the newly painted second floor above a mini-bazaar. The decor was sterile, and Jeff hoped the kitchen was too. The tables and chairs were white plastic lawn furniture. The room was crowded and smoky, and although the music here was better—old Beatles' tapes—it was also too loud, so they ordered to go. He saw Lance at one of the tables and looked away, but too late. His assistant waved, then stood up and came over.

Behind him trailed a lissomly beautiful young Kyrgyz woman. Lance's confident smile fell to a grimace as he approached. Sidling up to Jeff, he gripped his arm, miraculously picking the uninjured one, and whispered. "Hey, guy, you're lucky to be here. Things are getting heavy. Must be like back in Nam."

"Gettin' there," Jeff said.

"They got any word on who did it?"

"Not yet."

"Sons of bitches."

"Yeah."

Lance's blue eyes narrowed. "I'd like to line 'em up all up against the wall, pour gasoline on 'em, and toss in a match."

Jeff was silent.

The smile returned to Lance's face as he tipped his blond head toward his date. "Nice stuff, huh? We're just on our way out."

"Well, have a good evening," Jeff said.

Lance eyed Cholpon and winked at Jeff. "I see you're getting a little, too." He punched him on the shoulder, this time the sore one. "You old dog!"

"See you tomorrow," Jeff said.

He and Cholpon took the warm, fragrant box back to her apartment and ate at her living-room table. She pointed enthusiastically at her plate as she chewed. "What's name again?"

"Pizza."

"American food?"

"Sort of."

"I like it!"

He beamed. You pleased her! You did something right. But then he cautioned himself: Better watch it. You're going off the deep end awfully fast with her. You could be letting yourself in for another big hurt.

But this didn't feel like a rebound. He'd had those. She was so different, so fresh. A spritz of cheer in a heart he'd thought was dead.

She was like...everything was the first time with her. She was right here, all of her...interested but not needing anything. He'd never met anyone like her, in Kyrgyzstan or anywhere else.

Look how she paid attention to every bite of pizza. Look how pretty her face was when she chewed.

The light flickered—not the one inside Jeff but the one hanging from the ceiling. He looked up at the glass globe. A bus had just rumbled by on the street below; maybe the vibrations had loosened the contact. "Does it do that often?"

"Now yes," she said. "Since that first night you came here...it flashes off and on." She smiled at him. "Maybe it is trying to warn me about you: Dangerous man."

"Who me?" He raised his arms to show her he had no submachine gun tonight. "I'm not dangerous. But that could be."

"Really?" Now she was alarmed.

"Well yeah, if it got worse, it could short out."

"Short out?"

"All the lights would go out."

Cholpon raised her hands. "No, please."

"That explosion...it rocked the building pretty hard. Could've loosened some wires. I could take a look at it."

"Yes...please."

"Do you have a ladder?"

"No."

"Then...how do you change the light bulb?"

"The chair you sit in...it does not wobble too much."

She gave me the good chair, he thought with tender appreciation.

After they finished the pizza, Jeff stood on the chair and

106

took off the globe. The flickering increased as the wires moved. He handed the globe down to her.

She looked inside and said, embarrassed, "Always little bugs."

"Yeah, no way to keep them out. They always get in...I don't know how...or why. They work like crazy...just to get in there and die."

"Such bugs in America?"

"Oh yeah, gnats, they're all over." He wrapped his handkerchief around the light bulb—the clear kind where you can see the filament—and twisted it. It wasn't loose, and the flickering didn't get worse. So much for the easy solution.

He wiggled the wires going into the socket, but that too didn't increase the flashing. Probably it was up above. He swung the cord in a loop; the light flickered more and he heard the popping of shorts in the ceiling. He stopped the motion to avoid blowing a fuse. He'd like to be in the dark with her, but not that way.

Cholpon shrank back and stared upwards, small white teeth denting her lower lip.

"This is going to be complicated," he told her.

They cleared off her sturdiest table, padded it with blankets, dragged it into the middle of the room, and set the chair on top of it; that would get him close enough to the ceiling. She had a flashlight, but the batteries were weak, the light dim. They lit all her candles and set them on the table around the chair. At the electrical box near the front door he unscrewed the fuses, plunging the apartment into darkness except for the candles.

Jeff mounted the stack of furniture and examined the ceiling. The wires emerged from the center of a metal disc, which he unscrewed, revealing a hole into the space between the ceiling and the floor above. Dust sifted down.

Shining the flashlight into the cavity, he could see where these wires were spliced into the branch circuit. The splice was loose, barely making contact. Holding the flashlight in his mouth, he twisted the wires firmly together.

Cholpon didn't have any electrical tape, but she'd just bought a new roll of cloth adhesive tape to replace the one she'd used up on Jeff's wounds. Cloth wasn't ideal, but it would have to do. He peeled off a long strip and wrapping it around the splice. There...that should last...maybe as long as they would.

She peered up at him anxiously, candlelight lambent on her smooth ivory skin. This wasn't the typical candlelight evening, Jeff thought, but it was theirs.

"OK, now put the fuses back in," he said. "Let's see how it works. Here, take the flashlight."

She went into the hall and called, "Are you ready?"

"Ready!"

The lights came on; she came back; he wiggled the wires. The light shone steadily with no flickers. "You did it!" she said.

Her small smile lit him up inside. Her smiles were never big, but they radiated from every part of her and enlivened something in him that had long been shut down. He'd forgotten it was there until she'd beamed her light on it. Life springing up again.

"Turn off the lights...just in here," he said. "We should give it a rest." This had no logic, but candlelight would be cozier.

As they put the furniture back, Cholpon seemed to retreat into shyness. She took a chair by herself, and he sat on the couch. Don't rush her, he thought.

"When I was a little girl," she said, "that light seemed so big and far away as the sun."

"You grew up here?"

"Yes. Mother, father, I."

"And they are...?"

"Now no more."

"No brothers and sisters?"

"No...we were a modern family. The Party discouraged to have many children. But I would have liked...some others."

"Yeah, me too. I grew up with just my mother. Would've liked somebody else around...a sister to tease."

He decided against asking her if she'd been married, hoping she would do the same. He did, however, put his left hand prominently on his crossed knee to display ringless fingers. He thought back to when the eighteen-year indentation of his wedding ring had finally faded. It had taken six months, brought grief but also a touch of relief: if the mark faded, maybe the pain would too.

They talked about their lives. She asked about his scarred hand and forearm, and he told her about combat in Vietnam. She told him about going door to door as a child during that time collecting scraps of cotton cloth. The Young Pioneers, the communist youth group, boiled them to sterilize them, then made them into bandages for the Vietnamese.

They talked about how they both loved winter snows, shared memories of bundling up as children to go ice skating and build snowmen, and said they'd like to do those things together this winter. He explained bobbing for apples and she wanted to try it. They laughed about licking icicles and getting your tongue stuck.

He told her his mother, a retired school teacher, had wearied of Wyoming winters and now lived in Florida. She told him her mother, an engineer, had been killed in an industrial accident when Cholpon was fifteen.

As they talked, a familiarity flowed underneath their words. They each seemed to know what the other was feeling. Usually Jeff would rather fix a light socket than have a conversation, but with her it was easy to chat.

They sat without speaking for a while, enjoying each other's presence. Jeff could tell from the way her expression was changing—eyes a bit unfocused, lips parted—that if he put the moves on her now, he could make progress. But it wasn't the right time. They weren't really there yet. Better take it slow. Let her get used to it. Be a gentleman...for a change. Intrigue her.

"The Opera House has *Boris Godunov* this weekend," he said. "I thought if we went together, you could explain the story to me."

"You like opera?"

"Well, I don't know a lot about it. But what I've heard I liked."

"It is for me something I love. At university I studied music and English. Singing was my main music. It carries me away."

"You sang me a song that first night. I hope you sing it again...sometime when I can remember it better."

"After you have heard the opera, you will not want to hear me. They are very good."

"But they won't sing that song...especially the way you did."

"No."

"So...how about Saturday night...six-thirty?"

Cholpon nodded, smiling. "I will cook you dinner. But I will not sing."

"That's OK. I can wait...as long as it's not too long." Jeff

109

stood up. "Well, I better get going."

She looked disappointed.

That's good, he thought. Better that than the opposite.

"But this bomb," she said. "We did not talk about it."

"You're right." Jeff snapped his fingers. "For once I didn't even think about it."

"I know someone who might help find it. My teacher." She pointed to the picture of Djamila.

Jeff's mind reluctantly switched gears. Maybe the old gal had some contacts with al-Qaeda. "Good idea. Could you find out what she knows?"

"For eighteen years I have been trying to do that. It is quite a lot. For this bomb...she might be able to see where it is...in the mind. It is a Sufi way of seeing."

"You mean...like psychic?"

"Something like that."

Hm...a bit weird, but why not? he thought. The police use psychics. Could be interesting...worth checking out.

"Maybe you could get in touch with her and call me. Or let me know Saturday."

"I will do that," she said.

"Good. I'll see you then...or talk to you before." He took both her hands in his. "This has been fun...the most I've had in a long time. I really enjoyed it."

"I too."

He kissed each hand. Small, almost like a child's but strong. Short solid fingers, nails trimmed close; instead of polish, a thin crescent of dirt under them. She works with her hands in the earth.

He stared at her face to bring her image with him. Lively eyes, slightly upturned, wide set, look right at you. Small straight nose, nostrils just two little scallops on the sides...but they open out when she's enthused. Midnight hair.

"Take care," he told her.

"You too."

The Kyrgyz Army general staff had their offices near the presidential palace in a pre-revolutionary mansion, an unexpectedly civilian-looking building surrounded by a very military wall of cinder block and barbed wire. Carved sandstone balconies were graced with French doors, and massive umber walls were hung with ivy and topped with graceful turrets. Tall trees grew around it, and the twilight through their green leaves cast an attractive patina over the building, hiding its decrepit condition. Satellite dishes and antennas sprouted on the roof of this fading grandeur, insulting it like a silly hat on the head of a dignified dowager.

A Delta Force truck stopped at the entrance to the compound; two Kyrgyz guards saluted and opened the iron gate. The truck pulled in, and a dozen Americans climbed out. They entered the building to the salutes of more guards and walked up a wide curving staircase to the second floor banquet room. Banquets were frequent here, and the large room was well equipped. A long oak table in the center was flanked by side tables covered with chafing dishes, silverware, serving platters, and bottles of liquor. Three young women in military uniform stood ready to serve.

Wearing 9 mm. Beretta pistols in hip holsters, the officers milled around the table looking for their place cards. When Jeff found his, he picked up his shot glass and wine goblet and took them over to a side table, where he filled them with tea from a silver samovar. A full glass of something harmless was the only way to avoid alcohol at these events. The invitation specified military uniform or coat and tie, so Jeff was wearing his camel-hair sportcoat and a wild Jackson Pollock tie his daughter had given him for a long-ago birthday. He glanced out the window. The panes were the old rippled kind that he liked—they gave everything a mysterious wavery appearance. Down on the street the guards patrolled the sidewalk. The mountains glistened pink in the last rays of the sun; clouds shone mottled gold; the sky was a wash of violet, darkening in the east to a starry purple. In a nearby apartment building lights were being switched on.

What was Cholpon doing now? He'd much rather be having dinner with her. He pictured how she ate the pizza last night...dainty little nibbles.

General Osmonaliev, as the host, sat at the foot of the table and Colonel Hobbs, as the highest ranking guest, at the head. On

Hobbs' right sat the other Delta Force officers in descending order of rank. An empty chair with a helmet marked Justin Holmes' place. On Hobbs' left sat the US civilians now working on the bomb-recovery project: Creigh Townsend, Fred Garcia, Jeff, Bruce Watson, and Lance Abbott, most of whom were helping with supplies and paperwork. The sergeants, as enlisted men, had not been invited.

Osmonaliev, short and muscular with a uniformed chest full of medals, stood to formally welcome his guests. The somberness of his expression brought out a handsome strength in his round bronze face. His cheeks were flat, nose small, dark eyes narrow but bright. His black thatch of hair showed the indentation from his hatband. "I want to thank you all and the men under your command for coming to Kyrgyzstan. One of you"—he nodded toward Holmes' empty chair—"has already given his life in the service of peace and another is critically wounded. We mourn and honor our fallen comrades. As soldiers, we know that dying in the line of duty is a noble act. These men truly cared about making the world a safer place, as do all of us here. Now we will continue to work together to make that dream a reality."

As he sat down, the women filled all the shot glasses except Jeff's with Kyrgyz brandy. Colonel Hobbs stood up, about Osmonaliev's height but thinner. Deep-set eyes scanned out between a ridged forehead and high, prominent cheekbones flanking a blunt nose. He'd boxed at West Point, Jeff remembered hearing. Middleweight. The coppery tint to his brown skin spoke of a mix of Native-American and African ancestry. He raised his glass in a toast. "Thank you, General Osmonaliev. It's a great thing when former adversaries can become allies and work together to build a safer world...."

Jeff tuned out and let his thoughts drift back to Cholpon's smile. Slight, just a lift of her closed mouth, yet it filled him with cheer. She always seemed so happy—a grin would be superfluous. Just this little spilling over was enough. To kiss her lips while she was smiling, that he'd like to do.

When Hobbs finished his toast, the men raised their glasses to the group then turned to the two people sitting next to them and touched the knuckles of the hand holding the glass. They tossed down the shot, bottoms up. Jeff pretended to drink, wanting to keep his glass full to avoid the compulsory refill for the next round. An empty glass would imply the host was neglecting his duty.

The appetizer was garlicky slices of tomato wrapped with fried eggplant, tasty when eaten with chunks of flat bread. With it came a frothy mug of koumis, fermented mare's milk. Jeff took a polite sip; thick and sour, it fizzed with alcoholic carbonation.

The meal progressed in courses with toasts and down-the-hatch shots in between. Wine was served throughout, but the toasts were made only with brandy. Whenever Jeff craved a drink, he imagined Cholpon's image pressed on his throat like a locket. The urge remained, but now it was overshadowed.

A cucumber-dill salad was followed by potatoes and carrots cooked with chunks of mutton, then the main course, noodles with shredded mutton. Called five fingers, this Kyrgyz specialty was traditionally eaten by hand, but Jeff noticed that Osmonaliev used a fork.

The climax of the meal came when the women with a gracious flourish carried out a silver platter with a baked sheep's head, mouth open, teeth shining, tongue lolling. They stood proudly next to Hobbs, who braced himself for an ordeal. "I am indeed honored, General Osmonaliev," the colonel said. Smiling bravely, he took the silver spoon from the platter, scooped out one of the sheep's eyes, lifted it without looking at it, and swallowed it in one gulp. The ambassador must've briefed him, Jeff thought. Last spring a visiting US VIP had bit into one and thrown up over the table, a diplomatic faux pas. Hobbs washed the eye down with a shot of brandy, coughed, paused for a deep breath, then scooped out and swallowed the second one. "Delicious!"

He'll make general, Jeff thought.

Hobbs ate little of the dessert, an excellent apple cake with berry sauce. Champagne was served at the end of the meal, and Osmonaliev made the closing toast to international harmony.

By now all the men except Jeff were thoroughly sloshed. The women cleared the dishes, enduring a few fanny pats, and left quickly. As soon as they were gone, Creigh Townsend addressed the group. "Now that we can speak more confidentially, I have a few matters of interest to share with you." His grim yet eager tone riveted everyone's attention on him. He folded his arms across his chest, rumpling the vest of his three-piece suit and starched white shirt. Blue eyes flashed out from under a high forehead topped with receding black hair. "We now know—and I'm sure General Osmonaliev can confirm me on this through his sources—that the number of al-Qaeda in country has doubled in the past month...and they have armed units in Bishkek." The officers greeted this news with predatory mutters. "So we may be able to finish off what we started in Afghanistan: eliminate them. I'm sure you'll enjoy meeting up with them again, sort of a *jihad* reunion. These fanatics love to die...and you won't mind helping them out."

"Love to die," Hobbs repeated appreciatively. "That's true...they're worse than our marines."

The officers laughed, and Townsend continued, "The fact that al-Qaeda's here probably means the nuke's still here. So we've got a good chance of getting it back. If they didn't take it, they're looking for it. And we're going to be zeroing in on them."

"Like a laser bomb," Lance whispered.

Fred Garcia leaned his bulky frame back in his chair, a posture which gave him a double chin, and spoke to Townsend. "So you don't put much credence in those al-Jazeera reports...that this thing is already in the US ready to go off." His round, soft-featured face held darts of anxiety, and his crooked teeth chewed the fringe of his salt-and-pepper mustache. Jeff guessed he was worried about family back in DC.

"I've seen nothing—here or from Langley—to back that up," Townsend replied. "I think it's just to create panic."

"From the way the country's reacting...planning to evacuate New York and DC, it seems to be doing the job," Fred said.

Townsend nodded. "These guys know mass psychology. Also technology. Our tracking satellites haven't picked up any nuclear signature on this thing yet, so it may be shielded. That would also explain why our rad detectors here haven't found anything. If they've got it in lead, that makes our work harder...but all the more important."

"I still think the Chechens took it...to blast Moscow with it," Lance said, blue eyes glaring out of his blond, square face. "They know the only thing the Russians understand is force."

General Osmonaliev cleared his throat and spoke, very much in control despite the liquor. "Mr. Townsend's assessment conforms with our intelligence. All of our assets are doing everything possible to pinpoint the location of al-Qaeda. We have

114

also learned that they may detonate this weapon here in Kyrgyzstan...to punish us for siding with America. But I want to assure you that doesn't reduce our support of this joint effort. On the contrary, it makes it all the more clear that terrorism must be destroyed. Our own commando units also are totally committed to finding this terrible weapon. They are not as well equipped as Delta Force, but they are highly trained and disciplined, and they are eager to prove themselves as partners with you. We are looking forward to continuing with you in this new spirit of cooperation between our military and intelligence agencies."

"Thank you, general," Townsend said. "I regret to say I won't be personally continuing here, but I'll certainly brief my replacement on the need for cooperation. Unfortunately I'm being transferred back to Washington." Townsend paused and looked around the room. "It seems a certain lady has pulled some strings. The ambassadress, it turns out, has friends in high places. So I'll be moving on." His mouth pinched. "I wish all of you well...in our crucial mission."

"Aw, what a shitty deal," Bruce Watson said, fleshy face nodding in sympathy. Watson's knit tie was loosened, and the collar of his white short-sleeved shirt was open around his broad neck. A plastic insert with four ball-point pens filled the pocket.

The other men gave confirming murmurs, and Townsend managed an appreciative smile. "Thanks. So it goes...in the government game," he continued. "That's the bad news, but I've also got good news...great news. Sergeant Blake is off the critical list. Looks like he'll make it. He's one tough GI."

The group broke into applause and whoops. This dissolved the formality of the meal, and they stood and stretched.

With a well-brandied smile Lance edged his muscular torso into Jeff. "Hey, you old duck diddler. Who's that gal?"

Jeff turned his bad shoulder away from him. "My psychiatrist."

Lance did a double take. "They got those here? What's she charge?"

Jeff walked away.

Bruce Watson was staring quizzically up at Creigh Townsend as the taller man said with a trace of disdain, "What's my hunch? I don't deal in hunches. I deal in probabilities."

Watson's usually pink face flushed darker, and his steel-gray flattop seemed to bristle. He ducked his jowly chin and looked away.

Townsend turned and spoke to Colonel Hobbs, but the staccato hammering of an AK-47 out on the street overrode his words. Jeff froze in midstep. A cry from below, shouts of anger, then "*Allahu Akbar!*" and a longer burst of fire.

Watson gaped out the window and yelled in panic: "Bastards aiming a rocket launcher!"

Jeff, soberest of the group, dived under the table and rolled into a ball. Townsend fell onto Hobbs, pushed the smaller man to the floor, and covered him with his body as a flash of light and a crash of sound filled the room.

The exploding rocket's concussion battered Jeff and ice-picked his eardrums. Fire engulfed him for an instant, singeing his skin and charring his hair. His scream was silent, sucked from his throat into the vacuum. Incoming shrapnel tore through the table, shattering and splintering it but hurling it away from Jeff, which spared him most of the metal but left him open to flying glass from the window. Slivers of the panes he had looked through before embedded themselves in his back and head.

In a moment the flames were gone, burned out, leaving them in darkness. The building quaked and wobbled. Cordite smoke and the smell of burnt flesh and hair filled his nose. He coughed, flaring white agony, put his hands to his face and sobbed. Enough. Over. Let it come...ride the storm...into oblivion. But Cholpon? He saw her serene face and craved her presence. Wasn't she worth it? Yes. Stick around.

Someone crawled over his back, mauling him with knees and elbows. Jeff gasped in misery. That's what you get for sticking around.

Flashlight beams broke the darkness as men entered the shattered room. Al-Qaeda come to finish us off, he thought, then saw they were Kyrgyz soldiers come to help. One of them set up a lantern. The crawling man was Lance. Most of the skin had been ripped from his face, and his eyes were filled with blood; he groped blindly with hands in front of him. His mouth was moving, but Jeff couldn't hear if it was words or wails.

Coughing from acrid fumes, Jeff crawled to the hole where the window had been and peered over the edge. Two guards lay bleeding on the sidewalk; the street was empty.

He looked back into the smoky room. The lower half of Bruce Watson, shredded and burnt black, lay near the window. The upper half had disappeared—caught the rocket full in the chest. Bits of him were spread over the ceiling and walls. Jeff brushed a chunk off the sleeve of his bloody sportcoat. Bruce, you sweet dope, thanks for taking the hit. They couldn't resist aiming at you, you big curious American. They would've killed more of us if they'd shot past you—rocket would've burst in mid room.

Colonel Hobbs sat splay legged on the floor holding Creigh Townsend's hand and weeping. Townsend's back was ripped open to reveal broken sticks of ribs and a red but motionless lung from which protruded a jagged shard of iron.

Fred Garcia dragged himself toward Jeff, leaving a smear of blood on the floor behind him. His midsection had been blown open, now a ragged maw of burbling fluids, and his legs couldn't move. Jeff crawled to him, put his arms around him, and tried to give him what comfort he could.

Fred's chestnut eyes fluttered and darted, lips moved mutely, fingers scratched Jeff's arm. Jeff clutched him as his friend's liquid life flowed warm over them. Fred began shuddering, squeezed Jeff's hand, then stared at him imploringly. His lips parted as if to speak, but red froth bubbled out.

Groaning deep in his throat, Fred curled his body together, and Jeff cradled him in his arms until the face grew paler and the torso sagged, shivered with a final flurry, then stilled. When Jeff let him go he spread out on the floor.

Jeff cupped his hand to Fred's cheek and gazed down at him, biting his lip. He'd lost so many comrades in the war that his mourning was brief but full of feeling. Liked you, man. You were more than just a boss. A friend, simpatico to all my divorce pain, congratulating me on staying sober with a toast of your bourbon, sharing your job gripes with me. Thanks...good man...*amigo*.

Jeff closed his eyes and prayed: So be it, God. I know Fred's bound to be better off with you. But please help his family get through this.

Most of the Delta Force officers had been clustered around General Osmonaliev, who had been opening a fresh bottle of champagne in the back of the room. They'd been hit hard, but their eagerness had shielded him. The general had taken a chunk of

117

shrapnel in the cheek. Broken teeth showed through the hole as he struggled to his feet and began giving commands to the Kyrgyz soldiers, tears running down his face.

The Delta Force officers lay where they had been tossed about by the blast; some were moving, others inert. A captain was tying his belt around a lieutenant's mangled, spouting arm. Another man stuck his hand into a gash on his head, then gaped unbelieving at his bloody fingers.

Osmonaliev began wrapping the officers' wounds with cloth napkins. Jeff left Fred's body and helped him. They worked together, first making sure each man was still alive.

So much for zeroing in on al-Qaeda, Jeff thought.

The Kyrgyz general was crying as he stanched the wounds. When they ran out of napkins, Osmonaliev gripped both Jeff's hands in his, pressed them to his chest, and spoke, chin wrinkled, round face contorted.

"I can't hear you," Jeff said, but he couldn't hear himself either. That rocket...the last sound he'd ever hear? Listen to it the rest of his life.

Cholpon was brushing her teeth before bed when the doorbell rang. She slipped on her robe, went to the door, and peered through the hole. Jeff stood there, wobbling a bit. Oh no, maybe he was drunk. Last night he'd been drinking. She opened the door warily.

"Sorry to just stop by," he said. "Had a little run-in. Made me really want to see you." His head was shaved and half of it was bandaged. More bandages showed under the collar of his shirt. His face was haggard, the pupils of his eyes small.

She stared at him, her mouth hanging open, and wanted to wrap him in her arms. "What happened to you? Come." She stepped back so he could enter.

Jeff lurched through the door. "Al-Qaeda crashed the party."

She took his hand and led him into the living room, where she looked him over again, appalled.

"I seem to make a habit of seeing you when I'm bleeding. Sorry about that." Jeff managed a crooked smile. "Oh, before I forget...." He pulled a small bag out of his pocket and put it on the table. "I brought you some new flashlight batteries. Those others have had it."

They sat together on the couch, and she held his hand while they talked. He had just come from the Delta Force medics, who'd loaded him with painkillers, shaved his head, stood him under the shower to wash his wounds, plucked out pieces of metal and glass, and sewn him up. Thanks to the table above him, most of his lacerations were superficial. The medics had filled his ears with ointment and cotton, given him a packet of pills, and sent him home, where he'd changed clothes then grabbed a cab to her place.

"Sorry to barge in on you. I won't stay long. Just needed to see you."

"I am glad you came," Cholpon said, unable to take her eyes off his injuries. "Glad you are alive."

"And I'm glad I can hear you. I thought I was deaf for a while. I can still feel the explosion, like it's always going on...expanding out forever...taking me with it. Totally blown out...I'm hardly in my body."

"You will heal your body faster if you are in it," Cholpon said. "There is a way I could bring you back into it. Did you know your whole body is in your foot?"

Jeff shook his head and laughed but then winced as that stretched painful skin. "I'll never be able to predict what you say. You always come up with something different from what I'd expect. No, I didn't know my whole body was in my foot, but now that you mention it, it feels like it...like it's been walked on. Tell me about this foot business."

Nothing to be afraid of with this man, she thought.

Cholpon pointed to his feet. "Each part of the body is connected with a part of the foot...by the nerves. And if you massage that part of the foot, it helps that part of the body. Your head and back hurt too much to be massaged now, but I can help them from your feet."

"I'll try it. I'll try anything. What do I do?"

"Easy. Off the shoes and lie on the couch."

"And you do the work. Sounds wonderful." He scooted out of his shoes, and Cholpon probed and kneaded the soles of his feet. "Feels wonderful too," he said with a sigh. She concentrated on his big toes and the edges of his feet, and he responded with murmurs of appreciation. "Ummm...much better. My back...really doesn't hurt as bad."

When her fingers grew tired, she finished him off with light tingling strokes. She could tell he was relaxed because they didn't make him squirm. "Could you sleep?" she asked.

"I don't think so," he said, eyes closed. He curved his arm around her shoulder. "Thank you. Whew...that helped. This is the second time you've put me back together. You really have a way of cooling me out."

Cooling out...is that good? Cholpon wondered. From his expression it seemed to be.

While massaging him, she had felt her energy flowing into him. Now his energy was flowing into her through his hand, which had dropped down to the small of her back. She could feel its spreading warmth.

The hand fell away and his breath soughed in sleep.

Rest, my warrior.

When he awoke in the morning she fed him tea and melon. The painkillers had worn off, and he felt mangled, like a bone being chewed on by a big dog. His nerves were raw, the light too bright.

He took more pills.

Cholpon sat on the rug beside the couch, spooning slices of honeydew into his mouth. "I talked to my teacher. She said we should come there, she will help."

Jeff was too groggy to have much mind of his own. The idea of help was all he could process; he could use some of that. "When do you want to go?"

"After breakfast."

Forcing his mind back towards clarity, he mulled this over. After this attack, Delta Force would be bogged down in after-action reports and frantic but probably useless patrolling—just so much military tail-chasing. That aggravation he could do without.

Al-Qaeda were expert guerrilla fighters: they'd be hidden away by now—and come out again after the enemy relaxed. In the meantime the best way to find them might be from an entirely new direction...take off on a tangent to get a different angle on them. This old mystic woman might give him that. She knew something. Plus he could use a break...and Cholpon's TLC.

"Well...I guess we could," he said. "How long would we stay?"

"It is hard to say about time with Djamila. Maybe through the weekend."

"That means we can't go to the opera."

"Yes, but *Godunov* is a tragedy. I do not think we want a tragedy."

"No, not if we have a choice. Maybe there'll be something happy next week."

They drove in Cholpon's van to Jeff's apartment so he could pick up a few things. He suggested that she wait in the car—that way she wouldn't see what a wreck the place was, and he could hide the Heckler & Koch in his pack. No point in upsetting her. He pulled on a navy-blue watch cap to cover his shaved and bandaged head.

They stopped off at Delta headquarters on the Kyrgyz Air Force base, where he picked up a radio and survival kit. Most of the US officers were still in the hospital and a few in the morgue, so the HQ was nearly deserted, with one bandaged lieutenant and a sergeant manning the desks. Jeff wrote a memo to Hobbs saying he was tracking down a lead and would report in by radio.

"How about if I drive?" he asked Cholpon.

"This man is crazy," she said with a shake of her head. "Please you just drive yourself onto the back seat and lie down. You need resting."

"Well...OK."

Cholpon headed east towards Lake Issyk-Kul. On the back seat Jeff opened the survival kit and explored its contents with a boy's eagerness: laser pointer, signal mirror, compass, emergency rations, amphetamine pills, morphine Syrettes, antibiotics, bandages, water purification tablets, knife, can opener, fishing gear, all wrapped in a shelter sheet with a cord you could use for a snare. Great stuff.

He dozed.

Midway through the trip, atop the Bistrovka Pass, they stopped for lunch. The pass was arid, rocky, and windy, and the surrounding hillsides cut off the views. Drawn more towards each other than the scenery, they chatted while they ate the picnic Cholpon had packed: raw carrots, rice cooked with lentils and sprinkled with walnuts, soft cheese made from mare's milk, fresh apricots.

When they were finished, he moved closer and put his uninjured arm around her. The cap made his eyebrows more noticeable, grown together into one bent line on his ridged forehead, a reddish brown hawk flying at her. But she saw that the hazel eyes beneath them weren't predatory.

"I'm sure glad you opened your door that first night," he said. "Getting to know you...been one of the best things for me."

"I have enjoyed it too." Her face felt warm and she breathed deeply.

She flinched at the first brush of his lips on hers, but his touch was light, a nuzzle of seeking, and she yielded with a murmur. He held her face in the palm of his hand. Her lips responded timidly, but as he continued they opened more, and his tongue probed between them. At this, her body tensed and she pulled away shaking her head. "We must go."

His look told her, *We must go to bed!* Then he must have sensed her fear because his expression fell; he took her hands in his and gave them a squeeze. "OK. No rush."

She felt grateful...and a bit disappointed.

Jeff took more pain medication and slipped back to sleep on

the rocking, swaying back seat.

"We are almost there," Cholpon called a couple of hours later.

Jeff sat up drowsily, looked around the Issyk-Kul basin, and felt he'd come home. It was like Jackson Hole—a huge lake rimmed by sheer peaks. But here everything was even bigger...wilder. No end to the mountains. And the colors...so vivid—clear air. Blues of water and sky, greens of trees, and that red woodpecker's head drilling on a branch.

As they pulled into the farm, he saw an old wooden house, decrepit but stately, near the lake shore. Behind it, fields and orchards filled a narrow canyon rising up towards the mountains. Quite a place they had here.

Cholpon and Jeff unloaded the van, and the women came out to greet them. They ranged in age from young to elderly but most were somewhere in the middle. They all wore long, unbleached cotton shifts. Most were ethnic Kyrgyz but some were Middle Eastern and a few Russian. Their reactions to a male appearing in their midst ranged from curious to reserved to repelled.

Djamila was down by the lake, her secretary said, and wanted Cholpon and Jeff to join her there.

The two of them walked towards the shore, Jeff glancing around at the immensity of lake, mountains, and sky. The sun's omnipresent glare dissolved the scenery into variations of blue and white. Below him, whitecaps splashed the ultramarine; in front, snow fields sparkled on distant blue peaks; above, clouds dappled the azure. The vista made him feel small and huge at the same time.

They found Djamila on a wooden bench overlooking the water. Wearing the same simple clothes as the others, legs tucked under her, she gazed up at Jeff in the way Cholpon did, staring deep into his eyes then broadening her focus around his edges. "So this is the man...the searcher," she said in English accented from her years in India. She patted the bench beside her. "You sit here. We will see if we can help you find what you are seeking."

Jeff sat on the bench a little farther away and looked at the teacher. Her head was large in proportion to her tiny body. With almost unwrinkled skin, wispy white hair, and a toothless smile,

123

she was so old she was starting to look young again. She was like an elf. Jeff felt a stir of pleasantness and wanted to laugh.

"You are smiling," the old woman said.

"Yeah, I'm surprised. I feel good...in good shape. I've got some pain...but it's just staying where it is." He rotated his neck and touched his hands to his back. "It doesn't really bother me now...bother how I'm thinking."

"And do you know why?"

"No. It's strange. Before I hurt all over...and my head was groggy."

"We have made a special atmosphere in this place. Many people meditating here...many years...creates something in the air, a radiance," the *Shayka* said. "Your brain can feel that. It changes how you think."

"Well, could be. I do feel different here."

"You feel some peace?"

Jeff thought that over. It was a word that almost never occurred to him. "I guess that's what it is. Peace."

"Yes, that's what we make here. Not just for us...for everyone around us. All people are connected and share a consciousness, so what happens in our minds affects theirs."

Sounds occult, thought Jeff. But maybe that's how she can find the nuke, tune in to them somehow.

"There's something else I can feel around you," Djamila continued. "Quite strong."

Maybe I'm radioactive, he thought.

The *Shayka* closed her eyes. "You have a daughter...yes...who loves you very much."

Jeff shook his head, dumbfounded. "She does?"

Djamila nodded. "I can feel it from here."

"I wish *I* could."

"Perhaps you will."

Maybe she just made it up, took a guess. No, it rang true. But a surprise.

He looked back at her with new regard. "I'd be...very happy about that. It's wonderful news. Just your saying it helps. Thanks."

"Your marriage ending...this family breakup...can cover over her love. But it is still there," Djamila said.

How did she know about the divorce? He hadn't told Cholpon.

"Now you have come here...trying to find this horrible bomb. Maybe together we can find it."

"That would be great. What did you have in mind?"

Djamila leaned closer to him. "That's it exactly. You understand. We would find it in the mind. God made us so that our consciousness can encompass the universe. At the deepest level of our mind, we become the same as the universe, so all knowledge is available to us. But to look inside and find it, we need to be in that state where we *are* the same...where this is a reality, not just an idea."

Jeff glanced away dubiously. What she was saying didn't make a lot of sense to him. Too supernatural. But still...there could be something to it. Psychic power was probably real. He could believe this woman had it...she was remarkable...some kind of shimmer around her. Might be worth finding out. He looked back at her. "Well, if that's true...how do we get there?"

"By meditation. That is where we go when we meditate. Would you like to learn?"

Jeff mused. In the seventies in Boulder he'd taken a yoga class and meditated by staring at a candle. He'd liked it, it'd been relaxing, but after a while he let it go. He wouldn't mind trying something like that again. From Djamila's bright energy he could sense that what she had to teach would be more powerful. And this place had something special about it...a spark, a lightness. He could feel it, he wanted it—his way hadn't gotten him very far. This was an amazing person...and so was Cholpon. Maybe meditating was how they got that way. And maybe some of it would rub off on him. Couldn't hurt. "Well...I'll try it."

"To learn you must give something."

"Like money?"

"Not money. Time. You have to give your time. That is more precious."

"OK."

"That means twice a day, every day you have to do the meditation. Otherwise you should not learn."

"I'll do it," he said, and thought, I'll see how it goes.

The *Shayka* stretched out her legs, pushed herself up from the bench, and stood unsteadily a moment until her knees adjusted. "Cholpon, get the *puja* table ready. We will initiate this man of yours." They walked back toward the house, Djamila barefoot.

Inside the salon, Jeff saw the colorful fabric wall hangings and thought how much his daughter would like them. Dear Tricia, I love you too.

They entered Djamila's office, where Cholpon arranged roses and apples and a square of white cloth on a brass tray. She lit candles and incense and left the room.

Jeff wished she'd stayed, felt uneasy being alone with the *Shayka*. He hardly know her. She was a strange old bird. Did he really want to meditate? Back then it'd been the thing to do, now it seemed too mystical. But his life was at a dead end. He had to try another road, a new approach. An inner nudging told him he needed to learn this, it would be good for him.

Djamila asked him to sit in a chair next to her while she stood in front of a picture of a white-bearded man in an orange robe. "This is Brahmananda, Maharishi's teacher, who gave us this transcendental meditation. Now we will thank him for the knowledge." She began singing in a high little voice in a language he didn't recognize. She dipped a flower into a bowl of water and waved it around, spraying water here and there, then laid the fruit, flowers, and cloth in front of the picture. While she sang, a calm settled over him, and his face relaxed as tension dissolved. When she finished, the *Shayka* knelt in front of the picture and whispered a sound very softly, as if to herself, then gradually louder until he could hear it clearly: *Nivar-ti-tyam*.

She turned to him and said, "Say it with me."

They repeated it together, then she said, "Now close the eyes and think it silently."

He could see the word floating through his mind in curlicues—a Möbius strip turning into an infinity sign. It resonated through him, first with his heartbeat then with his breath, quieting them. His whole body relaxed, and he felt he was sinking deep into the chair, into the earth even, not sitting but floating. His thoughts started to space out, with gaps of silence between them. The silence grew into a delightful emptiness. At the center of it pulsed the mantra, a blend of sound and light. It grew fainter, finer, then disappeared like a bird wing-waving away, leaving his mind alert but without content, aware but not of any thing.

Then he heard noises from outside: a horse snorted and stamped its hoof, a cow mooed. Distracted, he drifted onto thoughts of Wyoming, the ranch in Sheridan where his father had worked, saw faded photos of his dad. His breath and heartbeat increased, sadness wafted over him.

No...don't get trapped in all that again. He brought his mind back to the mantra, which mixed with the other thoughts and eased them away. The calmness returned.

He inhaled lightly, tendrils of air curling into a vast space behind his closed eyes. As the sound continued, his mind became a darkness full of light, an emptiness that seemed to contain everything. Happiness welled up within him and he laughed.

The laughter brought him out of it, back to his body sitting in a chair. He opened his eyes; the room glowed.

I want to go back.

"Close the eyes and continue," said Djamila.

The sound now stretched out into a slow drone, then seemed to fold in on itself and turn inside out. He had a moment of deep silence, a plunging dive into rich, full nothingness, then thoughts rushed in and pulled him away.

Images and emotions from the past, burned deep into neural archives, flowed out as if from a film. He was a little boy tying a handkerchief to a toy soldier and throwing it up in the air. The handkerchief opened and his paratrooper dad came floating down to fight beside him. In his bedroom amid toy tanks and cannons, they had fought together from Guadalcanal to the Yalu River, and they always won. Above them flew models of Flying Tigers, Zeros, and Messerschmitts, and from his favorite power-diving fighter hung his father's dog tags.

Wails of loss rose within and surged over him. He pinched his eyes tighter and shook his head to chase the pictures away, but they ran on, needing release.

Now he was in a rice paddy, half crazy with fatigue and fear, pinned down by a North Vietnamese ambush. The NVA were firing a machine gun at them from a bamboo grove. Bullets flailed the paddy water, kicking up spouts, moving closer. John Randall, his team sergeant, answered fire with his rifle from behind a dike. Jeff was caught in the open, unable to move for lack of cover.

From out of the sky a plane dived and released a bomb that tumbled end over end to burst into an orange globe of fire engulfing the bamboo.

Driven out by napalm flames, a dozen gray figures with leaf-covered helmets rushed from the grove, yelling and firing their AK-47s.

Jeff panicked, jumped up, and ran back toward Randall. Bullets tore past him with dopplered whines.

The sergeant rose to his knees above the dike and shouted, "Get down, you fool!" Randall shook with spasms and fell back into the paddy.

Jeff's mind broke in a shriek; a bright, frozen glaze spread over his sight. The sergeant lay twisted in the mud, legs trying to move, two holes in his chest gushing blood. Jeff sank down beside him. "You'll be OK." He pressed his hands to the wounds, but blood throbbed through his fingers.

Jeff dropped his rifle and held Randall's twitching body. "I'll fix you up. We'll call a medevac." He clutched the sergeant while his M-16 sank into the paddy.

The plane roared back, so low Jeff could see rivets, and strafed the NVA, who crumpled into the muddy water.

He gathered Randall in his arms. Breath whistled from the chest holes and blood pulsed warm but slower now, staining both their uniforms ruddy brown. The sergeant gripped Jeff with dwindling strength, then stared blindly at him. A flicker of recognition lit his face. Jeff tried to draw the filming eyes into his, to keep their light as they faded.

Randall began thrashing and convulsing. He drew his knees to his chest; his jaw sagged, breath rasped.

"No!" Jeff held him and rocked back and forth. Why couldn't it have been me instead?

His inner voice lashed him: Because you're worse than worthless, a minus. This proves it.

Jeff dipped his chin in a cringe, sweating, feeling six years old, wanting to cry.

He opened his eyes to see Djamila gazing at him with calm compassion. "These are very sad stresses you have had," she said. "Now they are coming out. They are ready to be healed." She stepped closer to him and touched his head. "The meditation can bring up these old pains. Usually not so soon, but sometimes it happens. It is part of the purification. All this must come out. It is blocking your consciousness. We will give it some help...to release it. Then once it goes, it is gone. You are free of it."

As her fingers caressed his temples, his head jerked and his body shuddered. He closed his eyes again to filaments of light streaming between her hands. It blotted out the scenes, but the feelings remained.

He'd lost his dad again just when he thought he'd found him. He'd looked up to Randall, the older man's rare praise meant more to him than anything. The death Jeff's fault...his stupidity.

Djamila massaged in slow circles, making the light flow. Although her touch was gentle, the pain became more physical, turning into two clots of agony beneath her fingers. Jeff moaned, clenched his jaw, and gasped. The *Shayka* moved one hand to the back of his neck, the other to his forehead; she pressed harder than he would've thought possible for her; the pain compressed to a point, a hot spark. When she took her hands away, it disappeared.

The mantra moved into the space where the pain had been. Gradually it filled the raw, hollow pit inside him. He listened to it, he watched it, he felt better.

His breath and heartbeat quieted again, and the torment fell away, leaving him stunned, with no idea what would come next.

"Open the eyes," Djamila said.

Jeff blinked.

"How is the pain now?" she asked.

"Gone." His voice was a whisper. "That's really something."

"Was it easy to think the mantra?" Djamila asked.

"Yeah. It sort of thought itself. Took me on quite a trip."

"Usually it will be more peaceful."

"Even the pain...seemed right...needed to happen."

"Pain will not always be there. Now you should lie down and rest." She led him down the hall to an empty room where they had fixed up a cot for him.

He stretched out and looked up at the bright little woman. "Amazing stuff," he said. "What's with the song and the flowers and everything?"

"The ceremony, the chanting, that is what gives the mantra its power. It enlivens its vibrations when you first hear it. Without that, it would be just a word. It would not have the effect."

"Should I think it now?"

"No, it has done its work. Just rest."

The rest turned into an hour of black-out sleep. He awoke

confused, not knowing where he was, but as he came back to himself and lay there looking at the ceiling, he felt light and clear, freed of a weight he hadn't known he'd been carrying until it was gone. An old festering tumor had been pulled out of him. He gave a huge exhalation and knew with relief that John Randall was once again his friend.

Jeff wandered through the strange house and found Cholpon in the kitchen cleaning the beans, spreading them on a tray and picking out sticks and stones with her short, nimble fingers. Suddenly everything was beautiful to him—her, the speckled beans, the little rocks that could break a tooth. Life might hold something better than what he'd known so far. He helped her finish, and they took a walk.

A dazzle of sun greeted them outside. Strolling up the canyon and talking with Cholpon about what had happened helped him to leave the trauma in the past. They walked through fields of melons and vegetables, pastures with cows, sheep, and horses, and orchards of walnuts, apples, and apricots. The plants were ripening into a late-summer flourish of leaves, fruits, pods, and seeds. It seemed to him the perfect setting for Cholpon.

"I never thought I'd be here," he said, "with a beautiful woman...learning to meditate. Glad."

Cholpon smiled and lowered her eyes.

At the grape arbors, leaf-covered lattices offered a verdant shelter, a private place. They sat on a bench in green shade under vines hanging heavy with muscat.

He could feel her warm breathing body next to his. Sweat glistened above her lip, making him want to lick it, taste its wet salt. He started at her cheek, grazing over her fine-pored skin, then nibbling the corners of her mouth and pressing her full lips. A flush of delight ran through him.

She sat eyes closed, tense, breathing more heavily now. As he gave her more kisses, she relaxed and began returning them, her lips curious for these new sensations. She allowed his tongue to enter, even greeted it with her own.

Finally he dared a hand on her silk blouse, stroked her, felt the points of her breasts tighten and swell. He opened the buttons and caressed the mounded smoothness brimming above her bra.

Oh good, a front opener. He unhooked it and they flowed out to him, glad of release. She started to object, but he covered her lips again with his while his hands touched her urgently, touched her gently.

Needing to see them again, he broke the kiss. They stood out with curving fullness, dappled with green light through the arbor, nipples pert and alert.

There they are. So beautiful.

Within them ran tiny veins spreading liquid nourishment, like the translucent leaves around them. Everything was flowing with fluids of nurture. He kissed a breast, sucked it, and the tip filled.

Ah bliss. There is no better place than this.

Under his lips her tits grew taut. His own fluids began to rise, yearning to flow into hers. All of us frail wet creatures huddled together for succor.

Cholpon clutched him to her and stroked his head through his watch cap; he winced with pain from his wounds.

She gasped and took her hands away. "Oh, I have hurt you! No, I am sorry."

She moved her hands back towards him to comfort him but then stopped, afraid of hurting him again.

"It's OK." Jeff laughed to dismiss it. "Just a bit of masochistic spice." From her puzzled expression he could tell she didn't know what this meant.

"Your poor head. With the hat I forgot."

"Doesn't matter." He started for her breasts again, but the spell had been broken. Her hands covered them, and she glanced nervously around to see if anyone was watching. "We...cannot do this here," she stammered. "This is not what we do here. We must wait...until...I don't know...not now."

Flustered, she rehooked her bra. Grieved to see them disappearing, he put his arm around her shoulder to reestablish contact. "Well...I guess it is a little reckless out here. Maybe I can sneak into your room tonight. We could be alone."

She shook her head, unable to look at him. "No. Here we do not do such things."

"Oh well...you can't blame a guy for trying. Maybe...how about you sneak into my room?"

She managed an exasperated laugh. "If you don't stop, we will make you sleep in the barn with Talas."

"Who's Talas?"

"He's our other stallion. We don't let him in the house either."

"OK, I'll be good." He stood up to indicate his surrender. Worth waiting for, worth waiting for, he told himself. She likes you. She's quite special. She and the meditation could be a second chance for you.

That evening Djamila called the Sufis and Jeff together in the meeting room. Her secretary pinned a large map to the wall showed Kyrgyzstan and portions of the neighboring countries: Tajikistan, Afghanistan, Uzbekistan, Kazakstan, and China.

"We must see...what we can do," Djamila said in a lilting chant while looking at Jeff. So small, he thought, even frail, but she sparkled with power. "Somewhere it is here. We must see it...and find it. Now is the time. We must take the boys' toys away from them...these terrible weapons. These men...this bin Laden, this Bush, all these leading men...they have highjacked us all with their violence. They have turned the whole world into their suicide airplane. These men are too primitive to have such power. Too ignorant of the underlying reality. We must stop them."

Good luck, lady, thought Jeff. She was only speaking English, so it must be for him. The others must already know what she meant.

The teacher waved her arms commandingly. "I need room to move...room to see. Clear this out." She gestured to the cushions and prayer mats on the floor. "All of this against the wall. I will dance. And then we will see."

They cleared the floor and sat on cushions around the walls, leaving the old woman standing in the middle. She began to dance slowly, in little birdlike skips that circled in rings. "The deathmen have their fire...and we have our fire. Theirs burns the bodies of the people, ours burns only ignorance. We will see whose is stronger. We will dance down the deathmen, we will dance down their war." As the *Shayka* whirled faster, her hands rose above her head, her shift furled and rippled. "The deathmen have set us all in flames. But we have something more powerful, the transcendent. Their fire cannot destroy our immortality. We will whirl in the flames—we are the flames, we are the whirling, we are the still center into which the flames whirl and disappear." Her voice had turned raw and exultant. "Now sing to me...chant the *Shakti sutra*."

The forty voices merged into a chorus, sounding to Jeff like Gregorian chant but starker, less melodic, more resonant. Its grave elegance drew his mind inward, where it enlivened the contrast to his own inner silence.

Djamila sang with them while she spun, her flossy white hair a crown of sparks, her toothless mouth a cavern into the universe. The swirling patterns and intense colors of the wall fabrics danced with her.

"Now let the song continue in silence. All of you meditate, bring up the transcendent" she said, "and I will look into the diamond."

Jeff closed his eyes. Should he meditate, though? What old hurt would come out this time? But better that it came out...and left...than stay bottled up in there. Since the first session this afternoon, he felt unburdened, calmer, more balanced inside.

The singing stopped, and in the quiet he could hear Djamila's feet spinning in the dervish dance and feel the breeze she stirred.

The sound of his mantra volleyed around his mind, then gradually settled into a quiet hum. As it became fainter, his breath slowed and his other thoughts spooled out into dreamy meanderings then dropped away. The mantra faded, leaving a still, silent clarity of mind without thoughts but aware of itself—a static state like being suspended in a crystal, but also ecstatic, charged with joy.

Wonderful!

At the thought, it was gone. He took a deep breath; other thoughts poured in. These were about Cholpon, pleasant rather than painful, her presence now beside him, kissing her breasts beneath the arbor. The mantra weaved its way through and took him away again until Djamila's voice broke in:

"This bomb is in a valley. A town where two highways meet. Trees...near the mountains...on a strange looking truck...men with guns. It is metal. It is there." The *Shayka* stood still in the middle of the room, eyes closed, palms up, smiling. "Now I need your help. We must find where 'there' is."

For the next half hour the Sufis pored over the map, looking for highway crossings at valley towns, then narrowing down the possibilities based on what they knew of those areas. They came up with a short list of three:

Naryn in the south near China. Kyrgyzstan and China were distrustful and unfriendly neighbors, so the Chinese might've taken it. So might've the Islamic militants in northwestern China, who were getting more violent.

Sary Tash in the southwest near Tajikistan and Afghanistan. Al-Qaeda and Taliban units were active in this area, with a holy hatred of the US and its allies.

Kara Balta in the north near Kazakstan. From here whoever took it could wipe out the US oil drilling operations on the Kazak steppe.

"We will go. All of us. To these places. And find it," said Djamila.

"Then what?" Jeff asked.

"We will bring these men the gift of peace. We will do as in the ancient Vedic times. Every village had a group of meditators. They created coherence in the people around them...purified the collective consciousness. Violent thoughts would dissolve in this peaceful atmosphere, wouldn't come out into action.

"But I do not know if it will work now. This is a way to keep the peace, but the violence has already broken out. The negative forces may be too strong...they may have to erupt...into war. Then Kali's dance of destruction...could sweep everyone up.

"But we will do what we can. We have to try." The *Shayka's* glistening eyes sought out Jeff's.

He met her look and seemed to expand inside, as if their minds were a gateway into something larger. The sensation was scary but exhilarating. This woman really had something. If her way showed them where the nuke was, she'd have definitely earned that ten million dollars.

But could meditating affect other people? Well...it had affected him. Even before he'd meditated, just being around them, he'd felt better. Something in the atmosphere. He didn't know how it worked...but it did.

His first meditation had been powerful. Even now he breathed differently, deeper but less often. He was even...happy.

Everything he'd done before had been hard-line. Look at the result. He had to try another way...and so far Cholpon and Djamila's seemed pretty good. Give it the benefit of the doubt. He might even get to know God better. Something was happening here.

If she found the bomb, he'd radio Delta Force to grab it. No point in getting impractical.

Lake Issyk-Kul mirrored the dawn sky in a wash of amber and blue, rimmed by the green of pines along the shore. Reflections of trees shimmered on the surface as dew fell from needles to ripple the water. Cholpon and Jeff stood on the bank, enjoying a moment of solitude while the others loaded food, blankets, and cushions on the bus. Across the lake a swath of gray mist hid the far shore and the slopes of the mountains, but their snowy peaks floated pink above it.

"Thanks for all this," Jeff said. "Yesterday was...I don't know...hard to describe...a whole other dimension." He wore faded jeans, his green corduroy shirt, and the watch cap over the bandages on his head. His rucksack hung over one shoulder as he held her hand.

"I am glad you were open to it." Cholpon wore dark-blue wool slacks and a saffron sweater. Her almond skin contrasted with her ebony hair, which glistened with blue highlights in the morning sun. She glanced back at the others. "Time to go."

As they were getting on the bus, Jeff asked Djamila, "Should I drive?"

The teacher surveyed him and said dryly, "A steering wheel is not so heavy. We women handle that quite well."

Jeff felt foolish, then thought, Wait till you have a flat tire. You'll be glad I'm here.

Djamila smiled indulgently up at him. "You and Cholpon sit up front...beside me." She pointed a crooked finger at him and her smile turned wry. "So I can keep an eye on you."

She likes to rattle my chain, he thought.

The *Shayka* looked regal, wrapped in a purple velvet cloak. The other Sufis wore practical pants and sweaters, ready for mountain cold.

Jeff's wounds stung as if acid were eating them, but the pain was localized and less than yesterday. His mind was clear, without the wooziness and flush of infection.

Cholpon sensed Jeff's body struggling with its injuries as they sat with their sides touching. He had...fortitude. He was not one to give up. And he was off to a good start with the meditation. Already his aura had more blue and gold, less red. Djamila seemed to like him...the sisters at least accepted him...exotic visitor. They seemed inhibited from having a man along, though, not laughing and talking as much. But maybe that was fear of the bomb.

The bus drove along the lake shore, Acel at the wheel, past wisps of morning fog hovering in swales and ravines. In the damp barrow pits grew reeds and pampas grass. Oak trees overarched the road, creating a leafy canopy above them, and acorns clattering onto the roof of the bus. Acorns made Jeff think of Cholpon's nipples. Kiss them again. Maybe soon. All the inviting lushness of her...so close...tantalizing him.

Village women knelt beside the road filling wicker baskets with acorns for winter flour. They waved and so did the women in the bus. A red squirrel with tufted ears leapt between trees.

As they left the shore and climbed into the hills, the oaks gave way to poplars, leaves already turning yellow, sun strobing through the trunks as they sped along. This was orchard country, bent-boughed apple and pear trees laden with fruit. A picker stood on a ladder made from a single poplar trunk with pegs jutting out from either side, filling a horse cart while his horse munched windfall fruit.

Farther out in the field a man and woman dug potatoes alongside a grazing camel.

The bus drove through a village with square, squat houses of adobe and sandstone, built solid for insulation in minus-forty winters. Decorative carvings trimmed the wooden window frames and shutters, and mosaics of colored glass bordered the doors. The leathery smell of burning dung wafted from chimneys.

Yellow ribbons for good-luck wishes, the custom for greeting new-born babies, were tied to a shagbark cedar tree next to one of the houses. A brown cow with a yellow ribbon looped around her horns grazed in the yard. At her feet, black-and-white magpies nibbled on cow pies.

Welcome, little one, Jeff thought. Hope all the wishes come true.

Round-faced children waved and sang at the bus. Jeff imagined Cholpon and Djamila once being little girls like that. Now they were wise Sufi adepts. And they were changing him, both of them.

Sparsely whiskered old men watched impassively under round brown hats whose fur brims could fold down as ear flaps. Women in long skirts and dark shawls carried plastic water jugs on their shoulders to and from the communal pump, too burdened to

137

wave but not to smile.

On the outskirts of the village a man, his feet almost touching the ground, rode a small, trudging donkey down the road with two bulging loads of hay strapped to each side. The donkey's foal had dawdled behind and now trotted to catch up with mom.

In the fields farmers were harvesting hay with scythes and sickles. Golden clouds of straw dust hung in the air.

I don't want a nuclear bomb to destroy all this, Jeff thought. I really don't want that.

They turned south and entered the Tien Shan, the Sky Mountains, a young, sheer, jagged range like the Tetons but taller. Here they left the villages behind: the soil was too scanty for agriculture and the winters too harsh for human culture. They passed a few yurt encampments, though, where nomadic shepherds grazed their flocks in summer. The yurts—circular, domed-roofed huts made of gray felt and trimmed with brightly colored fabrics—were set along the edges of pastures.

At one point they had to wait while a herd of sheep crossed the road. The shepherd was on horseback and saw no need to hurry his flock for a mere bus. His dog frolicked in the stream beside the road, lapping water milky from granite particles. Pines and willows bordered the stream but couldn't climb the rocky slopes.

Traffic was sparse: trucks, buses, and a few rugged autos. The higher they drove the fewer people they saw until they were left with just Lenin's stern, fatherly figure staring down at them from the canyon walls and promontories. His bust had been chiseled into the stone, and his full standing form, arm pointing towards the communist utopia, was cast in bronze at overlook points. The two-lane highway, gravel with stretches of concrete, had been blasted and pick-axed into the mountainsides because the canyon floor was too narrow and too often flooded to tolerate a road. A tribute to dynamite, hard labor, and Soviet engineering, this was one of the few routes to penetrate the Tien Shan and was closed most of the winter.

Above timberline the slopes were bare except for occasional patches of emerald grass sparkling with red and yellow flowers. Gritty snow fields spilled onto the road; they had to stop several times to clear rockfalls.

The sun glared out of a deep blue sky and glinted the granite into coral. The barren landscape was drenched with light, the air dry and thin.

Every few hours they got off the bus for prayers and yoga asanas. In between they sang and snacked and napped and worried.

Evening was approaching as they dropped down into Naryn, one of the regions that matched the scene in Djamila's vision. The town lay at the bottom of a river gorge cut deep into the earth, its walls so sheer and the space between them so narrow that they confined the sky, shrinking it to a distant span of lavender overhead. The town was stretched along the river, its one main street already lit with neon arches because of the shadows.

Gloomy. They must only have sun at midday, Jeff thought.

Djamila looked about her with disappointment. "This is not it. The valley was wider. But we will spend the night here."

Jeff insisted on putting them all up in a hotel, but his generosity was mixed with selfishness. He whispered in Cholpon's ear, "A room just for you and me."

She lowered her eyes. Was she ready for this? Yes. She'd hardly slept last night from thinking about him. It was time. Scary, but yes. Some of the sisters might be scandalized, but that was their problem.

The only hotel that could hold them all was a stack of Soviet concrete on the central square. The most that could be said about the rooms was that they had high ceilings, which gave them a spacious feel and made the cobwebs more remote.

As they unpacked, Cholpon felt self-conscious; the room's anonymity reminded her how little they knew each other, at least on the surface. She glanced nervously around at the décor—Party moderne, as she called it. In Soviet times most travelers had been Communist Party officials, so the hotels had been furnished to their taste: chairs, table, and bed of square-cornered functionality without ornament but with a certain sleekness. The blond oak veneer was now peeling off to reveal pine underneath. Cigarette burns and vodka rings marred the finish. Her father the commissar would've liked the room. But would he have liked Jeff? And would he like her being here with him?

Jeff's maleness seemed to fill the space. Now she felt shy and reluctant about having left her sisters to be with him. For a moment of visual escape, she went to look out the window but

139

recoiled at the touch of the dusty net curtain, the gray of shrouds. She turned back to him, breath tight in her chest. She hadn't been with a man...in that way...for fifteen years. She hadn't wanted it...until now. She had to admit she did want him. Why?

Being around him...she felt solider, more complete. But she hadn't felt unsolid or incomplete before. Had he taken something away from her and was now offering it back...at a price...her independence? Or had she discovered something deeper about herself, urges that needed to be fulfilled before they could rest?

Will he be gentle?

"I like your friends," Jeff said, approaching her. "But I like better to be with just you."

She couldn't meet his eyes. What would he do now...grab her?

Jeff kept chatting. "Alone together. Do you like that too?" He stood behind her and encircled her middle with his arms.

She was too nervous to answer, but she swallowed and he seemed to take that for a yes. "Good," he said and hugged her.

Uh oh, here it comes. The pressure of his arms relaxed some of her tension. He kissed the back of her neck and rubbed her waist. She exhaled deeply, audibly, and was embarrassed by the sound, but with the breath another wave of tension left her. His lips brushed her ear then pressed her cheek as he leaned down and nuzzled the side of his head against hers. She felt a flutter of fear, then thought of Djamila's saying, *That which cannot be avoided is better met head on.* Seeing his head beside hers, she started to laugh, then couldn't stop as her nerves dissolved into giggles.

"What's so funny?" he asked, now contagiously amused himself.

"Head on," was all she could manage.

"OK, good idea." He turned her around to face him.

Uh oh, she thought, now you're in for it. And you asked for it. His eyes...beams of ardor scanning her. She tensed again, but another wave of laughter swept it away as his hands went up her quivering sides. She stopped laughing as his lips fused with hers and his arms drew her to him. Because of his height she had to raise her head and that raised her breasts; she could feel them rub against him with a tingle.

No...Yes. Wait...Now. She kissed him back, nudging her lips into his; then fear tightened on her again. She couldn't breathe or speak but couldn't stop kissing either. He rubbed his hands over her back, generating waves of warmth. He dropped one arm down to her legs; she could feel his muscles against her. As he scooped her off the ground into his arms and carried her towards the bed, the fear increased, clutching her like a metal band. Why was she afraid? Wouldn't she rather have his embrace than the fear's? Did she have a choice? Yes, give in. Let him.

He eased her down onto the mattress; she rolled away from him, facing the wall, her long hair splashing across her back. What was he going to do to her? How did they do it there? He lay beside her, one hand on her stomach, the other on her neck, rubbing. The bed, built for behemoths, was sturdy and hard. "Don't be afraid," said his voice in her ear, breath tickling. The front of his legs pressed the rear of hers, and his chest pressed into her back while he held her. Helpless. She could feel how much he wanted her.

Somehow it all made her cry, sobs that she knew were silly but couldn't stop.

"Hey," Jeff whispered, stroking the side of her face. "It's all right."

He put his hand on her breast with a touch that made her cry louder, but only for a moment as her fear fell into tatters while her heart began to pound. He rubbed the sides and slopes and tips of them, and as warmth swelled inside her she knew she was gone, his now to do with whatever he wanted, and this surrender made her cry again but in a long moan.

He was so much bigger than she was.

His hands were beneath her blouse and sweater now, plundering her, and his breath was faster and louder in her ear. She flushed with shame at how much she liked this. But she wouldn't like it with just anyone. It was him.

He turned her on her back and kissed her a long deep wet time while petting her, and she felt like a fountain bubbling up at him, offering herself. Then her arms were over her head, clothes coming off into his eager hands, his eyes searing her. "A cover...sheet...something," she stammered, covering her breasts with her arms. It was ridiculous, she knew, that she wanted him to touch her but not to see her. But it wasn't him...it was imagining others seeing them. She needed protection.

"Sure." He pulled down the bedspread, rolled her over onto

141

the cool inner sheets, got in beside her, and pulled the covers back over both of them; his hands and lips went back to work on her.

You must be crazy, part of her protested. Letting a man you hardly know do this to you.

I know him.

His own shirt came off, and they lay bare chest to chest, and her arms wrapped around him but flinched at the touch of his bandages. He was gazing at her breasts now beneath the sheet and murmuring deep in his throat as his mouth closed on them. The moisture and pressure of his lips seemed to fill them, making them fluid and heavy, making them want more of this.

For years...without even knowing it...she'd been waiting to present these to her true love...have him appreciate them, kiss them. They weren't any use to her, and he enjoyed them so much.

His hand moved up her legs with feathery strokes that made her shiver. Then his touch grew firmer, kneading her thighs, loosening her resistance as he moved higher. His half-clothed body was tense against her. He could hurt me. His fingers rested on her center, then delved in, touching her, fondling her delicately for a long time, sending shimmers of delight through her.

She closed her eyes as he took off his jeans. She could hear him panting and feel him trembling as he loomed over her. Afraid to look...but she wanted to look. He was putting something on it, covering it up. Oh...no baby. Then he was covering her with his long heavy body, and she seemed so small beneath him. A painful pushing at her middle. After years of chastity, her petals had closed into a tight bud. Now he was forcing them open, pressing in slowly, patiently, but insistently, spreading her inside, stretching her, sinking deeper in. Unaccustomed to this intrusion, she had to yield and yield more under his weight and size but there was a luxury in that. Gradually she unfolded, opened fully, blossomed out, petals clinging to this hard stem swelling in the softness of her center. He was touching something deep in her, filling her in a way that was so comforting, that she hadn't known she needed but was glad to find.

As she loosened, he moved in her in long thrusts, taking her. His power surged through her, overcoming her, freeing a wildness of acquiescence in her. Instead of just letting him, now she was eagerly giving herself to him, and the more he took, the more rose within her and flowed out to him.

He was petting her with his fingers as he moved in her, stroking her inside and outside. He riffled her tender node, fluttered around it, stirred it, roused it to a liveliness that built to an urgency of ecstasy.

Crying out, he was ramming her, enveloping her with his grunting body, now odored with a sharp appeal. Beneath him, she cleaved to him as he was cleaving her, riding her. His long ragged face was filled with adoration as he gazed down at her, his golden brown eyes moist. "I love you, Cholpon, I love you, woman. I want to do this to you always...I want to be with you always."

He was clambering over her, kissing her ravishingly. *Yes!* Her whole being seemed to rush together into one vivid point then explode out in seismic waves, contract again to a quivering quick then burst into effulgence, streaming in spasms, screaming in bliss, loving this man who was doing it to her.

At the peak her ego dissolved, her walls came tumbling down, and she merged with All. Her love expanded until she was one not just with Jeff but with creation. The boundlessness was like transcending during meditation but briefer, just a flash of unity. Then the walls came up again and she contracted back into duality—self and other.

As they clung together, Cholpon understood why people need sex so much. It's their only contact with unity. Sex did it by overwhelming us with sensations, and meditation by stilling sensations, but both brought us to the center of the universe where everything is one. With sex, the getting there was more fun...but with meditation you got to stay there longer.

They gradually swirled to a stop and lay hugging, floating in each other, murmuring shards of sound, unable to talk. They kissed. They slept.

Cholpon stole from their bed while Jeff was still asleep and rejoined her sisters for early morning prayer in a large downstairs room. She glanced away from their curious stares, her cheeks flushing. What were they thinking of her? Acel looked jealous, Zaryl offended. They knew she was no longer celibate. They knew...what she and Jeff had done. But they didn't know...what Jeff was really like.

But they wanted her to be happy. They might tease her but they were still her sisters. Whatever they were thinking, she needed to be who she was. And part of that now was Jeff's woman. It didn't feel unspiritual—it felt right. Djamila said the way to get enlightened was to meditate regularly then follow your deepest desires. Now they were for Jeff.

The ritual of *faqr*—bowing and praying to invoke the grace of Allah—brought her back into the group and showed their differences to be small compared to this bond they shared.

As she recited the verses, Cholpon imagined a *mullah* condemning her: *You have copulated with an infidel!*

She pushed the voice away. And I liked it! Stone me.

She went back upstairs and crept into bed. Jeff woke, blinked, smiled, murmured, "You...good...come here." He drew her into his warm embracing nakedness, and they cuddled together. "You have all your clothes on."

"Yes. You don't."

"How long have you been up?"

"Little while."

He yawned and stretched. "I guess I should do that too. Work to be done. But first." He snuggled closer and kissed her, stroked her forehead. "Last night...was great. It meant a lot to me."

She nodded into the hollow of his shoulder and neck, timid again but trying not to be. "To me too." The sight of his muscular body wearing only bandages made part of her want to blush and look away, another part of her to touch and surrender to him. Of the two parts, she now preferred the second—it was more honest. To be covered by his power, yes, all over her...carry her away. But not right now.

Red splotches had bled through some of his bandages; on others the tape was beginning to peel. "You need some new windings," she said.

"If you say so." He got up and took fresh dressings and tape from his pack.

She peeled off the old bandages, both of them wincing, he from the pain, she from causing it and from the sight of blood still oozing from the punctures. The bleeding was less than yesterday, though, and most of the holes were already scabbing over. She checked his first set of wounds, from the night they'd met, and saw the smaller scabs were already sloughing off. He seemed to heal quickly, a good trait in his line of work.

He looked so different from any man she'd known. Light-brown eyes set so deep...such a large nose, bent...wide mouth. And the scars...what he'd been through...and new ones coming pink and wrinkled. And down there he was different too—didn't have the cap.

His kiss...with the tongue. That was strange...but...stirring. The way he held her then.

She was starting to need him—he'd upset her yin-yang balance. All those years she'd been so stable inside, a balance of female and male. Maybe that made her a neuter, but it was comfortable. Now being around him, her inner male had fled, deserted her, and her abandoned female was clinging to Jeff. She was afraid he could make her do anything. She crumbled inside when he touched her. That had never happened before. This dissolution before his intrusion, his pressure, her opening—his solidity, her liquidity—this fearsome closeness.

She washed his wounds as he bathed in a tub with porcelain tiger paws for feet. "Your back...it looks like the tiger bit you," she told him.

Jeff gave a snorting laugh. "Rather a tiger than rusty old iron from a rocket. Tiger teeth are nice and clean...compared to shrapnel. I just hope whatever's left in there...that it works its way out...instead of deeper in. I don't want to set off metal detectors."

Cholpon dried his back and put on fresh bandages. "I want you to have not any more wounds. To be well and happy...not get hurt again."

"That sounds good...it even sounds possible." He drew her arms around his waist. "You've given me a reason to want that. Made me come alive again. *Spasibo.*"

"*Pajalsta*"—You're welcome. She kissed the back of his neck.

145

His voice turned awkward, hesitant: "We should stay together."

She tried to keep her voice steady. "I would like that."

"Good. I don't know how yet...or where...but if we want it, we could manage it."

Would we go to America? Cholpon wondered. What would it be like there? Maybe wonderful and rich. But she didn't think she'd like rich people...or maybe she didn't think they'd like her.

And how could she be without Djamila? The *Shayka* and her teachings—the center of Cholpon's life. But the teacher wouldn't always be here. Maybe when she left her body, Cholpon would leave Kyrgyzstan.

With Jeff? There was so much she didn't know about him. They were so different. Deep down the same, but on the surface—totally, intriguingly different.

The Sufis stocked up on fresh bread and apples from the open-air bazaar and set off for Sary Tash, the second possibility on their list. As they drove through Naryn, Jeff enjoyed the feel of Cholpon's leg next to his. Last night.... She was really amazing, all that vibrancy, the way she opened up and offered herself...drew it out of him. He'd never gotten that carried away before.

This wasn't like being swept away by a youthful crush. It was deeper, slower, calmer, not so overwhelming. Left him enough space to appreciate it.

A life together. She seemed to want that too. The last time he'd made a woman feel like that, he blew it. But learned a lesson. Maybe...just maybe...he got a fresh chance. They could be happy. It could happen. He wanted it so much he was afraid to hope for it.

At the Muslim cemetery on the edge of town the road to Sary Tash branched off to the west, and the one they'd been on continued south into China. Jeff wished they could keep going all the way from Tibet to Beijing to Shanghai. What was it really like down there? Some other time.

They turned and followed the river through a rocky gorge that gradually widened out into an agricultural plain. This road was narrower and all gravel, but they made better time because it was a gentle downgrade wending towards the Fergana Valley.

By now Jeff's novelty had worn off for the other the Sufis, and they accepted him with friendly nonchalance. They taught him one of their devotional songs by Ibn al-'Arabi, then asked him to sing a hymn from his religion. "Onward Christian Soldiers" came first to mind, but he didn't think it would set the right spirit, so he sang "Joy to the World." The women applauded with delight at his bass voice. Later, a couple of them asked him for help with their English. He was beginning to feel like one of the gals.

He took the binoculars out of his pack and scanned the mountains. "I still want to see a Marco Polo ram. Have you ever seen one?" he asked Cholpon.

She shook her head. "They are not many and they do not like people...because the people shoot them."

"That seems like a pretty good reason."

"A friend of my father, in the government, he told him there is a secret project. The government needs to get more money, and there are many rich men who want to kill a Marco Polo. It is the horns they like, the huge curve of them. They cut off the head...then put it on their wall. Can you imagine such a thing? Barbarians!"

"Yeah, people do that." Jeff winced, imagining the elk he'd shot in the Wind River Mountains. After tracking it for half a day, he'd brought it down with two rounds from a 30.06. He'd butchered it where it fell, fried the liver on the spot, and lugged the carcass out in sections. He'd hung the mounted head, with a six-foot rack of antlers, in his den. Who knows where it was now, since Valerie sold the house. He'd been proud of it, but now the killing seemed merely brutal. If a wolf had killed it, that'd be fine. But being a predator was losing its appeal to him. That must be more of Cholpon and Djamila's work. He was changing...in a way that was strange but felt right.

"And these men pay very much money," Cholpon said. "I have heard forty thousand dollars...because they are so rare."

"I believe it."

"So the government is breeding these Marco Polos in a secret farm. They take the seed from the...man sheep...to make many babies...lambs. Now they are still small, but when their horns grow big enough so the men want to kill them, they will let them go in the place where the hunters come. The men will think it is a great wild beast...but they just shoot a sheep."

"Hard currency," said Jeff.

Hours later they reached Osh, Kyrgyzstan's second largest city and a center of Muslim activity. Djamila had studied at the Sufi *Zawiya* here, and one of her classmates was now its *Shayk*. She gazed nostalgically at the sacred hill that crowned the town. "Up there was where I learned to dance the dervish rings," she said. "And many other things." The teacher turned to her secretary: "Do we have time to stop for devotions?"

After conferring, they decided no, they had to reach Sary Tash before nightfall.

Jeff remembered an embassy briefing on Osh as a haven for al-Qaeda and Taliban, so he was glad to just roll on through.

They began climbing again, lugging up into the Alai Mountains. The road crested at the bare, boulder-strewn Taldyk Pass, then dropped in a swooping series of switchbacks into the green valley of the Kyzl Su River and the town of Sary Tash. Across the valley to the south rose the jagged white peaks of the Pamirs, which marked the border to Tajikistan. The bus was headed straight for it, with Afghanistan close beyond. Another highway crossed theirs, running west also towards Tajikistan and east towards China.

"Yes. This is what I saw," Djamila said. "This valley, these roads, the mountains. And the bomb is there...somewhere." She pointed a crooked finger across the valley where the Pamirs began to rise.

"We will find it," said Cholpon.

But then what? wondered Jeff. Delta Force could helicopter or parachute in. But what if the bomb was someplace where they couldn't move right in on it? Soon as they showed up, whoever had it would run with it. Or blast it.

They drove through Sary Tash, a bleak settlement of adobe and tin where the local agricultural workers lived, then out into the wheat fields surrounding it. The grain flowed undulant and golden, stalks bending with kernels ready for harvest. Again Kyrgyzstan reminded Jeff of Wyoming: harshly beautiful land blemished with a few grimly practical towns. Fortunately both places had a lot more land than town.

One of the women, Radima, had grown up in this region. She told them smuggling was the main business after farming. Drugs, gold, and weapons flowed across these borders where too many countries lay too close together and national lines were less important than ethnic ones. Feuds often flared among the Kyrgyz, Tajiks, Afghans, Uzbeks, and Chinese living here. Her own brother had been a smuggler killed in a turf battle with Afghans who were trying to take over the drug trade.

As they approached the crossroads, Djamila said, "Stop the bus...it's too shaky. I don't know which way to go. I need your help...to clear the astral channels. Everyone meditate."

Acel pulled off the road, and they closed their eyes. Jeff took Cholpon's hand, wanting to hold it, but she took it back and scooted to the other side of the seat, saying, "Not now." She gave his knee a pat to cheer him up.

The sound of his mantra settled his mind like ocean waves gradually calming when the wind stops. The surface became smooth, thoughts came to rest, and he could see into the depths. Something glowed down there.

Go all the way to the bottom—find it.

This thought brought him out; he took a deep breath and was back on the bus.

Dive down again.

He drifted in and out for what could have been ten minutes or an hour until Djamila said, "Better. We go past the highway and take the next road to the right. Keep meditating. Jeff, you drive now. We need to have all the experienced meditators."

Feeling a bit put down but still glad to be taking the wheel, he traded places with Acel. The closer they got to the bomb, the more he wanted to have his eyes open. He was willing to give Djamila's way a try as long as it matched with common sense.

Jeff rumbled the bus west along an empty farm road bordered by wheat fields. The Kyzl Su River ran nearby, its deep pools looking like they would be great for trout fishing. Although he could see no people or houses, occasional tractor trails ran from their road through the fields up towards the ramparts of the Pamirs. The late-afternoon sun cast long shadows down the valley. Mount Lenin loomed sheer and icy above them, and farther across the border into Tajikistan towered Mount Communism. Both peaks soared majestically aloof to such names. Truly above it all, their granite palisades could even survive the bomb, but the life clinging to them—the Marco Polo sheep, ibex, and snow leopards, the lichen, lupin, and edelweiss—would perish, leaving them sterile, irradiated rocks.

That nuke got away from him once. This time he had to get it.

Djamila gestured toward the mountains. "In the vision...it was up where the hills start. Closer I could not see."

Pretty big area, Jeff thought. Miles of forest. How to narrow it down? Maybe campfire smoke. No, they probably wouldn't have a fire. They were hiding. But they had to drive it in there. Should be some truck tracks where they went in.

Jeff stopped the bus at each trail they came to and looked out the window for fresh tracks. He saw several, but they were all narrow, from tractors. Finally he saw wider marks of a large truck and chewed up ground. Take a closer look. In case anyone was watching, he drove a bit farther and pulled off the road.

Stepping off the bus, he shivered. Up here in these last days of August the chill of oncoming winter was already in the air. He ran back down the barrow pit in a crouch, lower than the tall wheat. At the trail he knelt in the dirt and saw tracks from a truck bigger than farmers usually have and fresh gouges from some other kind of vehicle, wider than a tractor. Not a lot of tracks—just one set of each. Whatever had gone in hadn't come out. He looked up to where the trail disappeared into the forest. Might be some sort of construction project. But no sign of anything like that. Just trees. Plus if they were building something they'd have a bigger road, more tracks. He shivered again, this time with the frisson of discovery. The bomb could be up there. Smiling crookedly, Jeff pictured it from the glimpse he'd got that first night. Djamila, you might have found it.

Back at the bus he told the women of the tracks. "How about if we go up the next trail? We can run parallel to this one."

"Yes, take it." Djamila said. "We don't want to get too close...just enough so our mind radiance can reach them. We are radiating peace...they are radiating something else. And we will see who is stronger."

"What if they catch us?" Acel asked in Kyrgyz.

"Well..." Cholpon said, "we're just a bunch of crazy Sufi women...come out to dance to the moon."

"But what about *him?*" Acel pointed to Jeff.

"Hmm." Cholpon eyed him wryly. "He's our Russian driver...unfortunately deaf and dumb, the poor man."

"What're you saying?" Jeff demanded. When she translated, he said, "OK...good plan," but thought, A bus driver with a submachine gun in his pack?

Jeff drove half a mile to the next trail, turned onto it, and bounced along the rough and rutted ground. Stalks of grain swept the sides of the bus. The uphill slant of the land increased until the valley soil yielded to rocks and the field and trail ended. Pines climbed the slopes from here up into the foothills and then the mountains. Jeff wheeled the bus around, in case they had to leave in a hurry, and backed as far into the trees as he could, enough to be out of sight. "We're here...wherever that is."

They all left the bus stiffly, glad to stretch and to visit the bushes. They then took turns massaging each other's shoulders and backs to relax the tightness from the long ride. After bundling into their coats and hats, they began munching bread and canned beans. When Cholpon offered him some, Jeff realized he was ravenous.

A butterfly, one of last of the season, perched on Djamila's knee and spread its gold and black wings. The *Shayka* pointed it out to Jeff. "See how alert and aware it is. Just looking at it you can tell how much God enjoys being a butterfly. The flying...drinking the sweet sap. Then when its time is up, God will enjoy how its body fertilizes the earth...for God is the earth too."

She was always teaching, thought Jeff. And he was her newest pupil. A rank beginner.

Djamila sipped tea from a thermos. "The whole universe is God. This butterfly, the earth, all this creation is God's personality, active in time and space. But just as you are more than your personality, so is God more than the universe."

Jeff held up a chunk of bread dipped in beans and said, "Does that mean God is the beans and the bread?"

Djamila nodded. "And you too. Never forget that. God is not some parent in the sky who made you. God *is* you. There is nothing in you that is not God. Everything is a manifestation of God. And when we meditate we go back to the junction point...where we are the same. This separation just appears to be real because the mind isn't fully developed. When you meditate longer it disappears...and you experience the unity."

Jeff was interested but also felt the need to taunt her a bit.

"That must mean God is the bomb too. Does He enjoy being that?"

"Yes, God is that too...and enjoys it all. But God will enjoy it even more when we save the bomb before it explodes. That will be a great adventure. God likes adventure stories, love stories, nature stories...even war stories. It is all God's play."

"What if it does explode?" Cholpon asked.

Djamila shrugged. "Then God enjoys being the explosion. But not as much as being the butterfly." She eased the creature onto her finger, raised it in the air, and watched it fly away. "Now I will meditate...to find out where we are."

The *Shayka* went off by herself and sat beneath a tree while the others finished dinner. In a few minutes she returned and said confidently, "This bomb is not far. I could feel the fear out there. Wherever fear is the strongest, there will be the most weapons. We are close."

She's like a Geiger counter, Jeff thought. But how accurate? If she was right, it should be on the other side of that ridge...somewhere. He stood up and said, "I'll scout it out while there's still light. Just take a look, see what I can find."

Cholpon tensed at the risk. "No." She wanted to hold on to him, convince him not to go.

"We need to know if it's there," he said. "I'll stay away from them."

"Then I can come along," she countered.

Jeff shook his head. "It's more dangerous with two people. More chance of getting spotted." He gathered his rucksack, then patted her head and pecked her cheek, feeling too inhibited by the others for a real embrace. "I'll be back."

Her eyes pinched shut, then opened to look at him desolately.

Jeff shouldered the pack despite the pain of his cuts and strode away with a wave. Part of him wanted to stay, felt torn away from her. Never see her again.... All of them might go up in smoke...whether they were God or not. But then he'd rather die trying to save it. The mission...find it! Their sentries would be watching the valley, so he'd come down from the other side. Recon patrol.

Staying near the base of the ridge, he followed a splashing brook through pines up towards the mountains. A covey of pheasants burst from the bushes ahead, the roar of beating wings startling him as if it were an ambush. Heart thumping, he followed them with his eyes, imagining squinting over a shotgun barrel, thinking of all the birds he had brought to earth. Would he really want to blast these? Terrible idea. Maybe he was getting more peaceful. Pheasants were so beautiful. And they'd rather not be killed.

Just before the ridge became too steep for free-climbing, he started up it. His fingers and toes sought niches in the stone, cracks solid enough to hoist his 190. At the touch of skin against rock, his mind dropped other thoughts and concentrated only on climbing, a total focus on the concrete present, body bristling with controlled tension. His arms hurt but they obeyed orders. The old running shoes were too slick to have much traction, so he had to test each foothold. Work close to the rock. Don't climb with your knees. Don't look down. Expect no mercy.

Jeff heaved himself up to the crest of the ridge, where a cold wind cut down from the mountains. He lay prone and looked below into a forested canyon, then with the binoculars he checked his ridge and the one across for a high-ground lookout post. Nothing. Scanning the shadowed canyon, he saw no sign of people.

The trail continued deeper into the Pamirs, but he could only get occasional glimpses of it through the pines. In the sky an eagle glided the updrafts; Jeff wished he had its eyes. Trees, trees. Finally a tiny spark within the forest caught his eye, then vanished. Maybe a campfire. No, too small. The flare of a match?

He adjusted the binoculars and examined the area minutely, following bits of the trail through the woods until he saw a camouflage-painted Kyrgyz Army truck. It seemed to be blocking the trail. Two men in Kyrgyz Army uniform were leaning against it, smoking. Jeff's stomach churned and he broke out in a sweat despite the cold air. Why the army? What was the army doing here? They didn't seem to be searching for anything. They were guarding the trail...stop anyone from coming up from the road.

But maybe...smugglers were paying them for protection. Could be. If it was the bomb, why would the Kyrgyz Army steal something that belonged to them? So they didn't have to give it up...to keep it from being dismantled. Definitely possible. But would the government risk breaking the Vienna Accords? The rest of the world would cut them off. They weren't fanatics...most of them weren't even religious, just the old communists who decided to go capitalist. They were too sensible to pull a stunt like that.

But the government wouldn't have to know. Could be a small group in the army...a fundamentalist cell.

Jeff looked farther up the trail until trees blotted it out. He needed to get closer...and for that he'd better buckle up. From his pack he took the submachine gun and web belt of ammunition pouches, strapped on the belt and checked the SMG—safety on, round in the chamber. The ritual wasn't as appealing as it used to be. Before, the Heckler & Koch had seemed a marvel...now it was repellent, an ugly chunk of black metal and plastic whose only purpose was killing. But it wasn't as ugly as the bomb. If he could use it to save the nuke, it'd be worth it.

Jeff had changed, at least a bit, and he wasn't sure whether to thank Cholpon and Djamila for it...or blame them. He used to be a real warrior...now he seemed to be turning into a peaceful old man. But not yet, not entirely.

That side of the ridge wasn't as steep, but directly below him lay an open scree slope that didn't offer any cover. To the right, though, up the canyon, were boulders and trees that could shield him. He dropped back to the side he'd climbed and scrambled along until he was about that far, then cut over and angled down into the canyon, staying behind cover except for a few crouching darts across exposed gaps.

He tuned up all his senses and let them spread out through the forest, his whole body becoming a receptor seeking a human presence. Covert surveillance—the old sneak and peek game. A trace of tobacco smoke in the air. It couldn't be from the guys at the truck—the wind was blowing down the canyon. Other people must be there, farther in. The good old nose, bent but still did its job. Saved him again. Vietnam, when he was point man on patrol, the stink of unwashed men in mildewed clothes—ambush ahead. He flanked them and hit them with rifle grenades. Dead, they smelled even worse.

Jeff clicked the safety off and followed the smoke spores, glancing at the ground before each footstep to keep it silent. The old excitement of being on patrol, a high-stakes game with his life wagered against others, crept back over him. He heard a distant cough. Homing in on the sound with the binoculars, straining to see in the fading light, he found the trail, then followed it until he saw men, maybe ten, lounging around some kind of vehicle. All in Kyrgyz Army uniform. The vehicle was tracked and low to the ground, ugly but functional—a snow cat. Used to support mountain troops and rescue avalanche victims, they would go just about anywhere. On the back, covered with a tarp, sat a large object—about the size of what he'd seen carried out of the armory that first night.

Probably not a big crate of hashish—it was pointed towards Tajikistan and the dope moved out of there. What else? The nuke.

Djamila, you're a wonder.

With the snow cat they could take the smuggler trails through the canyons and over the glaciers. And from there? Maybe blast the US base in Afghanistan. Or truck it down to the coast, sail it over to America into some nice harbor. Good-bye, San Diego.

But maybe the army just now found it. No, probably not—then there'd be more going on. At least they'd have a fire—too cold. These guys were layin' low, didn't want to be seen.

As he stared again at the tarp-shrouded shape, a thrill of certainty ran through him. This was it; he was finally getting another chance to save it. Don't blow it this time.

He could try to take them all out. No, there were too many. Not enough light left to insert Delta Force. He'd have to try Djamila's way...for tonight.

Heading back in the twilight, he stumbled and fell on the rocks, scraping the skin off his palms. He caught the cry of pain before it left his throat, but the submachine gun clattered against stone. Damnit! He got back to his feet and peered through the binoculars to check if the men had heard, but now it was too dark to see into the woods. He'd find out soon enough.

Jeff continued walking, looking for a place where the Sufis could spend the night. After searching high on the ridge, he came to an area of pines overlooking the canyon where the underbrush was thick enough for seclusion and the ground fairly level. From here the bomb was out of sight, blocked by forest, about 400 meters away. But could Djamila walk here?

The slope on this side of the ridge wasn't as steep and the

155

trail was easier going, so if they crossed over sooner, maybe she could make the hike.

A sudden flutter of bats made him duck his head; he flinched and waved his arms as a dozen flying mice buzzed him. Like a flight of Stealth bombers. He was getting spooked too easy. The bats flew on, hawking bugs in the evening sky.

When Jeff reached the bus, Cholpon smiled to see him stomping in. "I can tell you have good news," she said.

"I think so," he said and told them of his find.

Djamila nodded as if she'd expected it and told the Sufis to pack up for a night's work. "They are only twelve and we are forty," she said. "And when they sleep, their brains will open to us. They cannot resist us. They are ours."

"How's this actually supposed to happen?" Jeff asked with a skeptical lift of his eyebrows. "Those guys' brains aren't very open. They're a tough bunch down there."

"We will surround him...with a force field." Djamila spread her frail arms encompassingly. "Our meditation will create a radiance, a positive vibration that will cover them and flow through them. All night long. We will soothe their brain waves so their fear will disappear. Then they will know how useless this bomb is."

Sounded pretty idealistic, he thought. An awful lot was riding on what seemed just a theory. "But how does it really work?" he insisted. "On the practical level."

"It works like the radio," Djamila said. "What is that word for a radio sender?"

"You mean transmitter?"

"Yes, that's it. Everybody's brain is like a radio transmitter. It is always sending out vibrations. Most of these aren't very strong, like static...because they are thinking with just a small part of their brains. But when we use the whole brain and the thoughts come from the quiet part, from the transcendent, then they are much more powerful. And when a group of people are all operating from this level, the vibrations become strong enough to affect other people's brains...to make them calmer, more peaceful. It changes the consciousness. Maybe not forever, but while the group transmitter is sending...other people around them become less afraid."

Was this just a crazy idea? Maybe, Jeff thought. But science was proving all sorts of stuff they used to scoff at. In a way it made sense…just another kind of sense. Forty people meditating all night long might do something to those guys down there. He'd noticed his mind worked differently as soon as he got around the Sufis. It affected him, so it might affect the soldiers. For tonight there wasn't much choice. "Well…it's worth a try," he said. "Maybe it'll…tranquilize them awhile."

That could make it easier for Delta Force to take them out.

The Sufis filled pack baskets with blankets, cushions, food, and water, then set out. The trek there was an ordeal for Djamila, even though she wore sturdy shoes. As she walked behind Jeff, he could hear little yips of pain from the twisting of joints over rough, uneven ground. His offer to carry her was met with a withering stare, a dismissive wave of her hand, and the order to proceed. She was clearly the general leading her troops, in which Jeff was a lowly recruit. He slowed down whenever he sensed she was falling behind.

He was amazed by how silently the Sufis could move, even though burdened. In the dim evening light, they seem to be able to sense where obstacles were and to put their feet in the right place to avoid stumbling.

When they reached the grove, Jeff pointed to where the bomb and the guards were hidden by forest and darkness. "No problem," whispered Cholpon, showing off her American slang. "They don't have a chance against us. They won't know what hit them."

The women trimmed low branches from the pine trees, then propped cushions against the trunks for back support; another cushion went on the ground and a horsehair felt blanket on top of it.

Jeff didn't have any. Oh well. He'd been cold before.

Cholpon tossed him two cushions and a blanket. He looked to make sure she had some for herself, then took them with a grateful grin. "*Spasibo.*"

The women sat two to a tree, wrapped, hatted, and gloved, ready for their battle of peace. They ranged from twenty to eighty years old, from skinny to fat, from talkative to silent, but all had an inner light about them, an alertness.

Jeff didn't know if their kind of radiance would affect the

157

soldiers, but he didn't have a better plan, and he wanted to find out. If it worked, it could really change things. Instead of armies, we could have meditators. It could make guys like him obsolete. That actually sounded OK.

He and Cholpon found a tree at the edge of the group. She arranged the cushions so they could sit close but a little separate for meditation.

"It's going to be a long night...just sitting here," he said. "Let's take a little walk first, just you and me."

They left and strolled along the ridge; when they were out of sight of the group, Cholpon let him take her hand.

Now that they were alone, fears they had ignored before crept over them. Their bodies folded together as if hinged by their hands, and they clutched each other for protection.

This couldn't really shield them, Jeff knew, but what else could they do? They were just two little sparks in the darkness.

Their lips met, not from passion but helplessness. And it helped. They each drew strength from the other, embracing against the night, against the future. Whatever happened—they had this.

"Love you," Jeff whispered.

"I too for you," Cholpon murmured, her English crumbling.

They walked slowly back to the group and sat against their tree, shifting around trying to get comfortable. Jeff pictured the soft comforts of her body, so near yet so far, and all the warm beds in the world he wanted to share with her.

Some of the women's faces were strained with fright, others were calm, none looked cheery. They whispered occasionally to one another, then fell silent. Djamila sat off by herself in cross-legged lotus position without back support. She seemed the same as always.

As evening turned to night, the wind faded away, leaving the air still and crisp with a tang of pine resin. A wafer of moon, cool as a mint on the roof of his mouth, swam through wisps of clouds.

As Jeff thought his mantra, his breath slowed and his heart stopped pounding. He didn't realized it was pounding until it quieted. He shivered in his parka and blanket until he relaxed enough to accept the cold without resisting it. As he opened up to the chill, it ceased to bother him. It was just another physical sensation, and all those were superficial compared to this great empty peace. A few thoughts drifted by, butterflies on the breeze, but the spans of silence grew longer. Somehow the emptiness was lively, full of an energy that was his deepest self. It was not only his self but it linked him to the others, all of them together in a wholeness that was greater than their surface separation.

As the hours passed and their minds joined deeper, Jeff could sense this same underlying dimension in the atmosphere around them. The air had a quality, a flowing plasma that vibrated with their mental impulses. It must always be there, but now he was aware of it. His skin seemed more permeable, his body less dense, interpenetrated with the outside. He could feel his mind pulsating slow and strong in rhythm with the others, all of them mutually reinforcing. Then their brain waves merged and seemed to rise and spread out, covering and shielding them. Within this dome was total peace, everything was all right, nothing to fear. We can only be afraid of something different, and here everything became the same—multiplicity blended into the oneness of the unified field. He was part of an energy flowing in all directions, unbounded, without differences, one ocean of consciousness. It was alive, it was divine, it washed him with joy.

All the while he was sitting against a tree feeling pine needles drop onto his parka hood, his left foot falling asleep from being cross-legged too long, ears throbbing and cuts stinging. He could hear forest noises: burrowings and nibblings of mice; a woman's yelp of alarm as one scampered over her legs; the tread of deer approaching the thicket then trotting away as they smelled humans; the call of an owl.

These two different channels—separation and unity—were going on simultaneously, and he could shift between them, focusing more on one, then on the other. But they weren't really separate. The physical channel of the senses emerged from and was cupped within this empty, silent field. The still ocean of awareness was the source of everything.

His other meditations had never gone so deep; the group and the longer times seemed to make a difference.

Again the Sufis around him had changed the way his brain worked. Maybe this could reach the soldiers down in the canyon. Four hundred meters away didn't seem very far, judging from the power he was feeling here. But would it influence them enough to make them give up the bomb? It might just put them in a good mood for a while.

Realizing he was drifting off on thoughts, he turned his mind back to the mantra.

Jeff opened his eyes to first light. From beneath the horizon the oncoming sun flared white shafts into the blue, shining the clouds molten. Was that what the nuke would look like exploding? The last thing they'd see? He remembered light almost that intense last night glowing behind his closed eyes. That would be a better last sight.

He'd dozed off occasionally but mostly he'd meditated and the time had passed easily. Now he was cold and stiff but not fatigued.

Cholpon felt Jeff stirring but couldn't open her eyes yet. She needed to spend some extra time strengthening her inner shield this morning. Today was bound to take all she had. Sitting up straight in lotus while thinking her mantra, she gathered her energy together and concentrated it into a glowing sphere at the base of her spine. She raised it along the vertebrae past the solar plexus and released it where the ribs started. It flowed across her midsection radiating waves of power up towards her heart. From there the force resonated through her until she was tingling with readiness. She opened her eyes and smiled at Jeff. "Good morning," she whispered.

He smiled back, but his expression told her he was caught in worries. "I hope so," Jeff said. "We'll see."

They chatted about the night while taking each other in with their eyes to reestablish their bond. They both wanted to nuzzle in for a kiss, but with the others around that would have to wait.

The Sufis were stretching and murmuring greetings. Djamila was rubbing her sore knees with sesame oil. "No yoga this morning. We must move little...be invisible here," she said. "But we can still have morning prayer."

The women faced west toward Mecca, knelt to the ground, and chanted the Arabic *faqr*.

Feeling self-conscious as the infidel, Jeff went to the edge of the thicket, took the binoculars out of his pack, and scanned the canyon. He could see only forest below. That meant their group was less likely to be spotted, but he couldn't be sure if the bomb was still there.

Shivering and rubbing his hands for warmth, Jeff felt colder now than he had at night. The temperature didn't seem to bother the others. The Kyrgyz were cold resistant—after thousands of mountain winters in yurts.

From here, only the front slopes of the mountains could be seen; the peaks were hidden. This canyon cut deep into the interior and probably connected to trails leading to Tajikistan. Someone down there must know how to get the snow cat across. When would they leave?

Clouds were pouring out of the mountains like lava from a volcano, clotting the sky, turning its blue to gray and the sun to a silver smudge on the horizon. Snow began falling in little dry pellets that dropped swiftly and stung when they hit the skin. They weren't many but they were eager, glad to be the first of the season.

Snow in August! Jeff forgot their problems for a moment and raised his arms into the air. Like Wyoming again. Waking up that time in the Wind River Mountains in a tent that had become an igloo. Look at them coming down! He loved it here...and there. In one place or the other, he wanted to be with her.

During a breakfast of apples, bread, and cold water, Djamila described her plan for the day. "Cholpon and I will go down and help those men get free of the bomb. They do not want it anymore. We will make them see that."

"You're just going to walk down there? No! You didn't say anything about that," Jeff said, appalled. "They'll kill you...or...."

Djamila brushed off his fears with a swipe of her gnarled hand. "Now their hateful thoughts will not arise so easily. For a while at least, their minds are at peace. Their deeper self wants to be free of this bomb...and we will connect to that."

"But why do you have to go down there? It's...well...nutty to risk that. How can you be sure you changed them?" Jeff said. This is a madwoman, he thought. Radio Delta Force.

Djamila touched his arm; a wave of stillness passed through him. She gave him the full depth of her eyes, now stark and blazing. "I am not sure. We are just making an experiment. If I am wrong...they will kill us. And we will be free of them." She cackled with a humor that said in the long run everything was equal.

Djamila had a contempt for death Jeff had only seen before in combat soldiers. She had so many sides to her—she was either schizophrenic or a genius. The power of her presence and touch said it was the latter. But to walk into that kind of danger.... He put his arm on Cholpon's shoulder. "Hey, this is the woman I love."

"You can love her dead or alive...in the body or out of it. You don't love her just for her body, do you?" Djamila gave him a mocking, reproving look that became an octogenarian leer. "You're not that kind of a man, are you?"

"Well, no...but...." Rattling my chain again.

"So wherever you are, you can still love her...and she will love you. If our plan does not work...you can love each other in heaven...and next life. Don't worry." Her cavalier tone fell away and her voice turned somber. "You see, this experiment is the best we can do. If your soldiers come, they will not share the peace we have created. They will disrupt these vibrations we spent all night making. They will bring a violent consciousness...and drag the other men back into fear. Someone will set off the bomb." Her face, ancient with the eternal present, held neither dread nor optimism. "We must try." She stood up. "Cholpon, come."

"No," Jeff insisted. "I can't let you do this."

"We have to do it," Cholpon insisted back. "Who else is going to convince them to give it up...you? They'll be less likely to kill us. It's our best chance...a risk we need to take." She squeezed his hand, then left him and joined her *Shayka*.

Jeff wanted to drag her back. "Maybe we could work out a compromise. How about I come with you far enough so I can see how you're doing. I'll stay up on the ridge, but if there's trouble, I could...do something."

Now that she was separated from him, Cholpon looked more fearful. She nodded her approval.

Djamila wrinkled her toothless mouth into a grimace. "What would you do? Call your friends? They would not be much help. But if you would feel better, come and watch with your glasses."

"Good," Jeff said shortly and gathered his pack. The three of them set out, the old woman striding painfully, resolutely. The snow pellets had become flakes now, sifting out of the slate sky, melting as they hit the ground.

Cholpon drew close to him and stroked his arm. "We will come back." She tried to sound confident.

"This life or next?" Jeff asked. He stopped occasionally to search with the binoculars until he found the snow cat. It was about 300 meters away with ten men near it. They were shaking out sleeping bags, eating breakfast, smoking, but had no campfire.

In the forest back towards the wheat field, the truck still blocked the trail, with two guards there.

He could watch from up here. But watch what? Cholpon and Djamila getting killed?

Djamila took both of Jeff's hands in hers; his tension drained away like a grounded electrical charge. "Remember whatever happens will be right," the teacher said.

"I don't like that," he said. "There's too much at stake. If everything is right...it's as if...nothing matters...it's all the same."

"It ends up being all the same," Djamila said, "but it still does matter.

"How can that be?"

"In the field of matter, it really matters. In the unified field, it doesn't matter. There there is no matter, just energy vibrating....taking on different forms." The old woman tapped Jeff on the arm. "These forms do not last. But the real you is the energy, not the form. And that energy is God."

This didn't cheer him. He liked his form and Cholpon's form and what they did together. He asked with a shrug, "If that's true...then why do anything?"

"Because you want to! That is important. You are in the game...and you want to play your part...fulfill your desires. We want to save the bomb...someone else wants to explode it. Who knows who wins. Pretty exciting!" The *Shayka* threw up her arms with a toothless smile.

"But in the long run?"

"In the long run, there is no loss. God loves us and makes everything all right again. Then we have another game. That is what happens here. So we will do what we can. And if we fail...if it explodes...well, this radiation is only on the material level. Not so important. It just looks important...from here. We will have played our part...as well as we could." Djamila released his hands and stepped away. "Now we will go."

Jeff gazed at Cholpon, took her in his arms, kissed her lips, and hugged her to him, forgetting about being modest around the *Shayka*. "Bring this person back to me," he said to Djamila.

The old woman gave him an understanding nod. "That we will try to do."

Cholpon squeezed him then stepped away; Jeff tried to fix her features in his mind before she disappeared. Big eyes, so dark yet reflecting so much light...their flaring angle. Scant eyebrows, short lashes. That dear little nose so pert and dainty. Broad, high cheekbones slanting down to a rounded chin. Straight raven hair. Her face so open, even now with fear there...beautiful just by being hers. Standing with arms hanging down, hands cupped open in front of her. A mighty, small person. And she loved him.

Cholpon brushed her lips on his cheek once more, and the two women left. Jeff followed them with his eyes and then with the binoculars as they descended into the canyon, the student helping the teacher hobble over rough ground. When he lost sight of them in the trees, he focused on the men around the bomb. They were still leaning on the snow cat or pacing to keep warm, bored as soldiers usually are. Someone else was there too, whom he hadn't seen before, distinctive because of a white bandage on his face. Jeff twisted the ring on the glass and brought a familiar face into focus:

General Osmonaliev's.

Jeff's lost his breath and his mouth went dry. Why would he be here? What was he doing? Maybe the army did just find the nuke. No, it was too cold not to have a fire. Plus they'd have reinforcements by now, there'd be more going on. They didn't want anybody to know they were here.

Osmonaliev must've taken the damned thing. But how? Pondering, Jeff let the binoculars hang from his neck. The raiders would had to have been his guys. Could be. Plenty of Middle-Eastern looking soldiers in the Kyrgyz Army. He could've got a group on his side...with money...or religion, dressed them like Arabs, have them steal it. Or maybe he hired some free-lance mercenaries...out-of-work Mujahideen. Running the Kyrgyz search operation, he could make sure only false leads got passed on to the US. But why would he want the bomb? He was no fundamentalist—the way he drank. What was he going to do with it?

And why were they in uniform? If they stole it, you'd think they'd be incognito. Oh...this way if Delta showed up, he could claim he just found it. But as civilians, his guys would seem guilty. They also might get shot.

General Osmonaliev! Until now Jeff had sort of liked the guy. He had a certain flair.

How was he going to react to Cholpon and Djamila?

Deep in the pines Cholpon was trying to be brave. Don't think about dying, hold on to positivity. What you think is what you get.

Djamila startled her by singing aloud the peace prayer, "*Aum Shantih, Shantih, Shantih.*" Cholpon wanted to tell her to hush, the men could hear, but then she realized that was the point—to announce their presence. That which can't be avoided is better met head on. She joined her teacher in song, drawing the reverberant tones out from the heart *chakra* at the center of her chest. The sounds resonated through Cholpon, calming her fears, then spread out into the atmosphere.

She knew the universe was God's consciousness vibrating at different frequencies and manifesting into matter. Physics had finally discovered what the Vedas knew all along: the creation is all wave functions. By changing the vibration, it's possible to change the manifestation. Whether the Sufis had changed it enough to convince those men to give up their bomb...that they'd have to see.

A half dozen men approached, gaping in astonishment at these two women who were walking and singing into their secret camp. They seemed more bewildered than hostile. Djamila smiled in greeting as if she and Cholpon were expected guests.

Cholpon brought her awareness to her power center and drew a charge of strength from her inner shield. She took a deep breath and filled herself with courage. Feeling more protected, she looked at the men and saw their auras were mix of red and blue. These soldiers weren't the spiritual type, she knew, so the blue must be from last night's meditating. This and their peaceful reaction meant the Sufi radiance had gotten through to them...at least somewhat. Yesterday they would've probably grabbed their guns and shot. Today they just stared. That was progress.

Several other men stood near an ugly military machine that resembled a low bulldozer without a blade. A large object covered with canvas was tied down behind the driving compartment. The men glanced away guiltily, as if they had been caught at something by their mother.

Djamila strode directly up to one of them, older than the others with white bandages on his face. "I have come to bring you a Sufi blessing," she said him to in Kyrgyz. "Would you like that?"

The bandaged man spoke slowly, shaking his head in

amazement: "You are the one in the dream. How did you get here?"

"Did you like the dream?" Djamila asked.

"Where did you come from?" He touched his forehead. "You...you held my head in your hands...touched it all over...we were floating together in the light...you took my pain away...I was happy. It was the best dream I ever had. And it was you." His mouth stayed open.

The others spoke among themselves: "I saw her too"—"I had the same dream"—"She was floating above me"—"Who is she?"

"Last night was not a dream," Djamila said. "I came to you on the astral to heal your minds...to remove the pain that makes you hate."

The leader spoke still entranced in memory. "Maybe...it was real. Today I'm...better."

"What is unreal is the hatred you've had for so long. That is a dream, the nightmare you made of your life," Djamila said. "Now I gave you a taste of reality. What I brought you was the peace of Allah."

Slipping into suspicion, the man asked, "Who else is with you?"

"Allah is with us...and also with you." She reached out and touched his chest. *"La ilaha illa Allah."*

The leader's eyes closed for a moment, then opened warily. "Where did you come from?"

His men stood watching, no longer whispering among themselves.

"We came from Allah...to save you," the *Shayka* said. "Allah's peace, the peace you feel now, can stay with you. It can protect you from the misery you've had for so long. Wouldn't you rather have it...than *that?*" She pointed at the canvas-covered nuke. "To hold on to this peace, you must get rid of that. That thing is your great problem now, isn't it?"

The leader shrugged and stayed silent.

"Today you don't know what to do with it," she continued. "Before, you thought it would bring you happiness. Now you know it will bring you more pain. And you have had so much pain."

The bandaged man gave her a distrustful look. The others shuffled around nervously. One stocky soldier, younger than the leader but older than the rest, cleared his throat and stepped a few paces closer, the heel of his hand on his holstered pistol.

Djamila turned to him with a smile that dazzled despite her lack of teeth. "*Assalam alaikum*"—Peace to you—she said.

He looked self-consciously down at his hands.

The *Shayka* returned her attention to the general. "This morning you knew you did not want to kill any more people. You knew you would get more and more unhappy for each person you kill. But with this damned thing you must kill people. That is all it is for. And you don't know how to be free of it."

Osmonaliev stepped away from her in irritation. "I don't need to be free of it, I need to be free of you. How did you women find this place?"

"Your heart called out to us to rescue you. We are here to keep you from killing." Closing the distance between them, Djamila reached out and took his hand. "I can see you are not such a man to explode this bomb. You are too intelligent for that. It is something else." The *Shayka* stared at him; for the first time in eighteen years, Cholpon saw her flinch. "You want money...very much. That is why you have this bomb. But," Djamila went on slowly, now looking appalled, "you also plan to kill...to bring even more money. But this morning you know that will make you sadder...and you are so sad already, you've been sad all your life. You don't know what to do."

Osmonaliev took his hand away but kept looking at her.

"Call on the radio," she told him. "Tell them you found the bomb. The reward money, this ten million dollars.... How many are you here?" She glanced around. "You each have a million dollars. You are all rich. And you don't have to kill anyone else. You'll be heroes."

"It is not so simple." The general waved his hand dismissively and walked away.

The teacher followed him. "Are you afraid to hear what I say?"

"I have many things to do," he said brusquely, then pointed to his bandages. "They! Al-Qaeda! They did this to me. They did not know who it was, but they did it. Now I do to them. Yes, we will kill the al-Qaeda and take their money."

168

"That will make your life even worse," Djamila said with a shake of her head. "If those men hurt you, they were just delivering to you what you did to others in the past. What you do to others returns to you, the good and the bad."

Osmonaliev's hand cut the air. "So now I am delivering it to them...giving them their punishment. Is that not fair?

"There is no such thing as punishment. There are only the results of your actions, things you did before coming back to you. If you take revenge on these people, whatever you do to them will happen again to you. Let someone else give it back to them. There are plenty of ignorant people who like to do such things. Haven't you had enough pain? Let it go."

"They killed my guests...they disgraced me. That is reason to hate them."

"If they killed, someone will kill them in return. But don't you do it," Djamila said. "If you hate them, you hate yourself...and you hurt yourself. There really is no other person...we're not separate. The universe is only one thing interacting with itself."

"I don't see that."

"I will show you. But you must take the first step."

The general gestured impatiently. "I am busy."

"Come over here." Djamila took his hand and led him to a tree stump near the bomb. "Sit down...you will see."

Osmonaliev frowned condescendingly as he sat on the stump. The *Shayka* touched his chest with one hand and his forehead with the other. "Close your eyes," she told him.

As he did, his men looked on uneasily. After a minute his strong features wrinkled, pinched together, then sagged. The military tightness with which he held his body began to loosen; skin that had been rigid now quivered with vulnerability.

There went his body armor, thought Cholpon. He must be getting the full *darshan* blast.

The general began to cry, silent tears rolling down his bronze cheeks into his bandage. He tried to speak but then just shook his head, eyes shut tight.

"These old wounds we can heal," Djamila said to him. Chanting a mantra, she pressed harder and Osmonaliev shuddered. She moved both hands to his chest and massaged in time with his heartbeat, then took her hands away, drew closer to him, and blew several puffs of breath onto his heart. Osmonaliev exhaled with a groan. She reached to his head and pulsed her fingers on his temples, then puffed her breath onto his forehead. His shoulders fell and he sighed; the tears stopped.

"Now open your eyes."

He blinked, and his face relaxed but now looked older, frail.

"We all have such things inside us," Djamila said. "Now you can see why we must not make any more of them...for us or anyone else. Since we are all one, if you hurt someone else, you just hurt yourself."

"I need...need to think about that." His voice was tormented, almost pleading. "Maybe you're right, but...."

"Call now on the radio. You'll be rich...you'll be heroes. Ten million dollars is enough." She touched her fingers very delicately to his bandage. "No more pain...for anyone."

The general mulled this over before replying. "What would I tell the Americans? I was going to say we killed the al-Qaeda taking the bomb back from them. 'Here are the bodies...here is the bomb...now please the reward.' But if I don't kill the al-Qaeda, what do I say? The Americans know they wouldn't give it up without a fight."

"Tell them they carried their dead away. You surprised them and they ran...up there." Djamila gestured towards the mountains. "The Americans just want the bomb. They will be happy."

"But al-Qaeda wants it too. Enough to pay almost as much as the Americans. What do I tell al-Qaeda when they come? Not for sale? They will just take it."

"Tell them the Americans got here before they did...tracked you down. You had to give it up to them."

"No time. Al-Qaeda are coming now."

"Now?" Djamila gummed her lips in worry, then rapped her fist on the machine. "Hide this thing farther up the canyon. Then meet them down below. It is gone. The Americans already took it. That way you have the money and no more killing."

Osmonaliev put his hand to his forehead and considered this. "That would be a way...out of the danger." He spoke slowly, pondering. "Wouldn't be as much money...but it would be safer." He glanced up at the snowy sky. "We could do that. Better than...the other." He looked at the *Shayka*, his expression verging on friendliness. "Old woman, I don't know why I listen to you...a

170

crazy Sufi. But you are the one from last night. Just like now...your touch...it was wonderful. All night long you were with me...the light around you. And this morning everything is different. Yes, it would be better...if we did not kill anymore. Even better than more money. I will speak to the men." He stood up. "But half the ten million must be for me. They do not need so much."

Straightening into his military posture, he walked over to his soldiers, who were watching from a deferential distance. Djamila stole a hopeful glance at Cholpon. Osmonaliev spoke to the men with a commanding edge to his voice. Their faces showed confusion but also relief; no one objected.

They will go along with it, Cholpon thought. They all have had a taste of bliss from the transcendent. She sighed, almost cried, then smiled back at Djamila. Now Jeff and I....

One of the men climbed up on the machine and sat in the driving compartment while two others released the locks on the metal tracks. Their demeanor showed the cautious cheer of the reprieved.

From the valley came the sound of a motor. A truck was driving towards them up the trail through the wheat field.

Osmonaliev waved his arms at the soldier on the machine. "Don't start it! They will hear it. They will know." He turned to his stocky assistant, his voice full of urgent pressure. "Radio to the sentries. Tell them to stop them down on the trail. We will meet them there."

The truck had entered the forest and was now out of sight.

The major ran to a backpack radio hanging from the limb of a tree and spoke into the handset; he waited, spoke again. Someone answered; after a short exchange he put the handset down and turned to the general with a shake of his head. "They are already past...coming now."

Djamila's face fell into dismay, showing its age.

As the sound of the approaching truck grew louder, Cholpon could feel a crest of negativity reaching her. These new men...what were they? Such a powerful dark field from them. They'd been nowhere near the Sufi radiance. Cholpon's skin grew defensively tight, her jaw stiffened, and two points of pressure grew in her temples.

She watched the men change. Their faces turned sharp, eyes

skittered, limbs moved more abruptly. Back to their usual selves. She could sense their brain waves switching from coherence to chaos as the effects of last night crumbled away. The influence was too fragile. One night was not enough.

Now she could feel a current of aggression rising and flowing, increasing their separation—us versus them, kill or be killed.

The general was breathing heavily through his mouth, and veins stood out on his forehead. "Now—we must go back to the other way." He reached down and pulled a small pistol from a holster on his ankle, then turned a switch on the handle. "Pistols off safety," he told his men. "But wait for the signal."

Faces etched with stress, the soldiers also pulled out hidden pistols, released the safeties, and put them back.

Osmonaliev spoke to Djamila without meeting her eyes. "You must go. These men are.... Your way would have been better...but now it is too late."

The truck drove into view, a farm carryall with canvas covering the back. Djamila's features tensed with fear, an emotion Cholpon had never seen on her before. The *Shayka* gestured her to leave. The two women slipped into the trees as the truck pulled in and parked. Men began leaping out of a back flap in the canvas. They were dressed like farmers in brown overalls and brimmed felt hats but carried guns instead of harvest tools. Cholpon took one look at their black and red auras, the darkest she'd ever seen, and fled.

Jeff watched them from up on the ridge. His breath caught in his throat and his skin constricted. He clenched the binoculars tighter. If anybody chased them, he could at least put in some interdicting fire. It wouldn't be accurate at this distance, but it would make whoever was after them stop and take cover. But if they actually grabbed them or even get close, he couldn't do anything...just watch them die.

Jeff focused in on the new men. Most looked Middle-Eastern, but a few were Oriental. Many were scarred, some had missing fingers, others had patches of reddish, turkey-like skin characteristic of napalm burns. Al-Qaeda, Jeff knew in an instant. They all bristled with hostility. These guys had been under the gun a long time. They were ready to explode.

172

Jeff breathed faster through clenched teeth—the peacefulness of last night evaporated. Al-Qaeda were a hell of a lot worse than the Kyrgyz Army. They'd be merciless with Cholpon and Djamila.

The two women were into the forest by now, running until Djamila stumbled and fell. Cholpon went back and knelt beside her. Hurry, Jeff pleaded. The teacher was holding her knee. Cholpon helped her to stand, then lifted her onto her back and plodded on.

Jeff glanced back at the al-Qaeda. Maybe they hadn't seen the women. They were shaking hands with the Kyrgyz soldiers.

Time for help—Delta Force. Their bubble of peace had been invaded. What those guys brought with them was contagious.

Anger rose in Jeff, unpleasant but familiar—better fight than flight. He emptied out his pack, strapped on the ammo pouches, and made sure his SMG had a round in the chamber. Ugly or not, now he needed it.

He set up the radio transceiver, a compact electronic marvel that made the radios he'd used in Vietnam seem as primitive as crystal sets. He put on the helmet headset, wincing as it chafed his wounds, and flipped a switch to activate the satellite uplink that would let him talk to Bishkek. He set the frequency and twisted the fine-tune dial until he heard the Delta Force zero beat.

"Fiery Lane, this is three-nine, over," he spoke into the mouthpiece.

After a few seconds, the voice of the commo sergeant came faint but clear: "Fiery Lane."

"Three-nine. I need to talk to one-six. Urgent. Is he there?"

"I'll check."

While waiting Jeff scanned again with the binoculars but couldn't see Cholpon and Djamila for the trees. Someone had pulled the tarp off the bomb: it sat uncovered on a wooden pallet, a large metal cylinder.

Was that what he'd seen the first night? Too dark to be sure. It'd been about that size. A giant tin can. Or the god of death's radioactive rod.

Al-Qaeda were setting up a folding table near their truck while the soldiers stood around uneasily. On the table the al-Qaeda put a camp stove and then a big pot. What were they up to?

After a minute Hobbs' voice came over the headset. "This is one-six."

"Three-nine. I found Sonny."

A pause. "You sure?" Incredulity and hope mixed in the colonel's voice.

"I'm looking at him right now...but he may not be here for long."

"Where are you?"

"I don't have coordinates, but I can tell you how to get here." Jeff described the location and gave the number of enemy, but didn't mention that half of them were Kyrgyz military. Hobbs might freeze up and call in the diplomats to negotiate and by then the nuke would be gone.

"We've got a squad out in Osh on a search now," Hobbs said. "We can send them in ASAP...the main group can follow. But first we'll get an air strike in there."

"What? That'll set it off!"

Hobbs' voice came back irritated: "You think I'd order it if it'd set it off? This'll be low-explosive cluster ordnance—just takes out the personnel. That's our directive from DOD. This kind of LE cluster won't detonate it. Trust us."

Jeff said, "OK," and thought, What choice do I have?

"Let me check what kind of air support I can get you," the colonel said. "I'll be right back."

Combat again...but this time he didn't want it. That first night with the bomb...he'd been stone crazy. Back in Nam the fiercest fighters weren't the youngsters but the burnt out old guys with nothing left to lose. But now he did have something to lose. Jeff gnawed his lip. Cholpon made this pulsing mess of life seem not so bad after all. He'd better watch it.

He searched again for the two women and found them halfway up the ridge, Djamila still clinging to Cholpon's back, Cholpon struggling with each step. Jeff had to go help them. But what about the radio. Well...it was supposed to be mobile—he'd see.

He put the transceiver in the pack and strapped it on his back, leaving the headset on. Binoculars around his neck, SMG over his shoulder—ready. He started down toward them through the forest. Even if Hobbs couldn't reach him right now, he could get the planes on the way.

"Three-nine, this is one-six, over." The colonel's voice sounded as clear as before.

"Three-nine," said Jeff. A great piece of equipment.

"The air force is diverting a FAC out of Uzbek. It should be there in two-zero, coming up on the air-to-ground freq, call sign Longbow. And they're loading a jet now with clusters. We got the Osh team on the way, and we're calling in the rest of Delta."

"Good...I'll hold it down here. Look, if I get zapped before I can talk to the FAC, tell him we got friendlies all along the ridge line to the west. Don't put anything even close to there. But he can take out everything down in the canyon."

"Got it."

Jeff continued down the slope; Cholpon smiled with relief as she saw him.

"Thank God you got away," he said, taking Djamila from Cholpon's back and carrying her in his arms.

This time the *Shayka* didn't protest but just gazed gratefully up at him. Her voice, though, was full of disappointment: "Such a pity. Our plan worked...until these new men came. We had no chance to change their brain waves. They are...very negative."

Jeff's submachine gun and binoculars clattered against the teacher until Cholpon moved them farther around on his shoulders.

"Well, I think we're going to be OK." He explained that an airplane was on its way with special weapons that wouldn't explode the nuke but just kill the men in the canyon.

Djamila's eyes narrowed and her face tightened into wrinkles. "A war plane is coming?" A long sigh left her toothless mouth. "That will bring more violence. These men here, the new ones...when they see it, they can explode this thing themselves. We know these sort of men. They would rather to die by their own hand than by the infidels'."

"We got away," Cholpon told him reproachfully. "We don't need more weapons." She thought of the hungry children of Iraq and Afghanistan having their arms blown off when they pick up those little bombs they think are food packets. Grief welled within her and turned to outrage. Nothing can justify doing this to other human beings. Who do these men...these rulers...ignorant brutes...think they are?

Stung by her disapproval, Jeff said defensively, "Hey, we can't let al-Qaeda take that thing. They're gonna kill people with it...lots of 'em. That's why they want it. I had to do something. Delta Force are good guys...they want to stop the killing." Watching the snowflakes streaming down, he slumped into pessimism and imagined them as fallout killing everything, contaminating the land.

Busily unaware, a red squirrel scurried the ground searching for pine nuts. Perched on a bough, a blue jay pecked a snowflake from the air, hoping it was a bug.

"I'll tell you why I called them," he continued, voice strained. "I know it sounds cruel, but the worst that can happen this way is they set it off here. That'd be terrible—all of us die, Sary Tash too, couple of a thousand people. And the squirrel...lots of other nice things. Believe me, I don't want that to happen. But if al-Qaeda takes it, all of New York City could die. Millions. A lot worse. It's not that I'd rather have Kyrgyz die than Americans, it's the difference in the numbers."

Men see the world as a math problem, Cholpon thought, gaping at him. "Killing people because you think they might kill others? That way it never ends...just keeps rolling."

The *Shayka* patted him mollifyingly. "You did what you thought was right...from the level of duality. That is what is ruling again. The unity we made is gone. If we had big groups of meditators, they could prevent war. Enough of us could purify the collective consciousness...heal this sickness at its source...keep the fighting from breaking out. But we are too few, too late. So now Kali must have her dance." Djamila raised a frail, gnarled fist to the sky. "Goddess of destruction, it is yours. And we will see what is left afterwards."

They reached the grove with the other Sufis, and Jeff lowered Djamila to her feet. To try to mend their quarrel, Cholpon put her arm around Jeff's waist and said, "Stay with us now. There are still things we can do. We will work together on the transcendental level. Maybe we can keep the worst from happening."

Jeff shook his head. "I've got to work on the action level...have to guide the planes in, help Delta Force. Plus I want to watch in case anyone tries to come up here after you."

"It is better to meditate."

"They're counting on me. They're on the way. You meditate for both of us."

"You don't understand," Cholpon said. "Violence comes back on you."

Jeff overrode her impatiently. "You don't understand that I've got to be on the radio...so they know where to come. Otherwise the nuke will get away. I'm not going to let that happen again." Seeing the pain creasing her face, Jeff added, "I'm sorry. We'll work it out later. Now I've got to do this."

Cholpon nodded in resigned acceptance and touched the center of his chest. "You are a warrior. It is your way." She leaned against him, then forced herself away. "Take care, my soldier."

With an apologetic wave Jeff headed back to his lookout point. "I'll come as soon as I can."

He was just a beginner, she thought. She shouldn't expect more. Now the future had been set in motion, rushing down on them, sweeping them away.

Leaving her in mid strife, Jeff felt a stab of regret. Now she was disappointed in him. He might've botched it...lit a match to a short nuclear fuse. One last *Allahu Akbar* before blast-off for all of them. But at least he'd tried...done something to keep al-Qaeda from wiping out a whole city.

He spied down into the canyon again. The men were still divided into al-Qaeda and Kyrgyz Army, with what looked like strained attempts at conversation between them. Perhaps as a show of peace, they had stacked their weapons, al-Qaeda's against their truck and the army's against the snow cat. They didn't seem exactly friendly down there.

Jeff found a rock to sit on where he could brace the binoculars against a pine limb.

Most of the men now held cups in their hands. As steam rose from the pot, a man reached into a paper bag, pulled out a handful of something, and tossed it into the pot. Tea! Al-Qaeda had to observe the Muslim social ritual. Kept them warm too. Jeff shivered against the cold rock. He'd like a cup himself, thanks.

He noticed that General Osmonaliev was wearing a sergeant's uniform. What...why was he dressed as a sergeant? Didn't want al-Qaeda to know who he was. These were probably the same guys who rocketed us, almost killed both of us. And he was going to turn the bomb over to them? But he couldn't be on their side...then he wouldn't have been at the banquet.

The general was talking to one of the al-Qaeda. Jeff peered closely, hoping it would be bin Laden. How he'd like to have that man in his sights! An hour ago the idea of killing anything seemed repulsive. Now he felt the sour pump of aggression through his body. Not a change for the better, but it was where he was at. The guy looked Arab, but no, not tall enough to be bin Laden. Good old Osama must be lying awfully low these days—maybe under twenty tons of dirt in Tora Bora.

May this day be their last.

The men dipped their cups into the pot. One of them produced a jar of what looked like sugar and passed it around. How sweet—these killers sipping tea and chatting next to a nuclear bomb. The al-Qaeda were leaning against their truck, the soldiers standing across the table from them, both still wary but trying to be sociable. Before they could talk, they had to drink tea.

The al-Qaeda leader set a cloth sack on the table and dumped out bundles of bills. Osmonaliev picked one up and began to count.

Jeff groaned with a shock of revelation. The general was selling the damned thing! It had been business all along. Now the payoff. Enough cash to make them all rich. A dozen guys, just his personal cadre. Less chance of leaks, fewer ways to split the money. No one else in the government would have to know. What an entrepreneur!

While everyone was watching Osmonaliev count the cash, one of his soldiers pulled out a pistol and shot the al-Qaeda leader. The impact knocked the man against the truck, jarred off his felt hat; blood jetted from his chest—hit in the heart. The other Kyrgyz pulled out pistols as the remaining al-Qaeda dived for the ground. Before they could fire them, though, the Kyrgyz themselves began crumpling over. Jeff saw fire spitting from a slit in the truck's canvas cover and heard the hammering of an AK-47. On the ground the al-Qaeda now also had pistols in their hands, shooting at the Kyrgyz. Clutching his middle, Osmonaliev fell over the table, collapsing it along with the stove, pot, and cash.

Several Kyrgyz were firing at the hidden gunman in the truck while others dashed for their rifles and the cover of the snow cat. The al-Qaeda shot after them, their bullets pinging off the vehicle and the bomb casing.

As the Kyrgyz began returning fire from behind the snow cat, the al-Qaeda scrambled for cover, some behind their truck, others behind trees. Amid rifle and pistol reports Jeff could hear the cries of the wounded. Osmonaliev and the al-Qaeda leader lay next to each other, inert. Several Kyrgyz were writhing on the ground. The hidden gunman in the truck had apparently been hit; the canvas cover was riddled, and no more fire came from him.

Jeff sagged in bafflement against the tree limb on which he'd been steadying the binoculars. How...what? Must have been a double double-cross. They'd all stacked their rifles but had hidden pistols. Al-Qaeda must've set up the tea next to their truck so their gunman could mow down the Kyrgyz. But the Kyrgyz shot first, got the jump on them. Both sides wanted to rip the other off—get the bomb, keep the money. Thieves stealing from thieves again.

Several al-Qaeda ran deeper into the forest, apparently trying to circle the snow cat and flank the remaining Kyrgyz. One al-Qaeda staggered and fell, tried to crawl behind a tree, was hit again, kicked futilely with his legs, screamed a prayer, vomited blood, and lay still.

The gunfire became sporadic as both sides had to search for targets.

Jeff heard an airplane in the distance. The sound grew louder but stayed thin, a small plane. He scanned the sky and found it—single engine, bubble cockpit: their forward air controller. He switched the radio to the air-ground frequency, adjusted the mouthpiece on the headset, and called the FAC. "Longbow, this is Fiery Lane three-nine, over."

"Roger, this is Longbow, inbound. Do you have me visually, over?" The pilot had a Southern accent, maybe Georgia, its tones soothing.

"Roger."

"Request your location, over."

"We're to your southwest about two o'clock. Up on the ridge. I'll give you a flash." Hoping there was enough light, Jeff took the signal mirror from his survival kit, held it up, sighted on the plane through the center hole, and wobbled it.

"Gotcha," said the pilot. "You had any ground fire?"

"Small-arms fire going on now."

A staticky pause. Ground fire was always bad news to the air force. "Who's fighting?"

"Al-Qaeda and some other gang...both trying to grab the bomb." Jeff didn't mention Kyrgyz Army. Not the time for complications. Osmonaliev's guys were almost certainly a rogue group out for themselves anyway. A scheme like this had to be kept small.

"Any sign of anti-aircraft or machine gun?" the pilot asked.

"Negative. Just rifle and pistol."

"Roger. We've got a fast burner coming in with clusters. I'm going to need a sitrep from you to brief him with. First, where are your friendlies?"

"All along this ridge. The whole ridge is off limits. We've got forty civilians here. But anything down in the canyon is hostile and a target."

"How many hostiles?"

"About twenty."

"And where's Sonny?"

"Bottom of the canyon about 300 meters from me...southeast of my position."

"Can you get a laser on it?"

"I'll try." Jeff rummaged in his pack and took out the flashlight-sized pointer. The device was a little spooky to him, so he held it gingerly away and pushed the switch; a thin sparkling beam streamed out. So this was the new high-tech world of war, a magic wand. Wherever he pointed it, danced a tiny dazzle of light. What a great toy! He moved the beam towards the snow cat but stopped before it actually touched it. He knew a laser wouldn't trigger the bomb, but still....

"That's it," he told the pilot. "Can you get a fix on it?"

"Got it. I'll run it through the range finder and relay the coordinates up to the jet."

"And you're sure this won't set it off?"

"Affirm. This is just anti-personnel. Too diffused to set off a nuke...spreads out over 200 meters."

Hearing this again made Jeff a little more secure, but not much.

"I'm going to sitrep the jet," the FAC continued. "I'll be back with you in about five."

"Quicker the better. They might blast it if they know what's

180

coming."

"Roger." The pilot switched off.

Jeff moved his position. He found a boulder to sit against that gave him more cover and shielded him from the wind. When he looked back down in the canyon, Al-Qaeda now had the remaining Kyrgyz in a crossfire by the snow cat. The soldiers were huddled behind the tracks, unable to shoot at one group of al-Qaeda without exposing themselves to the other. Seeing their position was hopeless, the Kyrgyz began shouting and waving in surrender. Al-Qaeda shouted back, and the Kyrgyz stood up, arms raised, weaponless; al-Qaeda advanced on them, AKs aimed from the hip.

With a shuddering boom a jet flew over the canyon. The men looked up in panic. They must've been too wrapped up in their firefight to notice the FAC, but a fighter-bomber this low could only mean disaster was about to drop on them.

Several al-Qaeda sprinted for their truck while the others ran at the Kyrgyz. They held AKs to the soldiers' heads and gestured at the plane, as if accusing them of calling it. Dumbfounded, the four Kyrgyz shook their heads and gestured helplessly. The al-Qaeda shot one soldier; he convulsed and fell to the ground. They shouted at the other Kyrgyz and prodded them with their weapons. When the others only trembled and pleaded, they shot them too.

"Fiery Lane three-nine, this is Longbow, over," the FAC radioed Jeff.

"Three-nine."

"Falcon is going to make a dry run up the canyon. How's the ground fire now?"

"Just died down."

"Good."

Jeff stood up to get a better view and paced around to keep warm. The jet banked off the mountains and came roaring in toward the canyon. Al-Qaeda were probably shitting their pants, Jeff thought. Fine, he was glad. Finally they'd get some metal stuck in them. Come on, cluster bombs.

All this really won't help, said an inner voice that still clung to peace.

I know—but so what, he answered. Ride the storm....

He looked down in the canyon, hoping to see al-Qaeda with compasses in hand trying to find Mecca so they could say their final prayers. Instead they were unloading something from the truck, a long tube out of which they pulled a cylinder with fins and pointed tip.

He called on the radio: "Longbow, Longbow, they got a SAM!" No answer. The FAC must be talking on the air-to-air freq.

Hugely close, loud, and menacing, the fighter-bomber barreled in on its trial pass. With a protruding nose on a long silver fuselage, small delta wings set back, dual tails, and bomb pods underneath, it looked almost like a missile itself.

Moving frantically but efficiently, al-Qaeda set up a metal tripod and attached the SAM to it. The sound of the plane so low hurt Jeff's already lacerated eardrums. The men stepped back; fire burst from the base of the missile. It shot off at an angle to the oncoming jet.

A miss, thought Jeff, thank God!

As its heat-seeking sensor tuned in, the blazing dart twisted in the air and changed course.

Jeff was high enough on the ridge that he could see the pilot and weapons officer in the plane. Did they know what was chasing them? The SAM, now a laser-like streak of light, was right behind them, going faster. It sparked as it touched the jet's tail, then flashed with fire.

The plane shook; flames flared from the back; the fuel tanks erupted into a fireball that enveloped the fuselage.

Jeff let go of the binoculars and stared, mouth open, head shaking with helpless sorrow.

The pilot shot out of the cockpit, still strapped to his seat, clear of the blaze. The weapons officer must not have hit his eject button in time; he stayed in as the plane began to come apart.

What if it hits the nuke?

Flames gushed over the bomb pods, and the clusters exploded with a long brapping roar, spewing shrapnel in all directions. Jeff felt sharp stings on his face and a stab in his right eye; he flinched away and clutched his face. He couldn't see out of the eye—that side was dark. Was he blind? In one eye? Was his eye gone...or just wouldn't open? His hand came away covered with blood and clear fluid.

A globe of orange fire crowned with black smoke billowed

towards Jeff, generating wind as it gobbled air. He managed to turn just as flames fell on him, raining fire amid the snow. His parka, pack, and pants were burning. He inhaled smoke but no air. The pain in his eye was a searing lance surrounded by dancing needles.

As the jet disintegrated, the weapons officer—soaked in blazing fuel, trailing flames—plummeted through the sky. The rest of the plane impacted up the canyon past the bomb. The pilot's parachute began to open as he hit the ground with a thud.

The cloud of fire, its fuel dwindling, shrank away from Jeff and trailed to earth, igniting the pines. The trees were dry, their resin volatile—the fire found new fuel.

Jeff's clothes burned like a wick. He clawed off his pack, scorching his hands, then rolled on the ground trying to smother the flames. When his parka still burned, he tried to get out of it but in his panic only managed to jam the zipper. He stripped it off like a glove and pounded it against a boulder. No longer aflame, he reeked of kerosene.

He squinted into the signal mirror for a damage inventory. Blood mixed with vitreous fluid was running from under the twitching eyelid. He lifted it and revealed a grape pierced by a thorn. It was dark red and gave off a cooked smell—the hot metal must have boiled the eye. He thought of the sheep's eyes at the banquet. Would Hobbs want to eat this one? Would Cholpon still love a one-eyed geek? The pain was such a red-and-white glare that it was hard to believe the eye was dead. He doubled over, shaking with grief and agony. A cane and seeing-eye dog, tapping across the street. No, it was just one eye. He could still see. An eye patch...a glass eye fixed and staring emptily.

He moaned, then risked another look in the mirror. The skin of his haggard face was welted with burns and punctured with slivers of steel. With so many different kinds of pain, he couldn't tell which was from fire and which from shrapnel. His eyebrows, the only hair on his head, were now crisped.

Compared to the inferno of napalm, the jellied gasoline he'd called in on so many Vietnamese, he knew this was minor damage. Now he was getting some of it back.

Morphine...some Syrettes in the survival kit. He burrowed through and brought one out, a little tube with a needle on one end. Yes...relief. The poor Viet Cong didn't have much of that.

Hands shaking, he unscrewed the cap, pinched up his thigh, jabbed the point in, and squeezed the contents. He put another one in his pocket for later.

Peering through the binoculars with one eye, holding a bloody handkerchief to the other, Jeff watched the seven remaining al-Qaeda clapping each other on the back.

In the canyon flames were spreading in the trees, the snow just adding steam to the smoke.

In a chandelle the FAC soared up and away towards the clouds. Jeff radioed him, grieving for the fliers. These guys were probably his friends. To hell with all the call signs and code words. "I'm so sorry," he spoke into the mouthpiece, "I couldn't get you on the radio. They had a SAM hidden in the truck. I don't see any more, but there could be more."

He could hear the FAC breathing then finally speaking: "Roger." A pause. "It happens." Another pause. "But this changes everything. We might not be able to bring in Delta now. SAM could take the chopper out too."

Saving the bomb was all that mattered, Jeff thought. They couldn't let it get away. The mission! "I can keep an eye"—singular is right—"on the truck...warn you if they bring out any more SAMs. But you'd have to stay on this freq. If I see another SAM, you could have the chopper abort. There'd be time before they get it set up."

"I'll ask the pilot what he's willing to risk," said the FAC.

Jeff watched the al-Qaeda, still jubilant, returning to the snow cat and kicking bits of the fighter-bomber. One of them started to run up to the pilot's body, but the others called him back. No time for atrocities. They were getting out of there.

Hurry up, Delta Force.

A pall of fumes filled the canyon. Flames danced in the trees, accompanied by the crackle and hiss of burning pine. The air smelled of turpentine and kerosene.

The sodden languor of morphine began to creep over Jeff, not eliminating the pain but blurring it with numbness. At last.

The radio spat static as the FAC came back on: "What's happening on the ground?"

"Al-Qaeda's ready to leave...with the nuke," Jeff said. "No sign of a SAM."

"OK. The insertion is still a go. You got a gutsy pilot. He

was going to hover right over the trees, have Delta rope slide down. But that's too risky now. So he'll do a touch-and-go out on the wheat field—one pass, haul ass. But you yell if there's any change down there. I'll stand by on your freq."

"Roger."

The al-Qaeda seemed to be trying to figure out how to start the snow cat. They must've murdered the Kyrgyz too soon.

The snowflakes had increased into swirling white millions. What they lacked in size they made up in numbers. Shivering, Jeff tried to put the sooty, fume-stinking parka back on. He hurt his scorched fingers again opening the damned jammed zipper. He was so full of hurt and loss that he wanted to lie down and quit, just cry himself away. But there was too much to be done. He fought off opiate wooziness and braced himself for what might come.

Just an hour ago...that peace...now smashed. But he could get it back. He could still meditate with a glass eye...once they got the bomb out of the way. He'd recover from all this, go back to the farm with Cholpon, see that the Sufis got the money. They definitely earned it. Then he and Cholpon could figure out what to do, where to live. Would she like to ski? Maybe she'd let him teach her.

The increasing snow still wasn't having much effect on the fire, which was snapping, spitting, getting closer. It was a long ways from the women, though.

Jeff heard the whap-whap of a chopper and saw it near the entrance of the canyon, flying so low its skids skimmed the wheat. Al-Qaeda saw it too and sprinted back towards their truck. Blackhawk hovered, rotor wash flattening the grain, just long enough for twelve men to jump out. The aircraft gained altitude in a burst of speed and banked sharply away, long dark fuselage looking like a locust in flight. The Delta squad, laden with packs and weapons, began moving towards the canyon.

Al-Qaeda were taking something from the truck, but by now the helicopter was out of range.

"All-right!" Jeff called to the FAC. "Thank the pilot for me. This changes the odds."

"Good news. Glad to hear it."

Al-Qaeda had unloaded a wooden box, too small for a

SAM. Two men carried it by its rope handles as the group jogged down the canyon toward the field.

The FAC continued: "Our cloud cover is dropping. That's the bad news. Aircraft aren't going to be able to get in here with this low a ceiling. I'm going to have to go back myself."

Jeff stared up at the spotter plane, now almost lost in overcast. No air support. He hadn't realized how much he'd been depending on this voice in the sky until it told him it was leaving. "Isn't there any other way?" he asked, his mind scrambling for an alternative. "Can't you get a Stealth to drop those clusters from up above the clouds? You've got the coordinates."

"Negative. We can't high-altitude it with so many friendlies on the ground. Those clusters would blow all over the place."

"Well, how about this: Even if al-Qaeda drive it away, they're still going to be in this canyon. They don't have that many options in these mountains. We've got topo maps to see the routes they can take. We know how fast a snow cat goes. We should be able to figure out about where they are. As soon as they're far enough away...I mean, so none of us here on the ground get hit, your guys should be able to take them out."

"Hmm...that sounds doable. Yeah. We can even track them on infrared—the heat from the snow cat. With that, I think there's a good chance to get 'em."

"Well, that's better," Jeff said with relief.

"I'll relay that on up. In the meantime let's see what Delta can do. You keep us posted on the ground side. I think one way or the other, Sonny's safe."

Jeff hoped the FAC wasn't just trying to cheer him up with optimism before leaving. The spotter plane rocked its wings in farewell as it disappeared into the clouds.

"Fiery Lane three nine, this is zero five, over," a new voice called on the radio.

"That's your man on the ground," the FAC said to Jeff.

Jeff answered and briefed the Delta Force lieutenant, ending with, "Seven al-Qaeda headed in your direction. They've got AKs and a box of something...maybe grenades."

"How far are they now?" the lieutenant asked. He and his squad were forcing their way through the wheat, and his voice was strained with panting.

"About 500 meters and running," Jeff said.

"Where in the canyon?"

"About the middle."

"Let me know when the gap is 400 meters. We can rifle grenade 'em."

Through the trees Jeff could see al-Qaeda advancing, taking turns carrying the box in pairs.

"About now, I'd say," Jeff told the lieutenant.

"Good, give us corrections." One of the Delta troopers stopped and raised his rifle at a thirty-degree angle while the others continued running. An arc of smoke climbed from the weapon, crested, then dropped into the trees with an explosive flash and report. The impact was off to the side of the al-Qaeda, who kept running and spread out more. Good soldiers, Jeff thought. It takes a lot of training to overcome the instinct to stop and dive for cover.

"Almost," Jeff told the lieutenant. "Bring it in fifty meters to your right."

"Check. Here comes another one." The first Delta trooper ran to catch up with his comrades while another stopped, raised his rifle, and fired.

Jeff could see through the binoculars they had the M-5 carbine with built in grenade launcher. It had more range and accuracy than the Heckler & Koch, which they used for urban, close-in fighting. Jeff wished he had an M-5 now—he could reach al-Qaeda from up here.

Now that Delta Force was in action, Jeff was swept up in wild, tattered exhilaration. His comrades, the new generation of commandos. He could keep up with them.

This round exploded near one of the al-Qaeda, knocking him sideways to the ground. He rose to his knees, wobbled back and forth groping with his arms, then toppled over.

"You got one!" Jeff called. "Now bring it thirty meters closer to you."

Another grenade arced in, but Jeff had lost sight of the al-Qaeda in the trees. A minute later he heard their AKs; from the edge of the forest they opened fire on the GIs in the wheat field, dropping three Americans. The first was hit in the head and fell backwards; the second was clipped in the shoulder and spun to the side; another staggered in a circle until his knees buckled and he crumpled. The rest of Delta began fire and maneuver, half of them blasting out covering fire with their rifles and grenade launchers while the other half ran twenty meters then stopped and began firing as the others advanced.

One al-Qaeda fell and the rest took cover behind trees. The two carrying the wooden box dumped its contents on the ground. Moving with well-drilled speed, they fastened wires to several curved green rectangles.

Claymores! That could kill everyone in the wheat. Jeff radioed to warn the lieutenant. No answer. He called again. Nothing. The officer could have fallen...or his radio been hit.

The al-Qaeda attached the claymores to trees and aimed them towards the field at the level of the wheat. Each held thousands of steel pellets that would spray out in a lethal fan.

Hit by GI bullets as they worked, two al-Qaeda slumped to the ground. Their comrades crawled behind cover, unspooling wires as they went. They clicked the detonators; blasts snapped off three tree trunks; wedges of fire scythed out over the wheat. When the smoke cleared, the grain lay withered and the Delta soldiers had disappeared.

Three remaining al-Qaeda stood up shouting and shaking their fists in rhythm. Then they turned and ran back towards the nuke.

From out of the wheat field crawled a GI. Slowly he got to his feet. His Kevlar helmet was skewed to one side and his camouflage fatigues were splotched with blood. He followed the al-Qaeda, plodding painfully.

Good discipline, Jeff thought. He tried to reach him on the radio but got no answer.

He reported the losses to Hobbs, who took it hard. "Only one survivor...he's wounded. Two fliers dead...plane gone," the colonel recapped in a toneless voice. "And al-Qaeda's got the bomb. What a day."

"Could be more GIs wounded in the wheat," Jeff said, "if we can get a medevac in time."

"'Fraid not. The FAC briefed me on your weather. Air force can't fly blind through those mountains in a snow storm. We'll have to land Delta in Osh...truck them to you from there. Take hours."

Jeff gulped back a groan as this sank in. "Damn.

But...OK...there's still two of us on our feet. Only three al-Qaeda. Let's see what we can do."

After a pause Hobbs said, "Madsen, you're a good trooper."

"Thanks."

"Keep me informed."

"Roger." Jeff switched off the transmitter, glad of the praise but congratulating himself for not saying Sir.

He picked up the binoculars again: the al-Qaeda were loading equipment and supplies from their truck onto the snow cat. One tall middle-easterner was wounded in the arm and couldn't carry much.

Jeff found the Delta trooper laboring up the trail, hiding behind trees at each bend, peering ahead, moving again. With his wounds he must have found his assault pack too heavy—he stripped it off, then continued. Accomplish the mission...regardless of personal cost.

Jeff heard the grind of the starter on the snow cat, and his neck rippled with tension. Stop them! The soldier heard the sound too, and started moving faster. Jeff couldn't let him risk this alone.

An inner voice cried, All killing does is breed more of it. You have to stop it, break the chain. Go meditate with Cholpon.

But this was just a voice. His body was locked rigid, coursing with rage that demanded release. He breathed in rapid hisses, lips drawn back from his teeth.

If it hadn't been for them, I'd still have my eye.

The snow cat coughed to noisy life. Jeff angled down towards it, staying in the shadows of the pines, his breath pluming out into cold air. Meditation was fine, but he'd always been a man of action.

A long burst from an M-5 carbine made him stop and grab the binoculars. Another burst. Two AKs hammered back at it. One of the al-Qaeda lay tumbled next to the snow cat while his two comrades fired from behind the tracks. Jeff followed their tracers and saw the Delta trooper lean out from behind a tree and empty his magazine at them.

Short bursts, Jeff told him in his mind.

Jeff began running, and so did one of the al-Qaeda. While the trooper reloaded, the al-Qaeda gained an angle on him from the other side of the tree and raked the GI with fire. The American twitched from the slugs and slumped sideways, clutching his carbine. He tried to aim it but his arms collapsed; he tried to crawl but his legs thrashed. His body convulsed, and a howl retched from him. He brought a hand to his chest, crossed himself, and rolled flat.

If I'd only been quicker, Jeff thought. I blew it again.

The al-Qaeda raised his weapon over his head and yelled with blood lust, then started back toward the snow cat. His comrade began pulling levers on the rumbling vehicle. The metal tracks clanked into motion, and the machine lurched forward on the trail.

Now just within range, Jeff braced himself against a tree to steady the SMG. He put his right eye to the gun sight before he remembered and switched to the left. At the thought of his eye, a fresh wave of grief and pain hit him. His face broke out in a sweat. He clenched his jaw to stop trembling and followed the running man with the gun sight through a gauze of smoke while his inner voice cried, *Don't kill him—it'll just bounce back on you. That's why you hurt.*

So what, Jeff replied. I've always hurt.

Let the air force do it. You know the planes can track them now. You don't need to kill them.

They're targets of opportunity. Take them out. Jeff led the al-Qaeda by about a foot and squeezed off a burst. The man fell as he ran, pitching forward headlong, flailing arms and legs, rolling over twice, then sprawling still. Dark stains spread over his brown overalls.

His comrade on the snow cat picked up his AK and looked around for this new enemy.

"Up here!" Jeff shouted, wanting the guy to know where his death was coming from and who was giving it to him. Thinking of the Delta troopers, Fred Garcia, Bruce Watson, Creigh Townsend, and three thousand other murdered Americans, Jeff sent him single shots that jerked his body with each impact until he slid off the seat and out of sight behind the controls. The snow cat stalled.

Anybody else? Jeff looked around for other al-Qaeda. He saw bodies but none of them moved. The only sound was the snarl of the fire. It's over! Stopped them...dead. Won! Too numb for triumph, he felt only a relief so enormous that he wept from both eyes, then winced from stinging salt. Now...Cholpon...a life...finally.

The main fire was devouring trees and belching smoke farther up the canyon around the wreckage of the plane, and patches of flames also burned along the ridge where the aviation fuel had fallen. Jeff skirted them, welcoming the heat, coughing from the fumes, as he made his way down to the bomb. After all he'd gone through to save it, he needed to see it up close, to make sure it was real. And he had to check on survivors. Then call Hobbs. Another shot of morphine...squirt it right into the brain.

He walked past the strewn bodies of Kyrgyz and al-Qaeda. Relaxed now in death, most of them looked innocently youthful, boys out for adventure.

Approaching the snow cat, he saw the nuke to be a cylinder about five feet tall and a third that wide, encased in dull gray lead, dented but not punctured by the bullets. In lead like that, no wonder the detectors couldn't find it. A product of the Brezhnev era, it was built like the man: crude, squat, and solid. There was no doubt whatsoever that it would do its job.

Rest in peace, Leonid.

Around the ground blew bills of the payoff, US one thousands. He picked up a few Grover Clevelands, then gathered the weapons as he checked the bodies. Some had drawn themselves up into the fetal position before they died, their lives coming full circle. Some still showed dim signs of life, breathing but unconscious. He bent over Osmonaliev, who lay supine, uniform ruddy and soggy, eyes open but dull and fixed on infinity.

"This was your idea," Jeff muttered.

Straining under his load of AK-47s, he moved down towards the last Delta soldier. Please be alive. As if in answer, the GI's arm moved, then his head. Jeff's mournful face broke into a smile. Yes! The man slowly turned over. He was young, with a long, ragged face and deep-set eyes.

Vietnam...I was that age.

The soldier feebly propped himself on one elbow.

We'll get you out of here!

Through fading senses the GI saw motion...man approaching...AK-47. With his last strength he raised his carbine and sent the enemy a burst.

Jeff saw the muzzle flash and fell backwards as bullets punctured his chest, pierced his heart and lungs. He exploded

191

inside in concussive waves that carried everything—body, past, future—with it, dissolving it all in the last roar of his heart.

He tried to hold on to his life as it slipped away. All the things he'd never done with Cholpon. To leave her with only grief. He saw her now as she sat in meditation, her face grave but full of calm beauty. The face aged became Djamila's. The *Shayka* whispered, *Think your mantra, and it will take you where you need to go. It will be your boat to float to the sun. And the trip is all good.*

But Cholpon....

Next life...and the next. Nothing is lost, just delayed. Time to be with her, do all that, fulfill every desire. But not now. Now you need to rest.

His mantra became a gauze of light suffusing him. His pain stopped, breath stopped, thoughts stopped. In their absence came a void that held a winged exaltation. His being contracted to a tiny seed, a compression of all he'd been in his hundreds of lives, then left those boundaries and expanded out into infinite light. Jeff became a pure joy of greeting as he returned to unity.

"*Allah-aum.* It is over," said Djamila while the Sufis sat meditating among the trees high on the ridge.

The finality of her tone stabbed Cholpon. With a silent shriek of agony she bent over in full lotus, holding her chest as part of her crumbled to dust inside.

The Sufis came slowly out of meditation; some of them glanced at Cholpon, then looked away as they saw her grief.

Djamila stood up painfully and went to Cholpon. She put her hand on Cholpon's head in a *darshan* caress, but this time Cholpon could feel no comfort. My Jeff....

After a pause the teacher spoke quietly: "Now we must keep other soldiers from taking this bomb. We will go. Maybe there is time."

"What if they kill us?" Acel asked.

The *Shayka* moved her hand to Cholpon's shoulder. "No one is left. They have all killed each other."

Cholpon's last hope withered, leaving her ripped apart and crushed. Gone...so soon, barely begun. All we could have had...lost. Jeff...my man...my only man. Her thoughts wailed after him.

"But we must hurry," Djamila added.

Needing to weep and mourn, Cholpon resented Djamila's pulling her back into practicality. Everything was ashes...worthless. She craved to die, to join him. This tantalizing taste of love...so cruel. A door had swung open to show her a new world—a life with Jeff, maybe a child—then slammed shut in her face.

He was snatched away just as she was getting to know him again. No one could take his place...always an emptiness there. Djamila could talk all she wanted about how this had to be and was for the best. But it was just cruel. Even if her past actions did bring this on her, she couldn't love a God who would create a world run by such laws. This pain made everything else seem a sham.

The Sufis returned to the bus and drove back out to the road and over to the other trail, then through the wheat field and into the burning canyon, past the dead soldiers of three armies sprawled and twisted on the ground. The blazing hulk of an airplane lay farther into the forest, and pieces of wing and fuselage led to it in a trail of disintegration. Over the blackened bodies of trees, flames were advancing in their direction, still a ways off but close enough for the women to feel heat and smell smoke. On the slope a half-opened parachute billowed in the fire's breeze, and beside it sat a man in a chair.

They parked up near the hateful bomb. Cholpon took one look and glanced away. So ugly—metal skin around a radioactive heart, a man-made idol demanding human sacrifice.

"We will bury this thing...put it back in the ground...where it all came from," Djamila said. "There it will be safe."

"But the reward from the Americans," her secretary said. "We could—"

The *Shayka* cut her off with a wave of her hand. "No good can come of such money. It brings with it the karma of violence. They are killers too. When they dismantle their old bombs, they save the deadly parts to build new ones. I don't trust them not to use it someday. Bury it."

"But won't that poison the mountain?" asked Acel.

"No," Djamila said, "the poison comes from the explosion. If it doesn't explode, it is just uranium...even that will be held in by the lead. The earth can take its metals back. It knows how to handle them. Bury this thing...where people cannot find it. Drive it up the canyon...look for an easy place to dig. Under the ground it will be safe from the fire."

Acel gestured at the vehicle. "What do we do with this?"

The teacher surveyed the machine. "This crawling thing...it is not very high. It could disappear in the river. The water is deep enough to hide it. Can you drive it in...and not drown?"

"I can swim," said Acel. "But I can probably set the throttle so it will drive itself in."

"You are a wizard of skill," Djamila said. "Deep in water...deep in the earth. Gone. They will think the bomb was driven away. That's as good as we can do...to keep it away from the warriors."

The *Shayka* walked over to Cholpon and took her hand. "You and I will stay here." Cholpon nodded numbly.

The Sufis pulled the dead al-Qaeda from the vehicle, laid him on the ground, and chanted a brief prayer. Acel climbed into the driving compartment and stared puzzled at the controls. She flipped a few switches until the engine started, then pulled levers until it slipped into gear.

The women removed a shovel and some other tools that were attached to the frame, then pried the hubcaps off their bus to also use for digging. They followed Acel up the canyon until she found a sandy place where the trail crossed a dry stream bed. She stopped with the machine sloping so the wooden pallet with the bomb could be slid off.

They set to work in shifts, one group digging hurriedly, scooping sand, prying rocks out with tools and hands, while the other group rested, all of them singing the peace prayer when they weren't coughing and rubbing their eyes from smoke.

The blaze was moving nearer under clouds of gray fumes. Yellow sheets of flame hung in the pines; swirls of fire floated in the air. Pops of exploding resin added a staccato percussion to the gobbling roar. Burning branches dropped to earth, and the fire spread on the ground, slowed now by the increasing snow, the two elements at war.

Cholpon and Djamila walked among the bodies of the soldiers. Kyrgyz, Americans, al-Qaeda, hard to tell them apart. The snow fell with quiet evenness over everyone. Finally they found Jeff lying peaceful but vacant, eyes closed. Cholpon gasped and cried and extended her arms to emptiness. He was surrounded by rifles, ugly murderous things.

He really is dead. She sank down beside him. Your eyes, no more golden brown light. How I loved the way they looked at me.

To see him the way she knew him, she took off the radio helmet he wore.

I have nothing of you, not even a picture to remember you with, only this last sight of what isn't really you anymore. Large bent nose, wide mouth, head shaved and bandaged, strong body punctured now with even more wounds. You were the man I loved...for a little while.

Djamila knelt behind her and meditated, flossy white hair speckled with ashes.

Cholpon held his hand. They hurt you so bad you couldn't stay in your poor body. So many wounds, so much pain you must have had. I'm so sorry. She tried to wipe the blood from his face but found most of it had already dried. To prepare him for his funeral pyre, she straightened his body and lay his arms along his side palms up in the final asana position. She touched the crown *chakra* on top of his head where the soul departs, the last contact with the physical world.

Cholpon broke inside and cries tore from within as her chest seemed to rend. Collapsing against him, she wept out her loss.

My love. Don't worry about the fire. It is good and will not hurt you. Nothing can hurt you now.

Coughing and crying, face smudged with soot and tears, she sang him the Kyrgyz lullaby he loved so much.

The snowflakes melted on his face, but as the heat left his body, they began to cover him.

Life is a snowflake falling into fire.

Cholpon felt incinerated.

In desperation she clung to her mantra. Its sound enlivened an inner firmness that spread across her torso to become a band of power shielding her heart. She took shelter in it, still weeping but no longer overwhelmed.

When the women up the canyon had dug the hole deep enough, they loosened the pallet and slid it off with the bomb, holding with the tie ropes until it was too heavy, then letting it fall. As the nuke crashed down, they were afraid it would explode, but it just crushed the pallet and lay there on its side in dull inertness.

They shoveled the dirt back over it while Acel returned with the vehicle. Snow and soot were falling together now, thick and heavy, hiding the bomb's grave. Carcasses of trees would soon be covering it.

The group walked back to where Cholpon and Djamila were kneeling near Jeff. The others stopped a few paces away, hands clasped in front of them.

As Cholpon grieved, part of her stood beyond that in the refuge of the Goddess, watching it all with compassion.

The fire had spread along the canyon slopes; flames were closing in from three sides. Convection winds gusted them with heat and showered them with burning cinders, singeing their hair. Smoke fouled the air and stung now not just their eyes but their noses and throats.

"Let's go home," said the *Shayka*, "before more soldiers come. No one may know we were here. In Sary Tash everyone will be hiding in their houses...afraid bombs will fall." She coughed, then stood up with a wince of pain. "Now the fire of Agni will purify the bodies, burn out the violence. It will help Jeff on his way. Let us sing the *salat al-janaza* for him. That will also help."

Cholpon and her Sufi sisters sang the solemn but uplifting dirge, their prayer echoing off the canyon walls in an overlapping cascade of voices blending with the drone of the oncoming fire while ashes and snow piled up around them all.

Author's Afterword

A juggernaut of aggression continues to roll through our world, crushing multitudes of soft, breathing human beings, creating more counter-violence at every turn, lumbering towards annihilation. The brutal men who rule us are too ignorant for the power they wield, and we can't let them keep killing. Now none of us in any country is safe.

The transcendental meditation peace techniques described in *Summer Snow* can prevent terrorism and war. Scientific research has shown when large groups practice these techniques together, violence is reduced both in the local environment and internationally. Forty studies have demonstrated a field effect extending out from the groups of meditators into the surrounding society, neutralizing hostility and fostering calm, positive behavior. The techniques heal fear and aggressive stresses in the collective consciousness, where all humans are connected. Their peaceful influence can end this senseless cycle of wars and create global harmony.

Human nature is not essentially violent. God did not create us to kill each other. The violence comes from an overload of anxiety and stress, and that can be healed.

Peace is possible, but obviously not through force or diplomacy. Those means have failed, and now we must try a more fundamental method that solves this problem at its source in the collective consciousness that joins us all.

Although *Summer Snow* is fiction, the meditation and its effects are reality. To find out more about the scientific research on them, visit www.tm.org and www.invincibility.org.

About the Author

William T. Hathaway won a Rinehart Foundation Award for his

 first novel, *A World of Hurt*, which was based on his experiences in the US Special Forces in Panama and Vietnam. An anti-war activist, Hathaway is a member of Veterans Call to Conscience, which encourages soldiers to refuse to kill, and of a group of European peace workers that has established a sanctuary network sheltering US soldiers who have refused to be sent to Iraq and Afghanistan. He was interviewed for *Military Service and Christian Conscience*, a video production of the Episcopal Church.

Hathaway was born in Mississippi, raised in the Rocky Mountains, and educated at Columbia University and the University of Washington. He spent a year and a half in Central Asia researching and writing *Summer Snow*.

His fiction, poetry, journalism, and literary criticism appear in over 40 periodicals, and he wrote the introduction to *America Speaks Out: Collected Essays from Dissident Writers*. His third novel, *The Road Back*, will be published in 2006. He teaches college English and was a Fulbright professor of creative writing at universities in Germany, where he's currently living.

CPSIA information can be obtained at www.ICGtesting.com
Printed in the USA
LVOW12s2346120216

474924LV00001B/2/P